UNION:

An Abridged Version Of Love

Jason Dowdeswell

 FriesenPress

One Printers Way
Altona, MB R0G 0B0
Canada

www.friesenpress.com

Cover Art by Jeff Bartzis
Photo by MJ Davey
Edited by Jen Zdril

ISBN
978-1-03-915972-3 (Hardcover)
978-1-03-915971-6 (Paperback)
978-1-03-915973-0 (eBook)

1. FICTION, SCIENCE FICTION, SPACE OPERA

Distributed to the trade by The Ingram Book Company

For MJ, Harper & Rhys

A great toll has been endured to explore these flawed characters in detail. Thank you for being part of the process and believing in me.

Love,
Jay

Acknowledgments

I would like to thank MJ for accepting that I had written ninety thousand words of something of a teen science fiction tale onto pages of paper. And then for asking what comes next. MJ re-introduced me to our neighbour Jen, who little did I know at that time, has story superpowers.

Jen Zdril, I thank you for the help in the completion of this book. You took me under your wing after seeing the diamond in the rough of a draft manuscript.

Then through your deep care and patience, our friendship was forged through determination and partnership. Your blunt questions and fresh ideas in conversation ground even deeper truths for the characters of this tale. Your critical thinking and yet respect for my rules of this world helped refine a story that can appeal to the hero in all of us.

Though the principal theme has not waivered since the first idea, it took the span of years of living life and in observance of the human condition to understand the truer meaning behind the original principals. I expect this partnership too, was set in motion a long time ago. And our time to collaborate is just the beginning. You tuned the instrument and helped set a tone for this book. We joke about the material left out of Union. I know they will find their place.

I would also like to thank our editorial readers who offered time and critique: Maribeth Deen, Jonathan Dowdeswell, Jennifer Dowdeswell, Christian Trineer, Liana Yip, Jeff Bartzis, Gordon Rugg and Amy Martin.

I want to thank my father, mother, brothers and sisters for being both family and friend and constant supporter.

Through pride and greed, our superego blinds us from the answer we are looking for when it is right in front of us...

UNION:

An Abridged Version Of Love

CHAPTER ONE

The small drop ship could have housed a dozen or so infantry, but inside it was just the two of them. It was always just the two of them.

The battle-scarred vessel plummeted into the grey, stormy clouds then burst through over green grassy hills. It slowed, then stopped over a muddy area, covered in stone ruins.

Inside the command room, Day, tall and lean, bent over the overscan monitors, her keen eyes searching for warning signs.

"I've found the signal," she said. Her clipped, no-nonsense voice didn't quite mask her youthful exuberance.

"It looks like our intruder is in one of the old bunkers. There's a good landing point nearby with no sign of ground intrusion."

Mano, sitting at the helm, looked up and met her eyes.

Her fine features, which contrasted strikingly with the ugly scar running down from her left eyebrow to her chin, were alive with enthusiasm.

Day was happiest when a problem called for action.

"I take it you want to go meet our mystery guest," he said.

She nodded, and his hands danced across the control panel.

The landing gear stuck firm into the soft ground, and Day and Mano grabbed their gear and headed for the exit lift. As they arrived at the exit hatch, Day muttered, "I hate exiting by the top hatch," and she reached for the release latch.

"Yeah, we're going to be easy targets. We really need to repair the lower hold," answered Mano, clipping yet another of his various devices to his chest plate.

"I'll add it to the list. I'm sure we'll get to it by the next orbit," said Day, smiling wryly. She opened the hatch and scrambled out onto the dusty surface of her ship.

Coming to the edge, she braced herself and dropped to the ground below. With a squelch, her legs sunk to the knees in soft mud. She looked up to see Mano's amused face looking down at her from above.

He gestured in a way Day knew meant, "I think I'll try further down."

He chose to drop into a grassy area that looked more solid but found himself in the same predicament. She allowed herself a quick grin at the bemused look on his face, before scanning the horizon for activity. Slowly and as quietly as possible, she maneuvered herself till she was on her belly and able to crawl forward without sinking. Behind her she heard a whirring and a loud sucking sound as Mano extracted himself.

"Great. Real subtle, Mano," she murmured.

Mano twisted and rolled himself till he was beside Day. They looked around. On one side there were acres of green grass dancing in the wind, on the other a stone ruin with stairs going down to a metal door.

"That's it. Our visitor is in that bunker," Day whispered. "Let's knock."

Mano reached down and magician-like produced one of the small explosive devices that he always kept on his person. He handed it to Day.

Ahead of Mano, Day muddied through for another few lengths of tall grass until she found some solid rock. She lifted herself to her knees and surveyed the landscape through golden strands of hair that had broken loose in the wind. All was still lonely and silent.

Gripping the device she yelled, "You're on private property!" then threw it towards the bunker. The device plopped onto the roof then rolled and rolled down through the tall grass, but rather than landing outside of the bunker as planned, it bounced to the side, slipped into a thin visor window and disappeared.

"Oops," whispered Day.

BANG!

Day ducked down as the device did it's work then slowly looked up again. She saw smoke rising from the visor and bits of something fluttering in the wind and settling on the ground.

Mano caught up to her. "If you'd meant to do that, that throw would have been really impressive," he said, placidly.

"Well," said Day, sighing, "let's go see if there's anyone left to talk to."

The bunker was steaming and smoking, but it remained peaceful; the only sound was the wind whispering through the shaggy, green grass.

"What is that?" Day whispered, pointing to the fragments on the ground. Mano's eyes shifted, unnaturally, then he answered, "Parchment. It's an ancient form of documentation. You sort-of paint words onto it."

"Not dangerous, then. Alright, we just kicked a stinger's nest hard. Whoever's in there is likely to be grumpy. To be safe, you'd better rip the top off," said Day, firmly.

Mano paused. Day looked at her friend and though his dark, perfectly even features were expressionless, she could tell he was reluctant.

"Hey, I know it's exhausting. I don't like it either—it means I've got to put up with you looking your ugliest till we get back—but if you walk up to that door, you're likely to get your head blown off, and we don't have any spares."

Mano nodded. Day shifted back then forced herself to look at him. She had witnessed her friend do this many times, but every time it was hard to watch.

Mano stood up, his eyes shifting rapidly. His wiry, extra lightweight frame looked vulnerable standing there against the grey sky.

Suddenly, his eyes went dead, and his dark shaggy head rolled backwards grotesquely. At the same time, he collapsed at the knees, and his torso bent backwards in one quick motion. Swiftly, his shoulders rotated, his arm joints bent into alignment with his legs, and his hands extended to the ground. He now looked a bit like a table with a head under it.

Then came the part that bothered Day the most: Mano's face split up the middle from his chin to his forehead, so his eyes looked out the sides and various instruments burst from where his face used to be. It was a design flaw of Mano's particular model that his skin ripped every time he went into battle mode — aesthetics being a low priority of military designers. Replacing it was fast and easy, but it was unpleasant to see it tear and melt off his face.

Mano, now transformed, whirred quickly across the terrain. Out of the protrusion where his mouth used to be shot a beam that hit the bunker with a hiss. He began scoring along the bottom of the roof, whirling around the smoking bunker with great speed. When he finished, he crawled his now claw-like hands to the edge of the roof and gripped it. Then, bending his frame to allow him maximum thrusting capabilities, Mano tore the stone top off the bunker with a monstrous scraping noise, and shoved it onto the grass. When the debris settled, the contrasting silence was heavy.

Day scrambled up the hill till she was just behind Mano, next to the smoking edge.

Mano rolled onto his front, then his arms and legs rotated back into alignment, and he rose until he was upright again. Finally, his face reassembled. If it wasn't for the torn skin and clothing hanging limply from his face and body, he would have almost looked normal again. Day's voice rang out,

"This is a Wellspring outpost. Weapons will not be tolerated. Do you understand?"

The silence continued.

"If that is your crashed piece of junk there over the hill, we can help you fix it and allow you to be on your way, but if you want to live, you must do absolutely everything I say."

Still silence.

"Alright, let's take a look," said Day. She took out her hand pistol and stepped forward.

Looking down they could see sunlight shining into a large stone room. In one corner cowered a person, or person-shaped thing, wearing an odd, heavy-looking hooded robe. Day and Mano, weapons trained on the figure, watched carefully for signs of movement.

"Here's what you're going to do, if you don't want to end up a stain on the floor," ordered Day.

"You're going to slowly raise your hands, show us they're empty, and put them on your head. Then you can stand up."

The figure complied. Then the robed head tipped back revealing a gaunt face with large shining eyes. When the eyes met Days, the face broke into a smile.

/ / /

A time later, a sense of peace radiated from the robed, bald-headed man despite the bleakness of his surroundings. The dank, cramped cargo hold was designed to transport dangerous substances and not for comfort.

Day watched him on the screen for a while before opening the large round door and entering the hold.

"It's time for you to answer my questions," she said. After waiting a moment, she continued. "Do you understand me? You seemed to understand me earlier."

There was no answer from the man. He just looked at her with a strangely content expression. She continued, "You are not allowed here, and your ship has gone from junk to scrap. We can either send you home peacefully or kill you. What's it going to be?"

Pause.

"Can you at least tell me your name, so I know whose life I'm about to take?"

"Aha."

The man hadn't moved, and Day was almost unsure that the soft, high voice came from him.

"Aha." said Day.

After another pause, she asked, "Is that your name? Aha?"

"Aha, yes," said Aha.

Day took a deep breath. Patience was not one of her virtues.

"Your name is Aha? Pretty weird name. Where are you from, Aha?"

"The name was given to me by a Waxen. He saved me. He set me on my path."

Day looked at Aha suspiciously.

"Waxen don't have a reputation for saving people."

"Children don't have a reputation for violence and interrogation, but here we are," Aha responded, pointedly.

"I'm not a child, I'm seventeen," defended Day, annoyed at how her response made her feel even younger.

"Why are you here?"

"The Waxen. First, I'm here because of the Great Kayanai. He saved me from the Station."

"Kayanai Blu?" Day let out a short, disbelieving laugh.

"What station? Not, The Station?"

"Yes, the Station. You were just a baby when it fell out of the sky. It would have been my tomb, if not for the Waxen.

"The Station? You were on the Station?"

Wonder and disbelief-tinged Day's voice. Even on her distant outpost they had known the story of the Station and how it fell.

"On it, yes. Then off it, yes. Very quickly. We should not have survived. I did not think I could do it, but he knew."

Day shook her head. "I don't know what you mean. And I'm not interested in your war stories, I'm only interested in why you're here and…"

She paused and looked at him intently. "You flew off the Station? Are you a driver?"

Aha avoided her eyes. "I'm a disciple," he said rapidly. "Her disciple, though I think she's probably very angry with me. She'll find me, of course. It's alright. I'm here. I'm ready to die."

"Good! 'Cause I'm about ready to kill you," growled Day, exasperated, as she exited by the round doorway into the dark corridor.

"Get us up into orbit and turn off the gravity field. Turn down the inertial calmers for a moment too," Day commanded Mano, whose face was now back to its usual pleasant appearance.

"I think he's a driver. If I'm right, we've got a hefty award coming our way," she added with a rapacious smile.

Mano handed Day a small ball, tiny enough to conceal in a palm, then turned on his heel and headed down the corridor with quick, efficient steps.

Day called to his back, "Don't forget the warning this time!" then turned back and opened the large round door.

Aha watched Day as she entered. Once inside, Day closed the door, leaned against it and watched him back.

They held the stare as a jolt shook the room. Both Day and Aha reached out their hands to the walls to keep their balance, unperturbed. Aha continued to look at her with his small, contented smile, and she in turn looked back with a smile of her own. Hers was predatory.

For a long time nothing changed as they sped upwards. Then, a quiet signal chimed from Day's wrist. Seconds later, a whining noise started that was so loud it plugged their ears and set their teeth on edge, and there came a violent shake as if the room had been momentarily turned upside down. Day, prepared, had thrust one arm through the door handle, flattened her other palm against the door frame, and pushed her feet against the floor. Unprepared, Aha was launched up and slammed into the ceiling. He bounced off and began floating. They were in zero gravity.

Aha gazed dazedly at Day through the blood droplets orbiting his injured face like little red satellites. She met his eyes, revealed the small ball in her hand, made a mental calculation, then wound her arm back and threw the ball at the bulkhead.

The ball ricocheted and as planned, headed straight for Aha's head.

He ducked and watched carefully as the ball bounced twice, fast and hard, before it angled back towards Aha's torso. Aha quickly rotated his form and it shot past him. Again and again the ball rebounded and came at Aha in a blur of movement, and again and again he moved to avoid it.

Finally, the ball sailed near his arm, and he reached out and grabbed it.

Immediately, Day propelled herself up to Aha, snatched the ball from his hand, and kicked off him.

She landed skilfully back down and calmly regained her grip on the door handle. Then she put the ball in a pocket on her vest, leaned back, and watched Aha spin slowly toward the back bulkhead. Eventually, he put out his hands and came to a stop facing the wall.

"I knew it," she said with satisfaction.

"You're a driver. Only drivers move that way."

Aha righted himself and turned to face her. He waited impassively.

Day could see a cylindrical object now sticking out of his cloak.

"What is that?" said Day, warily, hand going to her pistol.

"I thought Mano searched you for weapons."

Aha looked down and said, "This is something infinitely more powerful than a weapon."

"Show me."

"You won't understand."

The hull vibrated again. The gravity field was re-engaged, and Aha crashed to the floor.

Day ran to him and grabbed the tube from his robe. It was a parchment rolled around a golden rod. As she slowly unraveled the pale crisp paper, Aha struggled to his feet and fumbled for it.

Day put out her hand and stopped him.

Aha stepped back and said, nervously, "Please be careful. It's irreplaceable. There was another, but your device blasted it to pieces just before we met—an act I would normally find unforgivable."

Day, ignoring him, studied the parchment covered in handwritten symbols. "I can barely make it out. It's odd to see letters drawn by hand. Did you write this?"

"No. She wrote it, the one I follow. I've been meditating on her words carefully for a long time—words she'd written and words she'd spoken to only me—and now I have nearly pieced together the whole picture. Enlightenment is within her grasp. May I have it back now, please?" Aha asked, politely holding out his hand.

"No. Maybe it will tell me what you're doing here, since you won't," Day replied, pointedly.

Aha, now holding both hands out imploringly, said, "I'm here to find you. She will find you too and discover your importance. You're the key. Now, may I have it back, please?"

Day held the parchment with one hand and with the other seized Aha by the collar of his robe,

"Me? You're here for me? Why? I'm not important! What do you know about me?"

The ship jolted again as the engines fired unexpectedly. Day furrowed her brow, confused.

"What is he-?"

Mano's terse voice broke in over the intercom.

"Ship approaching out of nowhere. Taking evasive action."

Aha's eyes widened, "She's found me!"

Day pushed him away, ran for the door, and as her hand reached for the handle, Mano's voice blared out,

"IMPACT IM—!"

A thunderous CRASH, and the room rotated and was showered in sparks.

There was a screeching sound of metal grinding against metal, then, suddenly, two long foreign objects burst through the wall. Like giant arms they ripped into the cavity of the room, and a hurricane wind sprang up as the air rushed out into the vacuum of space.

Aha was drawn towards the hole. He smashed into the edge and scrabbled at it frantically. Day caught one glimpse of his terrified face before he was sucked through and was gone.

Hanging desperately to the door handle, Day tried to turn back and pull herself towards the door, but the room shook again, and she was torn free. As she hurtled across the room towards the hole, she realized she was still holding the parchment. Just before reaching the hole in the wall, she turned the parchment sideways, thrust it in front of her, then lodged it across the top edge of the rupture and held on for dear life.

Though she managed to keep herself from whirling off into space, her legs slipped through the hole and out into the cold emptiness. Day's breath was torn from her lungs, and she could feel her limbs swiftly freezing. She closed her eyes, and an odd sense of peace came over her.

Suddenly, Day felt herself being pushed back into the ship with one powerful wrenching movement. She opened her eyes and watched with wonder as a huge shadowy figure held her with one hand and pulled at the edges of the rupture with the other. She looked down at the giant hand holding her and below it she could see her lower half covered in white frost. The room spun, and darkness overwhelmed her.

/ / /

The first thing Day noticed was pain. She slowly opened her eyes and found herself on the floor, leaning against the icy, damaged hull. Jets of hot air were blowing into the chamber, bringing feeling back to her frozen limbs and filling her lungs.

"At least I can breathe." She thought, wincing from the pain.

"The sealant system must have kicked in."

The steam and the flickering emergency lights made it hard to see, but Day could see that she wasn't alone. A giant was sitting cross-legged against the bulkhead opposite to her. The figure wore a long pale tunic, tall boots and a hooded black robe and appeared to be directing its gaze at the lower half of Day's body. Following their eyes, Day looked down. Her left leg, bent at a sickening angle, looked like a wet, tightly-wrapped rag of cloth, and her right leg was broken off from the knee down.

As Day watched the blood trickle from the stump of her leg, the pain and horror brought tears to her eyes. She tried to reach for her communicator, but her arm didn't cooperate, and the movement caused a wave of agony. She moaned and reeled back, falling limp against the hull.

She opened her eyes again, unsure of how long they'd been closed. Had she passed out again? Looking down, Day could see that her situation hadn't changed except that the pool of blood under her leg had grown. She also noticed her pistol was gone. She looked up. The shadowy figure was still there.

Day opened her mouth to speak, but only a croak came out.

She swallowed, moistening her dry throat, and tried again.

"At first I thought 'mech', since you can survive being in space without a suit. But looking at your size, I'd say you're a Waxen."

The figure's face was mostly hidden by the dark hood. Pale eyes glimmered at Day out of the shadows. The large head nodded.

Suddenly, the door opened. Hope filled Day's chest as Mano stepped in, illuminating the room with a powerful beam of light emanating from his eyes. Seeing Day, he began to rush to her aid, but she stopped him with a warning.

"We have a guest," she said.

He followed her eyes and spun around, but their guest had already moved with astonishing speed. Upright, the Waxen's size was terrifying. Mano tried to shift to gun mode, but before he was able to shoot, the Waxen wrapped its giant hands around Mano and hammered him into the wall so hard that pieces flew off him.

"STOP!" screamed Day, tears of fury springing to her eyes.

Mano managed to let out a quick blast at his attacker, but it had no noticeable effect on the Waxen other than to prompt it to smash him again, this time into the floor. The Waxen then calmly stepped on Mano's lower half, reached down and tore him in two.

As Mano's upper half smashed down next to Day, she sobbed his name and tried desperately to move towards him. Pain shook her body. Her legs and her right arm were in agony, but she blinked away her tears and reached out her left arm longingly at her friend.

A whizzing noise came from Mano as he tried to move, but he only succeeded in partially lifting himself on one arm. His eyes met Day's.

"Our guest appears to have an anger problem," he joked in an effort to lighten her sorrow.

A short, despairing laugh burst from Day. "Yeah, I don't like him either. Hey Mano, I don't think we're going to get out of this one."

"I'm sorry, Day," the mech said, remorsefully.

As Mano spoke, the shadow of the Waxen loomed over Day. Large eyes shone down at her, but Day still couldn't make out the Waxen's features.

"Day…" said a rich, deep voice, thoughtfully.

Day was startled. Though low and resonant, the voice was undoubtedly feminine. Waxen were rare enough, but female waxen were even rarer.

After a pause, the Waxen straightened and continued. "I could get you out of this, I suppose, but I don't think I will. Your suffering may be useful."

Thinking fast, Day responded, "A patrol will come when we don't make our report. We've got a medilab on this ship. If you help me into it, we'll contact them and tell them not to come."

The Waxen walked to the wall, leaned against it.

"Oh, I'm not worried about the patrol. If I were to leave, would they be here in time to save you? I don't think so. You're losing blood now that your leg is thawing."

Day groaned in helpless frustration.

"Tell me something I don't know. Why not just kill me? Are you just going to stand there watching me for your amusement?"

"Watching you suffer brings me no pleasure," answered the Waxen, softly. "On the contrary… I will watch you die because it suits my purpose. In return, I will give you what you wish, I will tell you something you don't know."

"Are you going to tell me who you are, who that idiot driver you blew into space was, or why you came here? Because I don't think I care at this point," rasped Day, exhaustedly.

"There is very little worth saying about Aha. He was a small man who wanted power that he could never wield or even understand. I tolerated him because he recognized me for what I am, but then he stole from me, making him intolerable." The giantess crouched down, looked deep into Day's eyes and held her gaze for a moment, then said, "No, instead I will tell you who you are, and why you're here."

Day was not expecting that, nor was she expecting the wave of emotion that the words woke in her. She dropped her eyes briefly, then looked up again and answered in disbelief, "Aha said I was important somehow. I know I'm anything but. I'm nobody."

"You did not come from nobodies, Day. Yes, I know who your parents were. I know your whole story."

A noise came from Mano as he shifted. The Waxen snapped her head in his direction.

"Even whole you wouldn't have enough fire power to harm me," she said, warningly.

"Stand down, Mano," said Day.

Mano was now propped up on his arm.

"I'm just getting comfortable for the story," he replied innocently, looking at Day with raised brows.

"I want to hear what she has to say, and I'd rather not watch you get smashed again," said Day, shaking her head slightly. She looked back to the Waxen.

"Tell me."

"I can tell you everything. Your story is intertwined with the end of the war and the beginning of the new era, and also with the lives of some of the greatest of all waxen—friends of mine, once. It will be a long story and you won't come into it for quite a while…"

Suddenly, the Waxen pulled out a small device and pointed it at Day's right leg. A beam flashed out and burned into the bleeding flesh. The beam stopped even before Day screamed.

"There. It won't save your life, but it will keep you from bleeding out before I finish,"

"You're all heart!" gasped Day.

The Waxen sat down against the wall and crossed her legs.

"It's difficult to know where to begin. Do I start back at the very beginning, at the birth of the waxen, or at the first Shriean attack? No, that's too far back. Perhaps I will start with Kayanai. Yes, I'll start with Kayanai."

CHAPTER TWO

In a landscape flat and wide, under a silver-pink sky stood Kayanai Blu. As far as the eye could see, the scalding ground of the metallic sand of planet Desigar shimmered and danced.

Kayanai stood pointing a gun at a kneeling man's terrified face. Even without the gun, the man would still have been afraid. To him, the Waxen must have looked like a terrible, beautiful giant chiselled out of an enormous hunk of granite by a master sculptor. Kayanai's muscles bulged from his leathery dark vest and boots, and his pale blue eyes bore into the man below him. The man tried to speak but only a wheezing squeak came out.

Behind Kayanai, the wreckage of a derailed maglev speed train burned. Among the plumes of smoke and goods scattered across the sands, were people, lying injured or just sitting. It was strangely quiet except for the small popping explosions from the flames.

Kayanai impatiently adjusted the hack, a curved pin which allowed his huge fingertip to activate the tiny weapon in his hand. The hack allowed him to use the smaller weapons of his fellow soldiers and his adversaries. The curve of this device was repeated again and again on the chest plate of his vest.

Weariness tinged his deep, resonant voice as he said, "This is a great opportunity for you to make a difference to your planet and your galaxy. What is your answer, driver?"

The driver swallowed and found his voice. "We are drivers of Jar Canon. We cannot—"

"Jar Canon is nothing compared to Waxman, and he wants drivers." interrupted Kayanai.

"Yes, but surely Wax Adoor understands the need for loyalty to one's leader…" His voice trailed off as the driver realized the backside of Kayanai's dark tunic was on fire.

Kayanai ignored the flames and answered, "Waxman does favor loyalty above all else—from his men. He doesn't care about loyalty to your jar."

A big blast of fire and smoke erupted to the left of them, and from the far edge of his vision, Kayanai made out a silhouette atop the wreckage of the train. The imposing sight looked like a huge statue of a conqueror erected to frighten its conquests.

Suddenly, the monument moved. It leapt to the ground and covered the distance to Kayanai and the driver in a few mighty strides. Upon reaching them, without pause, Waxman raised his foot and brought it down on the driver, crushing his head and killing him instantly.

Kayanai's face briefly showed shock, then went blank as he controlled himself. Keeping his voice even, he said, "I thought you wanted drivers."

Waxman, looming above even the great Kayanai, turned his dark smooth head and glanced down at his soldier before looking away, apparently satisfied at what he saw.

Then they both looked towards the horizon as Kayanai waited for a response.

Finally, Waxman said, "You're on fire," then turned on his heel and strode away.

Kayanai absentmindedly patted at his smouldering backside as he moved to fall into step beside his leader. His handsome features were hard and unreadable, but inside he was troubled; not about the burning clothing—waxen clothing, though hardy, was not as durable as their skin which was practically impenetrable—it was Waxman's actions that bothered him.

Cautiously, Kayanai glanced at Waxman and asked, "Did I misunder-stand your orders?"

The side of Waxman's grizzled cheek housed coloured communicator rings like tattoos along his jaw. He pulled one off and crushed it in his grip before letting the pieces fall, likely because there was no longer anyone alive on the other end.

Waxman brushed the pieces from his hands idly as he answered Kayanai.

"I said to find the finest drivers," his deep voice rumbled. "The two best among them have been found. The rest of the group is worthless."

They continued to march in silence, and Kayanai continued to mask his inner turmoil. As they walked through the scene of destruction they created, he thought, Once I would have convinced myself this is all for a grand cause. Now I know this is all just for Wax Adoor. He feels he needs a new army, now that he no longer has enough of us waxen…

Kayanai's thoughts drifted away. Once there'd been thousands of waxen, soldiers of the Wax—but they were gone, sent to fight the Shrie Shrie, lost… Waxman doesn't realize, even with the most advanced fleet helmed by the greatest drivers in the galaxy, it won't be enough to stop the Shrie Shrie if they return.

When Kayanai had first become a Waxen, it had been the proudest day of his life. He was going to be a hero, protecting the weak and fighting against tyranny. Like so many others, he had believed the propaganda that Waxman pumped out to all the worlds—Waxen are peacekeepers! Defenders of the galaxy! He had kept believing it for a long time, through-out untold battles and endless squashed insurrections, but now his leader's ruthlessness seemed to grow every day, and Kayanai could no longer fool himself. But he did have to keep fooling Waxman. Kayanai was Waxman's right hand and was probably the closest thing Waxman had to a friend. Disloyalty among waxen was the greatest crime. If he voiced his true feel-ings, he'd be a traitor.

What would he do if he knew? he thought. Kayanai didn't want to find out, so he kept his face like Waxman's: blank and hard.

They arrived at a fighter ship still somewhat buried in the sand from the ambush. A soldier waited outside; his hand clamped on the shoulder of an unhappy-looking woman. He approached them and said to Waxman,

"Here's one of your new drivers, sir. I thought you might want to test her abilities."

Waxman directed his flinty expression down at the soldier and growled, "She has never been raced. I use only proven drivers to pilot my ships. Put her in with the other one. Why have the cargo doors not been opened for us?"

The soldier leaped into action like he'd been struck by lightning.

"I'll get the mechs on it right away," he called over his shoulder as he marched away. Kayanai couldn't help being amused by the soldier's expression.

A good soldier only anticipates his leader's wishes if he's sure what they are. Instead of messing with the drivers, he should have realized there was no way for us to fit through the normal access ports and prepped the ship accordingly. Then Kayanai's amusement faded.

Our regular soldiers seem new all the time. We must be going through them quicker than ever. Another bad sign.

As they waited for the cargo doors, Kayanai turned to Waxman.

"So, the races you've been planning, they've already begun? Sounds like you're already testing drivers."

Waxman grunted an assentment and answered, "The races have been highly successful. The drivers are highly motivated to win, and the resulting races have become very popular among the soldiers. I envision one celebrated race that will weed out the unworthy while entertaining and distracting the masses."

"I'm surprised the drivers are motivated to win given how you've acquired them. They aren't likely to be very loyal given..." Kayanai gestured to the distant fires.

"Survival and prestige are very motivating," answered Waxman with the hint of a smile. "No, my drivers will train themselves to the limits of their potential. You'll see."

They finally entered the ship and were able to be seated in a large space behind the driver. There were few ships left that were designed just for waxen. Those that still existed were old—leftover from a time when there were more waxen drivers to pilot them. Since most new tech was made for regular-sized soldiers and citizens, ways had been found to adapt ships and weapons to accommodate the waxen.

Unfortunately for Kayanai, they usually involved them being cramped and uncomfortable.

Kayanai looked out the window as they flew low over the scarred deserts of Desigar. The landscape, though desolate, was made beautiful by the sun piercing the thick pink clouds.

The light made the sand shimmer and the metal plates beneath the sand sparkle. The area used to be a vast landing area for fleets of ships, but the sand blew over the old metal plating and nearly hid it from view. Before that, before the days of Waxman and his army of waxen, the land had been skinned in jesicore alloy.

When Kayanai was a child, he had seen images of this area of olden Desigar; the surface had been impossibly smooth and silvery blue as far as the eye could see, like a divine, endless lake. Now, the land was still flat, but its history had left it covered in broken shards of white rock and metallic sand mixed with jesicore dust. The ground no longer glowed but sparkled blindingly. Even the air was dazzling. High in the air hung particulates that had a cucoloris effect and reflected light like tiny mirrors, warping visibility and undulating like fog. It was a gorgeous but disorienting and confusing place to fly. Only well-trained drivers could navigate through the skies of Desigar.

As if in response to his thoughts, the ship swerved sharply, though as far as Kayanai could tell nothing had changed about their surroundings. Kayanai lamented never getting to see what the land used to look like before it was all torn up and plated.

Still, if it hadn't been mined, the jesicore couldn't have been used to create the strongest warriors the galaxy had ever seen, and I wouldn't be a waxen, he thought, wryly.

Sighing inwardly, Kayanai remembered how proud he'd been the day he was deemed worthy by Wax Adoor himself for the wax transformation.

The biochemical substance made from melted jesicore, known simply as 'liquid wax', was extraordinarily precious, and only the strongest, smartest, most courageous, most loyal soldiers were given the honor.

Except for the first waxen, mused Kayanai. There was no honor involved in what happened to them, poor bastards.

"Poor bastards?" Day interrupted. "We were told the first waxen were specially appointed." She coughed a bit, then continued, "That a worthy few were chosen by the fates... blah, blah... mystical mumbo jumbo. I take it that's not the real story?"

Throughout her tale, the waxen had been sitting cross-legged, back straight, her head raised enough for Day to see the movement of her mouth, but otherwise her face in shadow. Now she straightened her head, and though Day couldn't see her eyes, she felt the power of her gaze.

"You are young," the waxen said to her. "When time is a path that stretches behind you so far that you can't see the beginning, you come to realize how little the accuracy of such stories matter. One should only concern oneself about one's own story," she said, imperiously.

Day took a deep, painful breath and retorted, haltingly, "I may not have been around for hundreds of years, but I've learned when only winners write history books, perceptions are skewed, and those perceptions become reality. I prefer the truth."

A small chuckle came from the folds of the hood. "Stories evolve into legends, and legends are always preferred to the truth," responded the waxen, softly.

"But I will tell you briefly the story of the waxen, if you like." The waxen's voice changed slightly, almost as if she were telling a storybook tale.

"The very first waxen were indeed not treated honourably, they were, in fact, treated with complete disregard by the doctors and scientists working with them. Jesicore had originally been mined for strengthening the hulls of ships—no one cared about its organic properties until it was discovered that it had extraordinary similarities to skins cells. From that, the idea that it might be used to create indestructible soldiers was born.

Many creatures died before the scientists were able to create the first organically compatible liquid wax—one that could be introduced to a subject's bloodstream without immediately killing the subject. It seemed to not only make the subjects' skins as tough as armor, but it also had the extraordinary effect of making them grow larger and stronger. The problem was, though they didn't die immediately, the liquid wax always eventually killed the subject. Despite this, Desigar's military leaders were resolute. They wanted their indestructible soldiers. So, they found expendable human test subjects and brought them to the scientists—prisoners of war. The scientists experienced their first success in the form of a loud-mouthed prisoner named Jordi Tan who'd survived the latest process. The batch of jesicore infusion they used on him did not increase his strength and size, so he did not grow mad and burst like the others before him. Instead, only his skin took to the jesicore bonding completely, and he became armoured head to toe in a metallic wax—a very hard, very shiny, reflective material. But the scientists were greedy; they wanted the size and strength too. So, they continued their experiments. Still, on and on, every subject's brain would swell, causing them to go mad, then finally their organs would burst. In the end, they found a surprisingly simple solution and developed a new procedure. Confident that they'd found the answer at last, they carefully chose the biggest, strongest prisoner they had and infused the wax deep into every cell of his body. His skin hardened and he grew stronger and taller, slowly and moderately. He survived. The prisoner became everything they had dreamed of: the *ultimate soldier*. They were fools. As soon as the prisoner realized his strength, their dream soldier became their worst nightmare. He attacked, and in the end, no one in the lab or the surrounding headquarters survived. That soldier was Wax Adoor.

He freed the other prisoners, they learned the secrets of the liquid wax, and they became the first waxen, led by Wax Adoor, later known as just "Waxman". Waxman immediately saw the potential of his army to become a powerful force for peace and order."

Day's scoffing cough interrupted the flow of words, and a spray of blood flew and landed near the waxen's feet as though in protest.

"Powerful force of peace…" Day croaked. "Everyone knows waxen are brutes, imperialists interested in peace only if everyone does whatever they say."

The giant leaned back against the bulkhead and shrugged.

"There was a time when waxen were genuinely seen as defenders of peace. When Waxman approached the trade leaders of the splintered factions who ruled the galaxy— eventually called jars—and pledged that he and his army would work with them to stop the endless warring between planets, the leaders were happy to accept their help. Rebellions were brought under control and trade deals were kept as no one wanted to face the waxen army should they break the rules. Then came the real shift in power. The jar who controlled Desigar, then the central trade hub and richest planet in the galaxy, suddenly died.

"Convenient," said Day, pointedly.

"Very," answered the waxen, wryly. "Many called for Waxman to take the throne, but he humbly declined. Instead, he used his influence to have Jordi Tan take over the position of Jar of Desigar. The other jars became convinced that Tan would be the perfect bridge between the waxen and themselves and that he would look out for the interests of both. They were wrong, of course. Tan was Waxman's puppet from the first, existing only to be the target of the citizen's outrage as Waxman's every cruel act was made in his name. Tan declared himself Jar Emperor of the Galaxy, and through him Waxman established the Galactic Alliance which he ruled from the shadows with an iron fist. Waxman no longer spoke of bettering the small lives of regular people, instead he spoke only of eliminating threats and maintaining control. He extended his reach as far as it would go and tightened his grip at the slightest resistance. Any planet that tried to pull away was punished, and any leader that didn't agree with his vision was replaced."

"So that's how Desigar fell into the hands of that maniac," said Day, softly. "I hear it's a ruined mess now."

"Let's get back to Kayanai," said the Waxen, noting Day's grey complexion. "You don't have the time for us to get too far off topic. He was about to meet with Jar Tan, the Illustrious Jar of Desigar, who at this point was, as you said, a maniac. Kayanai was not looking forward to it."

Mano cut in again. "You seem to know a lot about what Kayanai was thinking and feeling all the time. How could you know what was going on inside him?"

The Waxen paused, considering how to answer. Then she said, "I learned his thoughts and feelings from Kayanai himself. I experienced every moment…" Her voice trailed off and she paused again. Finally, she shook her head. "I've learned many things I once thought impossible to know. Listen now, and no more questions."

CHAPTER THREE

Far off in the distance, Kayanai could see the ruins and towering spires of an old, great city, one of many left on the now mostly barren planet of Desigar. Though no longer packed with people and thriving cities, Desigar was still situated at the center of the galaxy and an important stopover for trade ships, and it was still home to the emperor of this region of space, Jar Tan. The towers of his great palace grew rapidly as the driver moved the ship lower, made a couple of deft maneuvers, and took them down.

Waxman and Kayanai walked out into the blinding light and bustling activity of a large makeshift tent city. In every direction, there were tent poles being raised, tarps being mounted, and machines and people moving crates, boxes, and an eclectic assortment of items. In the distance, at the edge of the tents, the low, flat-topped pillars of Jordi Tan's new palace rose. High above, partially shrouded in the hazy atmosphere, was a line of spaceships waiting to land and deploy their cargo.

The crowd parted automatically as the waxen strode along the dusty road. The sun beat down on Kayanai's muscular chest. A memory of being sunburnt as a child flashed in his mind.

At least I don't have to worry about sunburns now, he thought, wryly. Waxen were, of course, impervious to harmful sun rays.

"We'll be needing new clothing again soon," he said to Wax.

Waxman said, "Will you be volunteering?"

"I am always ready to give my blood as needed," replied Kayanai, stiffly. In his mind he added, "As you well know."

Palatial guards passed them, struggling under the weight of an enormous, outrageously ornate throne. Waxman and Kayanai glanced at each other, and their mouths twitched with amusement. The moment gave Kayanai a surge of nostalgia. Sharing a light moment with Waxman was rare these days. At the edge of the tent city, the air above the tents shimmered and obscured a towering shape in the sky. As they approached, it came into view the way a camouflaged creature seems to appear out of nowhere. It was a ship, a colossal cruiser docked perpendicular to the ground, so vast that the stern was hidden in the misty clouds and swirling air.

From out of the shadow directly underneath the cruiser, stepped Iran Crowne. He stood motionless in front of them like an advertisement for Waxman's army etched into the side of the ship's hull.

They were all still as statues. Waxman had taught them all the art of conserving energy.

"Wax is not wasteful," he would say.

"Be still until you must not. Move slow unless you need to attack, then move with all your speed and might to deliver your blow."

Conserving energy helps waxen achieve enormous sizes and keep from growing too fast. It was Waxman's utmost self-discipline that allowed him to maintain a height and size greater than all other waxen.

"Was that it? That was the secret the scientists discovered would keep the waxen from growing too large—conserving energy?" asked Mano.

A hiss of impatience escaped the Waxen's lips.

"No. It was simpler even than that. I suppose I can tell you; neither of you will be telling anyone else. The scientists discovered two things: first they found the perfect ratio of wax to blood to keep the subject from growing too quickly, and second, they discovered a method to slow down and even reverse the growing when it got to dangerous levels. The solution was outrageously simple: regular submersion in water. It allows Waxen to regain their strength and control the enlarging effects of the wax."

"So, all the waxen have to do to keep from growing too large is take a bath?" said Day, incredulously.

"Yes. It's a carefully guarded secret. The waxen see it as a point of pride to spread out their submerges in order to reach as large a size as possible. The key to that is to remain calm at all times and conserve energy. No one ever surpassed Waxman's height—no one dared—but Kayanai got very close. Although at this point in our story, Kayanai was bathing more often making himself the smallest he'd ever been."

"Why?" asked Day.

"Enough," said the Waxen. "I said no more questions. Listen and all will become clear."

Kayanai stood comparing Iran and Waxman's heights. Iran is past Waxman's chin, he mused. He's taller than me by quite a bit now. A tinge of shame pricked Kayanai, but he shrugged it off.

Iran even looked a bit like Waxman with his broad chest, steely eyes and very closely cropped hair, though clothing wise they couldn't be more different. Iran had taken to wearing a white shirt and dark pants, and it had become his signature look, while Waxman always wore combat fatigues and armor. Kayanai liked to joke about how far away Iran could be seen coming in his elegant attire, but he knew the shirt was a badge of honor for Iran. It showed that he wasn't scared, and it set him apart from the other waxen. Or maybe it's just that he knows it looks good on him, Kayanai thought, wryly.

The three waxen stood in a line and looked out at the pandemonium around them.

"Jar Tan has the whole place in an uproar," remarked Iran. "He ordered this place to be built in less time it takes to land a skimmer."

"Why all these dusty tents? Why isn't he in his palace? Is he bored of how fancy it is?" Kayanai's voice rose to a high whiny pitch. "These jewels are too bright! My eyes are tired! Take everything outside!" he said in an excellent imitation of the emperor.

Iran snorted with laughter and said, "Something like that. He said he wanted to be nearer the landing pads so he could get his gifts faster. Apparently, they couldn't all fit in the palace and it was taking too long for them to get to him. I have to say, people are loving the tents though. The whole thing has turned into a kind of festival with food stations popping up and— "

"Where is he?" asked Waxman, cutting Iran off and scanning their surroundings.

"There," said Iran, pointing.

They turned and saw a sort of amphitheatre made of silky, gaudy coloured fabrics larger than the other tents.

"He's really going over the top with this, isn't he?" said Kayanai.

"I don't think 'over the top' is in Jordi Tan's vocabulary," replied Iran.

"True. For him, this is normal," said Kayanai, chuckling.

Waxman was moving towards the amphitheatre before they had stopped talking. Kayanai and Iran shared a meaningful glance and followed.

As they entered the amphitheatre, they could see workers positioning decorations and palatial furniture, including the elaborate throne they'd seen earlier. As if they were doing a strange dance, the throne handlers were moving around the space in half steps left, right, forward, back...

"STOP!" A voice from behind them shrieked. The workers all froze, nervously.

"LEAVE IT!"

The workers clomped the throne down with palpable relief, and stepped away, some stumbling in sheer exhaustion.

The three Waxen turned toward the source of the voice and of the worker's anguish. As he turned, Kayanai squinted his eyes in readiness.

The Jar of Desigar, was blinding to look upon. Though his transformation had made him impervious to injury and highly resistant to disease and aging, the prototype liquid wax did not take on the colour of his skin, nor did it cause him to grow larger—in fact, the ruler was rather impish now due to his extreme age—but was still a spectacular figure. Light bounced off his shiny, silvery-blue jesicore skin, and created a radiant effect, making him sparkle and glow. The dazzling effect was magnified by the jewels with which he vainly adorned himself.

Through the slits of his eyes, Kayanai could just make out Jordi's smirk. Next to him, Iran had his hand up to block the rays. Waxman appeared unaffected by Jordi's brilliance and merely frowned down at him.

"I've had to move my chair outside!" Jordi bellowed as if he were speaking over loud machinery.

"I have decreed that all merchant ships must bring me gifts now. There are so many ships and so much imperial cargo to receive that I got sick of waiting for it to be brought inside —and with all my gifts it was getting far too cramped in there anyway—so I've moved the palace outside!

It's fun, isn't it?

Do you like it?"

He turned to Waxman with a hopeful look on his face. As emperor, he enjoyed bullying others, but Jordi Tan was fully aware who held the real power, so his voice took on a fawning tone when he spoke to Wax Adoor. Waxman acknowledged his words with a slight nod.

"Crowne! Blu! Come see me open my presents!" Jordi gamboled over to a pile of chests and crates being opened by two assistants.

As he gestured them impatiently out of his way, the light bounced off him and danced around the space like light reflecting on a tree over moving water. When Kayanai looked back at Jordi from the dazzling display, he saw that the emperor was looking down into a crate with a maniacal grin.

Uh oh. That look… thought Kayanai.

"Come see these!" Jordi hollered, excitedly. Then he gingerly pulled out two huge, wet, writhing eels and held them aloft, proudly. Seeing no response from the waxen, Jordi shrieked and threw the eels at their feet. The waxen glanced down at the eels floundering in front of them but stayed motionless. For a second, Jordi looked furious, then he broke into wild laughter.

Suddenly, his face turned angry again as he screamed, "Someone better get over here and clean up this disgusting mess!"

Instantly, two cleaning mechs jumped forward and started clearing the eels away. Jordi stalked over to his throne, threw himself into it, and began barking orders to have his presents be opened and brought to him. More huge boxes and items were carted in by more labor mechs, and the noise inside the amphitheater became cacophonous.

Eventually, Waxman raised his voice over the ruckus. "Jar Tan."

It was all he had to do. Under Waxman's unflinching gaze Jordi paused, clapped his hands and yelled,

"We're going! Move people!"

Then the party moved out into the long line of crowds, and they set off towards the new makeshift landing area created for the fleet ships returning from deep space.

Kayanai, exasperated by the whole process, let his mind wander, as he so often did in those days.

Why does Waxman bother keeping Jordi as his puppet? he thought. When he was first emperor, Tan was extravagant and full of himself, but at least he was stable. Now, he's a complete madman. If Waxman wants a figurehead to hold office while he leads campaigns against dictatorships, uprisings and Shrie Shrie attacks, why not instate someone who isn't completely insane? Looking at Waxman's proud profile, Kayanai answered his own question in his mind. Because Waxman loves that he is seen as the people's protector while Jordi is seen as an evil tyrant forcing his cruel will upon his subjects, that's why. But surely Waxman must realize that by now the stories that are told about him.

The truth that Wax Adoor controlled the emperor was a favourite narrative of insurrectionists, and rebel groups had spread the fact far enough that most planets in the Alliance considered Waxman as much of a dictator as Tan. Kayanai knew this from the conversations he'd had with countless captured prisoners.

Kayanai broke out of his thoughts and was dismayed to realize that Jordi had ripped a huge gun bigger than himself from the top of an armoured tank mech and was now wielding it unsteadily. He turned all his attention towards keeping an eye on Jordi in case he decided to suddenly start ᴊlasting everything with his new toy—easier said than done now that Jordi was out in the sunlight. He was so bright it was nearly impossible to look at him directly.

Jordi slowed down, obviously straining under the weight of the weapon. Thankfully, he stepped into the shade of a tarp reducing the glare off his skin, then lowered the end of the gun and rested it on the ground.

Kayanai breathed a sigh of relief. The three waxen were able to follow him under the tarp as it rose as high as the giants, though Waxman's head brushed the top. Kayanai watched to see if Waxman would break his own rule of moving only when necessary to reach up to stop the top of the tarp from flapping at his smooth head. Waxman stayed still as a stone, though his face showed his annoyance. Kayanai looked at Iran to share in the amusing moment, but when he saw Iran's worried expression, he looked back at Jordi.

The cannon gun was suddenly back in Tan's hands and pointing at the line of gift givers, and with a squeal of laughter, the emperor fired a volley of white fire at the crowd. The fireballs vaporized everything down the centre line and left people and crates at the edge on fire. Instantly there was chaos as crowds of people tried to flee screaming through the smoke and flames.

The falling bodies and escaping people exposed a row of cages full of exotic creatures that had been affected by the blast. Their roars of pain and fear were so intense they could be felt as well as heard.

"A captive audience!" yelled Jordi with glee, and he aimed at them and fired again.

The containers were built for space travel and impact, so were able to absorb the blow of the attack, though several of the unfortunate beasts were set on fire. One of the cages was knocked over from the impact, causing the gate to become unhinged and allowing the large creature inside to break free. Its thin body moved on six heavy legs ending in sharp claws, and its long neck and head snaked quickly in different directions flashing its narrow eyes and long fangs. It clawed its way off its back using surrounding people to regain its footing. Once it was up, it continued its assault on those nearby, slashing and tearing in its fear and fury.

Jordi Tan loved the bloodbath. He cackled and cheered and insisted his entourage of toadies and lackeys join him in the revelling.

Kayanai stepped forward next to Waxman, waiting for a signal that would allow him to interfere. Waxman was a statue. Then, he made a tiny movement—not a signal, but a slight stiffening.

Kayanai followed Waxman's gaze and saw a patch of small figures who were in dangerous proximity to the rampaging beast. They were wearing drivers uniforms. That was why his interest was piqued. Regular citizens dying didn't bother Waxman, but drivers were a different story.

"Surely he'll give the signal now!" thought Kayanai. But Waxman had relaxed again.

Another Waxen was already taking action.

The creature had a handful of drivers cornered against a tower of crates. One tried to dash away, and the creature pounced, chomped down the driver's head, and shook him till his body flew away and fell headless leaving a smack of red on the dusty ground.

Jordi shrieked with laughter. His shaking body caused the light bouncing off him to dance across the chaotic surroundings.

He stopped suddenly.

There was a newcomer on the scene.

The beast was running again, and behind it, moving even more swiftly than the creature, was the new Waxen. In a flurry of movement, the Waxen jumped, wrapped his arms around the creature's neck, dug his heels into the ground, then twisting his arms he snapped the creature's neck. Bodies, blood, and fur rolled to a stop as the creature's killer released his hold and stood up to full height. There was a pause… then the sudden silence was broken as the crowd burst into applause and cheers.

"Genjai," thought Kayanai, "of course he shows up just to save the day and drink in the accolades."

Genjai's long dark hair fluttered in the wind as he walked towards them, all the while smiling charmingly at his adoring audience. His face took on a more stoic, Wax-like expression when he arrived before Waxman. Though much younger, he was nearly as tall as Kayanai. Waxman gave him the honor of a slight nod.

Jordi smashed the gun to the ground in frustration and stomped over to them.

"Can't you at least let me have some fun?" he whined, angrily.

Ignoring the complaint, Waxman said, "This mess can't be here when Kolorov arrives."

"Doesn't matter. She's not coming," Jordi said, looking at Waxman smugly.

At Waxman's steely expression, Jordi's thin smile dropped, and he looked down and began fiddling with his robes, clearly avoiding Waxman's eyes.

"Jordi," said Waxman, his voice soft and menacing. "Did you not recall all the fleets? Where is Kolorov?"

"There's no room!" squeaked Jordi, defensively. "Have you seen The Station? Since it, apparently, needs repairs so badly, half of it is shut down, and the other half is crammed so full of ships, you couldn't fit a Kitlen fighter in there! I have enough angry commanders grilling me about why the station is under repair and why we have recalled every fleet in the Alliance to Desigar, and I didn't want to add Kolorov to the mix. Can you imagine telling Chief Commander Kolorov to land all her ships down here in the dust with all these others? She'd bite my head off. Besides, my palatial grounds look like a parking lot as it is!"

Waxman appraised Jordi for a moment, then he reached out his enormous hand, placed it heavily on Jordi's shoulder and said, "Let's have a conversation about this." Jordi winced as Waxman's hand gripped his shoulder painfully.

"Uh yes, we can step into—." Jordi's voice rose to a yelp as Waxman shoved him into a nearby tent and followed him in, menacingly. Kayanai and Iran looked at each other.

"Gengai and I'll keep watch out here," said Iran.

"Yeah, you'll fit in that little tent better than us," grinned Gengai.

Kayanai ignored Gengai. "Fine," he grunted and ducked under the entrance.

The tent was empty inside other than Tan and Waxman. Kayanai stood blocking the entrance, entertained by the sight of Waxman holding Tan by the throat while the emperor babbled nonsensically. Waxman cut the babbling off with a squeeze. "I told you to recall the entire fleet," growled Waxman, "and I specifically mentioned Kolorov. I don't want to hear about your complaints. You have all the might and wealth of the Alliance at your fingertips. Get your underlings to solve the problem. I want Kolorov here."

Jordi, eyes wide, opened and closed his mouth like a fish, and Waxman released his grip.

"I'm trying to tell you that it was Kolorov herself who didn't want to come here," Jordi sputtered. "She told me that she protested being recalled for no apparent reason, as her fleet was needed in the Raderak system—a breach of the Wellspring Accord, apparently. Kolorov's prime directive is to defend the Wellspring Accord, and there's no room here so I thought—"

"Your thoughts are not why I made you emperor. Recall Kolorov immediately."

"But the Wellspring Accord—"

"I do not need you to explain to me the Wellspring Accord. I wrote it. Recall Kolorov. Or Desigar will need a new jar."

"I can see you're plotting, Waxman. Just remember who the citizens bow to. You know you need me to keep my reputation."

"Tend to your flock, Tan. We are just passing through," murmured Waxman, dismissively.

Waxman issued a hand signal to follow as he walked away from Jordi. The waxen followed one by one. Last to leave, Iran said over his shoulder, "Don't worry, Tan. We couldn't possibly tarnish your spotless reputation."

They chuckled as they walked away, knowing Jordi was glaring at their backs.

Moments later, the four waxen were standing in front of a cargo ship still splattered with blood from the victims of the gun blasts. A soldier ran to greet them.

"Sir, I made sure to raise the shields when the shots began firing. The cargo is intact," he said, proudly.

Waxman responded with a stony stare.

The soldier laughed nervously. "Of course, you probably guessed that from the fact that we're all still alive."

Without appearing to move, Waxman's expression turned threatening. It was clear the soldier had said something he shouldn't.

Kayanai turned to question Waxman, "What—?"

"You'll be tired after leading that ambush," interrupted Waxman. "After you and Iran deliver this ship to the Station, you must get some rest. Genjai, you're with me."

As they boarded the ship, Iran and Kayanai shared a look. Waxman was keeping things from them. It was clear they were taking some dangerous cargo to the Station—but what, and why?

CHAPTER FOUR

"I accept all that you have told us except one thing; no way Waxman wrote the Wellspring Accord." Day's face twisted skeptically.

The giantess cocked her head. "Waxman has been the true power behind the Alliance from the beginning. It is our most important, most sacred agreement, signed by every planet in the Alliance. Why would you doubt his hand in it?"

"Because it was written to protect families. Are you telling me deep down Wax Adoor cared about mothers, fathers, children… ?"

The Waxen gave a small, amused snort. "No," she replied. "The Wellspring Accord was not created out of concern for citizens' safety. As the waxen gained power, fear of them grew among regular citizens. This was not what Waxman wanted. He wanted the waxen to be seen as protectors of the people, he knew it was safer to be loved than hated. Waxman sensed the people's growing distrust and became aware that leaders were considering backing out of the Alliance to address their citizens' concerns. He concocted a plan to have the council put forward a peace accord that would allow Alliance members to mark planets and territories as areas untouchable by violence. These regions would become safe havens for child-rearing and would be separated from areas of trade and production where skirmishes and fights were more likely to break out. The Wellspring

Accord was enthusiastically received among leaders and citizens, and the waxen's pledge to uphold the accord gave them the reputation as peace-keepers that Waxman was looking for. Attacks on Wellspring planets became abhorrent to all, and the waxen's swift justice against any who breached the accord turned them from monsters to heroes in the eyes of the people."

"You expect me to believe Waxman created the Wellspring Accord just to improve his reputation?"

"Is it so unbelievable? By creating the accord, Waxman not only cemented his army's place on the side of good in the collective conscious-ness of the citizens of the Alliance, he also used the accord as an excuse to quash rebellions in their infancy. It was very easy for Waxman to attack a planet and afterwards accuse its citizens of breaching the accord with very little evidence."

"Whoa, that's…" Day paused, her mouth open as she contemplated the implications of what she'd just heard. "I can't even deal with that. Go back to Iran and Kayanai. They'd just figured out that Waxman was having them ferry some kind of explosives up to the Station."

"Yes, Kayanai had just added this to his list of things that were troubling him. Let's continue."

/ / /

Iran shifted uncomfortably in the flight chair that had been cobbled together for him.

"They could have done a better job adapting this junker for us," he said, irritably, as his huge hands worked the tiny controls with surpris-ing delicacy.

Next to him, Kayanai was checking readings in his own makeshift chair.

He replied, "Could be worse; Waxman could have asked the show-off down there to drive, and we'd be crammed in here with him," he gestured with his chin, "swaggering around." They both looked out to the tarmac below and saw Genjai leaning on one of the torn and twisted command chairs next to him. He smirked at them and gave them a little wave.

Iran made a noise of disgust. "Did you notice how much bigger he's gotten?"

"Yeah, especially his teeth," observed Kayanai.

They both chuckled.

"Let's get out of here," said Iran as he manipulated the controls.

The carrier lifted off, and immediately, one of the other ships vying for the prime landing spot moved in to grab the empty space on the deck. Iran directed the carrier up and over the vast parking lot of fleet ships, and soon in front of them they could see the Umbilical Tower.

The tallest structure ever built; the great Umbilical Tower stretched from the surface of the planet all the way to the outer edge of Desigar's atmosphere. Its outer cylindrical casing was constructed out of a light, yet extraordinarily strong, transparent material that allowed observers to marvel at its inner mechanism. In the center was a thick cable around which an endless series of spiralling platforms moved in a rising cork-screw. The direction of the twisting depended on whether items were being shipped to or from the planet. On each circular platform were massive sphere cargo containers filled with precious supplies. These spheres moved up the turning screw making it unnecessary to go through the bother and expense of having every cargo ship land and take off from Desigar. Instead, they mostly docked at The Station.

Iran and Kayanai could just make out The Station above them as the last tendrils of pink atmosphere faded to the black of space.

One couldn't help but be impressed by the view. A marvel of engineering, the Station was the main refueling port for ships visiting Desigar and the biggest and busiest station of its kind in the Galactic Alliance. It's round shape and tight orbit made it seem as if Desigar had a small moon covered with small, evenly spaced craters. Each round "crater" was, in fact, an entry point to the station. Ships flew into them and waited to be pulled into one of the many connecting corridors, each of which led to a docking area. This was a complicated process as the outer shell of the station remained still while the inside was in constant rotation to create artificial gravity. It was an outdated system — The Station was very old— but it still worked.

It's ordered entry points and complex tunnels always gave Kayanai the impression of a home for tunneling creatures.

With nothing to do till they were assigned their entry port, Iran sat back and sighed.

"Jordi Tan is right, you know," he said.

Kayanai raised his brows in surprise. "That's probably the first time anyone's ever said that. What is that idiot right about, exactly?"

"Waxman is plotting something," answered Iran, putting his hands behind his head and his feet up on the console. "I'm telling you, something's coming. Four of us back from off-world and just as all these fleets are coming in to resupply... I've got a nasty feeling that we're about to be shoved back in the mud."

"Speaking of mud..." Kayanai nods at Iran's dirty boots on the console.

Iran scoffed. "Really? We've junked this ship already. What's a little dirt gonna do?"

"Are we waxen or are we a bunch of careless, filthy mercenaries?" Kayanai balled his fists in frustration. "Is this who we are now, Iran?"

At Kayanai's outburst, Iran looked at him, both eyebrows now raised, then slowly dropped his feet. "Yeah, alright. I hear you."

He sat back and sighed. "Being a waxen used to mean something different. Now... heck, I don't know. Something's changed."

"We used to understand why Waxman gave us the orders he gave us! We used to be like brothers, fighting side by side, killing only when we had to... for the greater good." Kayanai got his voice under control. "That's what's changed."

They avoided each other's eyes and looked out the window. The Station loomed overhead.

Iran huffed and shook his head slightly. "You think so? Yeah, maybe. Or maybe it's us that's changed."

Thinking the same thing, both men's eyes trailed downwards till they found a sinister black shape floating in space off in the distance. It was the Infidel.

The outpost, christened the Infidel by those who feared it, hung in near Desigar space like a black spider in a web of stars. Dark now, only its silhouette against the light of the stars behind it betrayed its presence. Back at the beginning of the Shriean war, the Infidel had appeared out of nowhere.

It wasn't there and then it was. For a long time it had been a bright hive of activity, with Shriean ships bursting forth from it seemingly endlessly.

Then, on the day Cal brought Kayanai and Iran back from Gengaru, it suddenly went dark. The Infidel appeared to be dead.

Appearances, however, can be deceiving. Though time passed and it remained quiet, the Infidel also maintained its constant position on the edge of Desigar space. The lack of orbital decay meant that it wasn't truly dead, just dormant. Now the station served as a constant reminder that the Shrie Shrie were still out there somewhere, watching and waiting.

"Do you still think about it?" asked Iran, quietly.

"Every time I close my eyes. And sometimes even when they're open." Kayanai cleared his throat and nodded towards the black shape in the distance. "That place better stay dark."

"I don't think Waxman wants it to. That's what scares me." Iran looked at Kayanai, worriedly. "We both know he'd love to finish that war."

Kayanai met his eyes. "If the war starts up again, it'll be Cal who finishes it. You and I both know that too. If Cal returns, he'll kill us all."

The console beeped.

Iran broke the gaze and said, "We just have to hope we never see him again, I guess," He pressed some buttons. "Time to dock. Let's go deliver whatever it is we're delivering and go get some rest."

"Yeah," said Kayanai, strapping in. "At least that's one order I'm happy to follow."

The light from the stars and arriving ships poured into the dark room and fell on Kayanai like moonlight. He was alone.

Iran had disappeared saying he had better things to do than rest. This was fine with Kayanai. He was grateful for any moment of peace.

It appears his chamber had been made just for him. The massive room was dominated by the view of the endless arrival of ships outside, and a long rectangular pool that stretched the whole length of the transparent wall. The expanse was so great that the ceiling disappeared into the darkness. These things, along with the water surrounding him, made Kayanai feel like he was floating in space among the stars. To some this would have felt intimidating, but space had never frightened Kayanai. The bright stars, the warm swirling colours of nebulae, the vastness and emptiness had always felt welcoming to him.

After gazing out for a long time, Kayanai looked down to rest his eyes. He saw a splash of blood across his chest. He knew it wasn't his. Jordi's rampage? No, he'd been too far away. Then he remembered the driver Waxman had crushed.

In his mind flashed the image of the driver's head trembling while he pointed his gun at it. At one point the man had bravely looked up at Kayanai—it was when he'd talked about loyalty.

Kayanai tried to remember his eyes, what colour and shape they were, but he couldn't.

He submerged fast and swam hard, willing the water to wash away the reminder of death from both his body and mind. When he reached the other side of the pool, he felt better.

Water stopped the ache of his constantly growing limbs and cleared his mind.

Kayanai tried to focus on the black space between the stars to quiet his thoughts, but his attention was caught by the elegant dance of the ships. Most of the movement was automated and happened along well-ordered paths, but there was one ship that zoomed in past the others and executed a complicated maneuver that allowed it to dock ahead of the others. Kayanai watched in admiration.

There's the difference between a driver and a mere pilot," he thought. I can pilot a ship if I must, but what real drivers can do is incredible… like Gengai. Kayanai sighed. He didn't want to think about Gengai.

As annoying as he was, Kayanai grudgingly had to admit that Genjai was talented. No one else could have managed the Gengai Maneuver.

/   /   /

"The what?" Day cut in again. "I've heard of Kayanai, but not Gengai." Day wanted to ask more, but she stopped. Talking was exhausting.

Her guest's eyes focused on her.

"You've never heard of Gengai or the Gengai Maneuver?"

Day's blank stare was her answer.

"That's disappointing. There's an appalling lack of education among young citizens these days," sighed the Waxen.

Day could still roll her eyes. "Where I grew up, we learned how to stay alive. No time for much else."

"Clearly, you did not learn enough," said the Waxen, looking at Day's ruined body, pointedly.

From the corner, Mano's sudden voice surprised them both. "If you hadn't slammed into our ship and Day had been taught how to fight waxen, you wouldn't be here right now. Day masters anything she's taught."

Day smiled briefly at Mano's loyalty.

"Well then, be quiet and allow me to teach her some history," retorted the Waxen, never taking her eyes off Day.

"Before the Shriean War, the only threat to the Alliance was the occasional uprising. Then came the day we found out we are not alone in the universe. Without warning, the Shrie Shrie: a faceless warring species of great technological advancement, struck deep at the center of our trade routes. Desigar was nearly laid waste. Our forces were decimated. We were losing so badly it was near impossible to keep up the illusion that we were winning. But there was no way to change our defensive position. We needed to find a way to go on the offensive, but we didn't know where they were coming from. As they could phase immediately from one place to another, we had no way of tracing their route back to their home system."

"Then came Cal. He was one of the best drivers we had, despite being wild and reckless. He was flying with Kayanai and Iran, and, as usual, they were doing well. They had already destroyed two ships and were right on top of another and firing at it mercilessly, when suddenly the ship phased. When the Shrie Shrie blip out of being and pop up somewhere else, a vertical shaft of light almost like a blade of energy surrounds their ships. Well, Cal, Iran and Kayanai were so close to that Shrie Shrie ship that when it phased, they got caught in that shaft of light and disappeared with it. Waxman was furious that he'd lost his best fighters, but he also felt he'd been shown how they might be able to turn the war around. He hatched a plan: He would order a driver to purposely fly close to an enemy ship, get phased back to the Shrie Shrie planet, and then find a way to communicate the planet's location to the fleet.

"Many thought it was a pointless suicide mission without Cal, their so far best driver. But Waxman had Gengai up his sleeve. Gengai was a talented young driver, cocky and brave, and what he wanted most of all was to be Waxen. Waxman had very little of the Liquid Wax left, and he'd been saving it for a long time, but he promised Gengai that if he brought back the location of his enemy, he would make Gengai the very last Waxen. Gengai agreed.

Not only did Gengai successfully phase out with a Shriean warship and find the Shrie Shrie home planet, he was able to stay alive long enough to piggyback another enemy warship and return to Desigar space in one piece. Waxman greeted him with honors, gave him the last of the Liquid Wax. Gengai became the last of our brothers."

"Is it true?" asked Day. "Will there never be another Waxen?"

"It's true," answered the Waxen.

"Good," said Day, sourly. "It means nothing to me if the waxen die out. They have become as ineffective as with the Wellspring accord itself. But enough of this. Back to Kayanai. We left him soaking and shrinking in his pool of self-doubt. Let us return there now."

The peace of Kayanai's surroundings was doing nothing to calm the commotion in his mind. Now it was thoughts of Gengai that troubled him.

"He acts like he's bigger than me already," thought Kayanai. "He's slowly moving into my position as Waxman's right hand. Waxman suspects my feelings. He senses my loyalty wavering."

But it wasn't just this that bothered Kayanai. Gengai was also a reminder of what Kayanai used to be: strong, loyal, and most of all, fearless.

His mind swung to unwelcome thoughts of Gengaru, the Shrie Shrie home planet. It was among its purple jungles, oppressive heat, and within its endless mud that Kayania's nightmares were born.

He breathed deep as he felt angry pride swell in his chest. Gengai thinks he's stronger, but Iran and I survived that jungle. He doesn't know what strength is, he thought, balling his hands into fists. Anger. Fear. They were always with him now.

"Enough!" he growled, aloud.

The sound jolted him out of his turmoil and with great effort he pushed the thoughts away and breathed deeply to try and regain his old calm.

"With stillness comes wisdom." The old Waxman saying was exhaled softly from his lips.

Outside, the returning fleets of ships continued to pour in. It seemed impossible that even The Station could hold them all.

A beep in his ear from his com broke the silence. He touched one of the circles on his cheek and a grating garbled noise filled Kayanai's right ear. Finally, the encryption decoder kicked in and Waxman's low blunt voice filled the room.

"Find Iran and get on the Crimson Axel. She's fueled, loaded and docked for you at The Station. Then pick up Genjai and I. I have a surprise for you."

Kayanai was already surprised. Waxman's voice held an unusual hint of suppressed excitement.

As he rose out of the water, he pondered, A surprise from Waxman... what's he playing at? And why do I get the feeling I'd rather not know?

CHAPTER FIVE

Like a teary eye, the bright blue water planet Anavah shimmered bright and lonely in the surrounding black emptiness. There was very little land on Anavah, but what land it had was extremely fertile, making it well suited as an agricultural outpost. Its tiny population grew food of such quality and quantity that they were "strongly encouraged" to join the Alliance. It was a sad, but beautiful place. The light from its great distant sun reflected off its vast oceans, swirled into golden clouds, and shone in through the viewport of the waxen's ship.

The Crimson Axel was truly a pleasure to pilot, and Kayanai was enjoying the flight despite his misgivings about what they were doing in what was essentially the middle of nowhere. It was surprisingly agile and responsive for its age and size. Since it was built for waxen, it meant that he didn't need any hacks to fly it—a real treat. The powerful war carrier, one of the few remaining ships built for their size, was a threatening-looking ship, with batteries of cannons, a menacing gun tower atop her armoured camo deck, and spiked fins that ran down the length of her hull. Through the signature V-cross pilot vest he wore he could start and stop the vessel at his whim, and with his voice and body he could make the ship execute any movement he wished, though he kept his maneuvers simple, given he was no driver. Behind him sat the real expert, Gengai, sulking that he wasn't driving, and Iran, enjoying Gengai's irritation.

There was no need to switch control to a driver as the flight plan was well within Kayanai's capabilities: fly to Anavah and land at the coordinates. Anavah was remote, and the landing area was expansive; a child could manage it.

To his right sat Waxman, whose quiet excitement was electrifying the air in the cockpit and adding to the overall sense of occasion. Waxman being in such a good mood was unusual, to say the least.

Kayanai shifted his weight and slid the ship through the thick atmosphere, then shifted again to keep the vessel level as they descended. Genjai leaned in and said, "You should increase the descent speed whenever you hit those hot zones."

Kayanai ignored the comment knowing it would irritate Gengai further. He could feel Iran's amusement behind him. They broke through the clouds and below them stretched a coastline with craggy cliffs over a long, black sand beach.

"Land in that space beyond those trees just before the ridge," ordered Waxman.

With a series of quick efficient movements, Kayanai brought the ship down. It landed with a light thump that tore ground and plants under the Axel's weight.

Through the ship's bridge viewport, all they could see was blue as the distant horizon of the ocean faded into the sky.

They followed Waxman out of the ship and onto the rocky cliff. Without pause, Waxman began to descend a gully down to the beach. With bouncing steps, he made his way quickly down the steep hill. This exuberance was not something the others had seen in him. Gengai immediately jumped behind him, keeping up by sliding recklessly. Kayanai and Iran followed cautiously. Kayanai touched a portion of his vest which set the Crimson Axel into standby mode. Her wing flaps settled in unison as if a beast going into deep sleep.

As he stepped down onto the glittering black sand, he heard Iran in front of him take a deep breath. For a second he was surprised—though the climb down was steep, such a feat would never normally wind a Waxen

— then Iran stepped aside and Kayanai realized the reason for his sharp intake. The beach was hauntingly beautiful.

The sun was beginning to set, and the sky ranged from golden orange to cobalt blue. Rushing waves left delicate patterns of white foam stark against the black shoreline, and the silhouettes of flying creatures swirled peacefully overhead.

Three waxen stood shoulder to shoulder: Kayanai, drinking in the beauty; Iran, alert and wary; Gengai, impatient and skeptical.

Waxman stood slightly ahead of them, exultant with expectation. They stood and the time drifted by like the salty wind tousling their hair. Kayanai could see how much taller Iran was than him now, and Gengai was gaining on him.

I'm shrinking, he thought. Too much bathing.

The waiting continued. Cold dread began creeping up his neck. He tried to will it away.

Waxman said softly, "Wait for it. It's coming."

Kayanai could see the hairs rising on the back of Iran's neck.

He senses it too, thought Kayanai, something is coming. Something is wrong.

Then he saw it. Out in the ocean, a small wave grew larger and rounder. But it was not a wave. Slowly, it lifted and took the shape of his nightmares.

From the deep, a Shriean warcruiser began to take shape, a dark, lean, oval-shaped tech large enough to carry a fleet of deadly warships in its belly, and from whose bow a mass energy weapon could erupt at any moment. To Iran and Kayanai, there was no more horrible sight in existence.

Time stopped.

In what felt like slow motion, Kayanai dropped to a knee, reached for the rifle cannon on his back, pinned it with the hack, and brought his eye to the sight. He hunted the horizon line till he saw the dreaded black shape. The rifle itself was useless, but the telescope confirmed the threat. Out of the corner of his eye, he saw Iran turn.

The Axel, thought Kayanai. He dropped his weapon and lunged back towards the hillside. Next to him, Iran was moving with similar speed. They stretched their enhanced capabilities to the utmost and bounded up the cliffside in a series of powerful leaps.

Unaware of the panic of his soldiers, Waxman watched with a growing smile as the wave broke and the sinister shape of the Shriean war cruiser rose silkily from the sea. Gengai stood stock still in shock as Waxman laughed in delight at the sight of the sleek black ship dripping water off its hull like drool from the jaws of a monster.

Kayanai and Iran burst over the hill and pounded their way to the Axel. As they reached the side gun port entry, Kayanai touched his vest to activate the ship's defense mode. The side gate ramp lowered, and a heavy caliber side cannon locked into place, while Iran, who was a leap ahead of Kayanai, jumped into the operator position. Kayanai bolted in through the dark entrance and sprinted for the control bridge.

As he reached the helm, he tapped the controls on his vest to engage the engines and power up weapons, then he locked himself into pilot position. The viewport chimed on and showed the overlay readout over the view outside, and he lifted the ship off the ground. His heart was slamming in his chest, but he didn't notice it. His fear was background. Like the ship, he was now in battle mode.

Through the viewport, Kayanai could see Waxman and Genjai down on the beach standing defenseless with a Shriean threat hovering in front of them. He yelled into his com, "They're sitting ducks down there! Be ready!" and began bringing the Crimson Axel into attack position.

The moment they were in range, Iran opened fire with the side cannon. A continuous volley of flashing energy blasts hammered into the nose of the Shriean warcruiser. Then when they reached the right altitude and position, Kayanai let fly a series of hydra-torpedoes.

If they had been fighting a warcruiser like their own, it would have been a devastating attack, but despite the fact that every blast landed on target, there was no discernible effect.

"Just have to keep them off the guys down there till I can hit them with an atomic," thought Kayanai.

Suddenly, Waxman's voice came over the com. "Stop firing! It's not an enemy ship!"

"The hell it's not!" yelled back Iran, keeping up the assault.

"Get down!" added Kayanai, "I'm launching an atomic!"

"Kayanai, stop!" roared Waxman.

But Kayanai would never stop; not while his enemy was out there. He fired the atomic. It launched vertically in order to target from above for most effect. Then Kayanai shot off some more hydra-torpedoes to keep it busy till the atomic found its target.

Up to this point, the Shriean cruiser had done nothing to defend itself. It just hovered there motionless above the waves. Now the nose of the ship lit up and a single beam shot out and effortlessly obliterated the arriving torpedoes before they hit.

"Cease fire!" came Waxman's voice again, but Kayanai and Iran were so focused and strained they were only dimly aware of the sound.

At this point, realizing he'd lost control of his men, Waxman's finger reached for the small white comms ring on his cheek, switched channels, and yelled over the comms to the alien ship, "Atomic above you! Take care of it! Protect my ship at all costs!"

Switching comms again he roared, "Kayanai. Get down here and pick us up!" He then signaled Gengai and they turned to make their way back up the hill to close the distance.

"Heading your way," answered Kayanai. With perfect aim, Iran kept peppering the Shriean warcruiser while Kayanai brought the Axel about and made for the cliff.

Just as he began descending, a vertical beam shot from the bow of the Shriean ship and met the atomic and there was a noiseless flash. Then a ringed ball of light blossomed in the sky, and moments later a thunderous sound filled the sky.

The blast caused the Axel to veer off course and knocked Waxman and Gengai off the hill bringing them crashing down onto the burnt sand. Kayanai fought to regain control of the ship and managed to stop it from spinning and brought them around.

Over his comms he cried, "Iran! Are you alright?"

"I'm okay," came Iran's strained voice, "I had time to duck in."

With no time to feel relief, Kayanai looked out to see what had happened to Waxman and Gengai. He could just make them out far below on the beach. Their clothes were mostly burnt off, and they were slowly getting to their feet.

Iran's voice came over the comms. "The side cannon was damaged in the blast. Do you want me up there?"

"We're landing on the beach. Stay down there and be ready to help them in," replied Kayanai.

He could see the Shriean ship was now turning back towards the beach, and he let go another volley of torpedoes, then lowered the Axel abruptly down to the beach. From his perch outside the ship, Iran reached down his hand into the swirling sand and gestured for Waxman to jump. Waxman ignored the hand and launched himself up with a tremendous leap. He landed next to Iran and pushed past him into the open entryway while Iran grasped for Gengai's hand.

Tattered and blackened, his expression deadly, Waxman thundered full speed toward the command room and Kayanai.

In the command room, Kayanai raised the Axel up and away from the incoming enemy ship. Just as he was bringing the Axel around to fire another atomic, Waxman burst into the bridge and slammed into him.

Kayanai was taken by surprise and knocked out of his chair. But still in battle mode, he grasped at Waxman and yanked him off his feet as well. They both tumbled and smashed into the control screen, which cracked, and the display flickered. Kayanai jumped to his feet and tried to throw himself back into the command seat, but Waxman gripped him and thrust him hard at the back wall.

"They're coming!" screamed Kayanai as he tried to body check Waxman out of the way to get back to the helm. Waxman was able to keep his balance and wrap his giant hand around Kayanai's neck. Kayanai ignored the hand, pressed a button on his vest and reached for a control on the helm.

Finally, Waxman lifted Kayanai in the air and yelled, "That's enough!"

Kayanai's crazed eyes snapped up and focused on Waxman.

When their gaze locked, Kayanai could see himself reflected in Waxman's furious eyes. He saw the hand tight around his neck. He reacted.

Kayanai's hand shot out and wrapped around Waxman's neck. They held the position for a long moment, their faces reddening, muscles flexing, fingers curling. Then slowly, Waxman lowered Kayanai back down. There was surprise in Waxman's eyes. Kayanai's mad determination gave him strength to match Waxman's own— something neither of them had imagined possible.

His eyes still burning into Waxman's, Kayanai suddenly shot his free hand out and hit the controls, launching another volley at the Shriean cruiser.

Waxman growled and strained violently at Kayanai to get him away from the controls. Suddenly, he froze, and his expression changed as his eyes focused on the viewport beyond Kayanai. In Waxman's eyes, Kayanai could see a great glowing ball of orange light reflected and growing bigger.

There was a blast, the floor spun under their feet, and they were tossed about amongst smoke, fire and chaos.

When the movement stopped, they looked up and saw the Shriean warcruiser directly ahead. Its nose began glowing orange with building energy. Waxman reached for his comms as Kayanai rose and attempted to make for the command controls, but they were too late. Another energy blast hit the Axel making it shoot back and slam down onto the edge of the cliff. It paused there, creaking and groaning. Then it teetered for a moment.

Then the ship slowly, inexorably, slid off the edge and crashed down heavily onto the beach, collapsing like a great wounded beast.

/ / /

The blackened Crimson Axel was camouflaged against, and partially buried in, the black sand. The scarred hull sizzled and steamed.

In the pile of twisted metal and wreckage that was once the command bridge, each Waxen breathed heavily and waited. The noise of wrestling metal had ended, and all, now, was quiet. The air was thick with the smell of burning material, and smoke glowed in the daylight streaming through a crack that split the ship lengthwise along the top. Kayanai found himself blinking dazedly at a shaft of light from the setting sun shining across his leg. His eyes adjusted and he gazed up through the crack into the sky.

"It's still out there," he thought. For a moment, he waited for the shadow of the enemy ship to block out the light. Then he tore his eyes away and scanned the room for the others. Through the sparking, dangling cables and smoking debris, he was able to make out the large shape of Waxman shifting his weight against the far wall.

Suddenly, he noticed the hull was vibrating against his palms. The hum turned into a loud cracking noise as a large plate of the top hull broke free from the rest of the ship and crashed down on him from above.

Kayanai found himself on his back with an extremely heavy chunk of metal pressing down on him. He tried to call out to his friends, but all that escaped him was a strangled grunt.

"Kayanai!" he made out Iran's voice. "Where are you?"

He could hear shifting and clanking as Waxman and Iran moved around in the debris, and Waxman's voice calling to him on his comm.

"Kayanai. Can you read me?"

Kayanai couldn't move to activate his comm, and he couldn't call out, so he did the only thing he could— he strained at the wreckage, raising his knees enough to free one of his arms slightly so he could push his hand against the metal and unpin his other hand. Now both arms were able to push upwards. He took a deep breath and heaved with all his might. He could hear the voices of his companions, but he couldn't make out what they were saying through the sound of the blood pumping in his temples. Slowly, agonizingly, the metal panel began to tilt upwards. Finally, with a roar Kayanai straightened his trembling arms, and above him he saw the large hands of his friends grip the panel and lift the hulking slab of metal off him. It crashed onto a pile of rubble.

Kayanai squinted against the dust and sand blown into the air, and the reddish gold light streaming in from the widened crack in the roof above them and saw Waxman's granite face glaring down at him.

"If you want to stay alive, do what I say," Waxman said, quietly.

They locked eyes, and finally Kayanai nodded. Waxman held his hand. Kayanai grasped it and was yanked to his feet.

"Glad you're okay. Now let's get out of here," coughed Iran.

"We'll climb out," said Waxman. By piling various debris onto what used to be the control panel, they were able to create foot holds that allowed them to scramble up and out of the wreckage of the Crimson Axel.

Outside, the sun had just dipped below the horizon. Kayanai glanced back at the Axel; what had long been a flying fortress for them was now a hulking mass of garbage. Feeling no time for regret, Kayanai looked forward across the water, and froze.

The beauty of the view was now marred by the Shriean warcruiser hovering over the water directly ahead. It was some distance out, but well within firing range. Iran and Kayanai were about to take a mighty leap down to the beach to find cover when Waxman bellowed, "Stop!"

They stopped.

"It's our ship," said Waxman, emphatically.

There was a long pause while Iran and Kayanai looked at the ship in wonder as they struggled to process Waxman's words.

"Follow me," said Waxman. Then he leaped off the edge of the wreckage and floated down, down until he landed heavily onto the sand below. One by one, his waxen followed suit, starting with Gengai, then Iran, then finally, warily, came Kayanai.

CHAPTER SIX

Down on the beach now, they stood shoulder to shoulder, watching the ship. All was still. All was cobalt and indigo except the black of the sand and the line of gold where water met sky.

A question rose to Kayania's lips, but before he could speak, Waxman raised his arm and said, "Look there."

Looking like a tiny insect, a figure could be seen moving along the top of the enormous Shriean ship. Then it moved to the very tip of the smooth bow, and stood for a moment, silhouetted against the sky.

Kayanai's breath caught in his throat. Who the hell is that? he thought.

Iran asked, his voice full of wonder, "That can't be a Shrie Shrie. No way they have curves like that."

Whoever it was dove gracefully off the bow and slid cleanly into the water with barely a splash. Moments later, the figure surfaced and began swimming towards them. Without realizing it, Kayanai stepped towards the water, his eyes fixed on the person swimming towards them. "Who...?" he thought, his brain unable to complete the thought. He moved forward as if something tugged at him. The figure was close enough now that they could see it was a woman. A very tall woman.

As the woman found her footing and her torso rose out of the water, Kayanai let out a gasp. He knew that pale skin and that long, long dark hair.

He knew that beautiful, powerful body that he'd fought next to so many times—though it had grown taller and slighter. He waded out to meet her and they both stopped, their eyes drinking in the sight of each other.

"Jevan," he whispered.

She smoothed her wet hair back, cocked her head and said,

"That was some welcome, old friend."

Her green eyes flashed at him. It was always hard to tell if she was amused or angry. The waves crashed around them. Kayanai tried to bring words to his lips, but finally gave up, shook his head and reached out to her. Jevan stepped into his arms, and they clasped each other tightly.

Kayanai lifted her up and growled happily. In response, she slipped from his grasp, kicked his leg out from under him and flipped him underwater. Through the water, he could see her grin as she pressed her knee against his chest. He quickly grabbed her arm, swung himself up and pummelled her down into the water. He held her there a second then pulled her out again and held her up over him. He paused with her above him, enjoying the way the water dripped from her hair and lashes and the mix of happiness and annoyance on her face.

"Better put me down, old buddy," she said.

"Or what?" he said, jokingly, then changed his mind. He knew how quickly she could move when she was furious. And he was tired.

"Okay, okay," he said, and he lowered her down respectfully. Their eyes didn't waver once.

Jevan stood back and finally broke the gaze and walked towards Waxman. She extended her palm to him. He reached out and pressed his palm against hers, then nodded approvingly.

"Sorry about the Crimson Axel," she said.

"When I said, 'defend the ship at all costs', I didn't mean at the cost of our lives," he responded, wryly.

"Still getting the hang of that thing," she replied.

Iran voice cuts in. "Impossible! Khran!? How… ?"

Jevan turned to Iran and slapped him hard on the shoulder.

"Good to see you too, Iran," she said, looking him up and down and noting his torn and dirty clothing. "That white shirt... Maybe it's time to update your wardrobe."

She came next to Gengai who was standing with his arms crossed and an irritated look on his handsome face. He clearly didn't have a clue what was going on, he just knew he was not the center of attention, and he didn't like it.

"Look at you, Genjai!" she said, admiringly. The last time I saw you, you were the finest driver around. And now, you're one of us!" She stepped forward and threw her arms around him, taking him by surprise and nearly overbalancing him. She was similar in height, though Gengai was bulkier.

"Thank you for your sacrifices," she said. "I'm honoured to have you as a brother." He fumbled the hug awkwardly, but when Jevan stood back his face had softened.

"Enough," said Waxman. "We've made enough noise for the whole planet to notice us. Let's get off this beach." He turned to Jevan.

"Hide her."

Jevan tapped a command onto her vest and raised her arm towards the sea. A moment later, a great monster of metal rose from the water next to the Shriean ship. The alien warcruiser, which had felt large and ominous, was now dwarfed by a ship many times its size. Despite its enormity, the appearance of this ship filled Kayanai with wonder instead of alarm. Firstly, it was so damaged that the fact it was still operational was astonishing, and secondly because it was a ship he knew.

"Kolorov'son's command ship!" exclaimed Gengai.

"Or what's left of it," said Kayanai, ruefully.

Jevan gestured and the Regent moved till it was hovering overtop of the Shriean ship. She tapped her vest again. "Open cargo door 2," she commanded, and with a loud clank and whirring hum, a huge opening appeared on the bottom of the Regent.

Then, as she lowered her arm the command ship descended, and the alien ship disappeared inside her.

"Close hatch." Jevan tapped her vest again, and the Regent was now hovering directly over the waves.

"Let's go," said Waxman.

Jevan immediately turned, waded out into the water and dove towards the command ship. The other waxen dove in after her.

It was dark under the water. Jevan activated a light on her vest and suddenly Kayanai could see sea grasses rippling around them and a large-eyed creature swimming in and out of view.

They swam fast and hard till the command ship loomed above them.

They surfaced and Jevan opened a small entry hatch into a cargo room. Jevan led them out and they ducked through a series of small, dark, battle-scarred hallways.

As they came to a lift, they passed a blood-splattered wall. Kayanai suppressed his urge to question Jevan about what happened. He knew she would tell her story when she was ready.

Gengai was not so patient. "What the hell happened here?"

Ignoring him, Jevan said, "There's no way we'll all fit in the lift."

"You and I will go up first," said Waxman to Jevan. To the rest he said. "Head to the bridge."

They stepped into the lift and were gone. A moment later another lift arrived. Iran and Kayanai stepped in. It barely fit the two of them.

"Hey!" said Gengai. The door closed on his angry face.

Through his laughter, Kayanai managed to speak the command to take them to the bridge.

"He's so beautiful when he's angry," said Iran. They both laughed again. Kayanai said, "I can't believe we're laughing."

"Why not laugh? Everything's crazy."

"What do you think happened here?"

"I don't know. But Jevan does, and she better tell us, 'cause I'm sick of not knowing what's going on."

"I'm with Iran." Day's voice was a hoarse whisper. "This story of yours is damned confusing."

"It's your story," replied her guest.

"My story! None of this has anything to do with me." The effort of speaking caused Day's head to spin.

"It has everything to do with you." The Waxen studied Day for a moment. "You are going to lose consciousness soon."

"I won't," said Day, determinedly. "What could I possibly have to do with Jevan Khran?"

"What do you know of her?"

"Not much. She used to be a big deal. No one cares much about her now. No one's seen her for eons, as far as I know." Day said, haltingly. She paused and looked at the Waxen curiously. "Maybe you have? Sounds like you know her well— she still alive?"

The Waxen hesitated then answered, softly, "I knew Jevan once. She was strong, resolute, unwaveringly loyal… Then her loyalty changed…" Her voice trailed off. She reached down, unclipped a flask from her vest, popped the top, leaned over, and placed it by Day's hand.

"Drink this and stay awake. I will tell you of Jevan Khran."

Day looked at the flask dubiously, but then thirst overrode her misgivings, and she lifted it feebly to her lips and drank. Immediately a delicious warmth spread about her body and her mind became clearer.

"You could make one hell of a living selling this stuff," she said appreciatively.

The Waxen ignored her and continued.

"When Kayanai and Iran disappeared to the Shriean planet Gengaru, Jevan made a promise to herself that she would do everything in her power to find them again. So, when Gengai returned with the coordinates of the planet's location and scanning data that suggested her friends had survived the jump through space, she volunteered to head the mission to Gengaru.

"It was the largest fighting force of waxen ever assembled. Every Waxen able to reach The Station before the launch date was ordered to join the fleet. There were nearly ten thousand of our soldiers, all assembled in our greatest ship, The Shiva Axel.

Chief Commander Kolorov assembled a fleet of her best and brightest and put her own son in command of the flagship, The Regent. They felt they couldn't lose.

"At first, all was well. They travelled fast and far—farther than any of them had travelled in their lives. Then while travelling through a dark zone, they hit a nebula that caused all the ships' circuitry to go haywire, and suddenly they were hit with communication blackouts, sensor failures and, most worrying, a malfunction in The Shiva's water recycling system.

Soon there was only a small amount of water for thousands of waxen to bathe in. Pain and madness were on the horizon. Fights broke out, and a power struggle turned to a mutiny. Waxen are famous for their constancy and loyalty, but take away their water…

"A battle for control of The Shiva began. Jevan saw what was coming and tried desperately to contact Kolorov's son for help, but communications were still down. She tried to take a small transport ship to The Regent, but before she could one of the mutinying groups got the sensors back up and attacked The Regent—apparently the idea was to steal their water—but in their madness they reduced the fleet's flagship to a ruin. Jevan was on her own. But she was a survivor, so she devised a desperate, terrible plan."

"She crept through the ship, collecting provisions and equipment and avoiding the frenzied fighting, and made her way to the holding cell area. It was full of dead waxen. They'd been locked up and left to grow mad and kill each other or burst in agony. She barricaded herself inside, alone with hundreds of corpses. For a long, long time she waited there, staying alive the only way she could…"

The Waxen paused. Day, her imagination alive with images of horror, waited impatiently for the story to continue until eventually she said, "What? What did she do?" Finally, in a sharp, flat voice, the Waxen continued.

"She drained the corpses and bathed in their blood. That's how she stayed alive." The Waxen took a deep breath. "She stayed in that nightmare for a long time till slowly the sounds of battle outside quieted, then ceased. She exited her refuge and made her way to the bridge. Once she reached it, she tried over and over to contact Kolorov's son and the rest of the fleet, but she was met with silence."

"Jevan was alone in a crippled ship, lost in deep space, and surrounded by the torn and mutilated corpses of her people. She had nothing to fight, and no one to fight for. So, she despaired. Slumped in the command seat, Jevan looked out at the endless stars with dead eyes, feeling as empty as the corpses she'd drained."

"Then, slowly, her emptiness was filled by a longing for battle. With every fibre of her being, she wished she'd fought to the death with the others until it was as if her body had dissipated and all that was left was an image of the enemy."

"Jevan blinked and saw a marker beep on her console. The viewport lit up and scanners revealed a Shrie Shrie warcruiser. It was dormant and floated as if abandoned. As she clasped the arms of the command chair to rise, Jevan blinked again, and she was inside it. Instantly, the ship was hers. That is how Jevan escaped her floating grave and acquired the ship that would change her life."

"Wait, what?" Day's voice broke the silence that followed the Waxen's tale. "That an enemy alien warcruiser appeared out of nowhere, I can believe— they do that—but how could Jevan just be inside one suddenly? And how could she control it? Why would the Shrie Shrie do that??"

The Waxen spoke slowly, almost to herself. "I don't believe the Shrie Shrie did anything. I think Jevan did it herself. She willed that ship to appear, and she willed it to carry her."

"That's impossible."

"Your belief in its impossibility doesn't make it any less true. Jevan could not only pilot the enemy ship, she was also able to communicate with the fleet that had disappeared and discovered that Kolorov'son was still alive. He had been rescued from the Regent and had moved the rest of the fleet away from the Shiva Axel to keep it safe. They had recovered most of their systems, aside from long range communications, and were continuing to Gengaru as planned. She was able to contact Waxman and tell him all that happened. In return, she learned from him of the Shriean ships blinking out suddenly and The Infidel going dark, and of Kayanai and Iran reappearing on Desigar, much changed and full of tales of trying to survive in alien jungles. According to them, it was all because of Cal. They had been half dead when Cal had swooped down in a Shrie Shrie ship and picked them up out of the jungles of Gengaru. He told them the war was over and that he was taking them home, but that if they ever tried to find him or the Shrie Shrie again, they would all be killed."

"So, this Cal was actually responsible for the cease fire?"

"Yes. While Kayanai and Iran were fighting to stay alive in the jungle, Cal somehow made contact with the Shrie Shrie, and became... like them."

"What does that mean?"

"Cal could fly their ships, he could phase in and out, and he understood them… knew them somehow."

"He was a traitor then."

The Waxen tilted her head as she considered, then said, "Cal no longer answered to Waxman, so in that way he was a traitor. But Cal was something else… something different… something new."

"Enough! I'm tired of being confused. Get back to Jevan. I see now that Jevan must have returned with the Shriean ship… and Kolorov'son's ship as well."

"Yes. The fleet had abandoned it as it was too damaged for battle, so Waxman wisely told Jevan to use it to transport the Shriean ship in secret back to Desigar space."

"Huh, he should have told Jevan to keep it hidden in the Regent when he showed up with Kayanai and Iran." The thought made Day suddenly bark a short painful laugh. "Waxman was like, 'Iran, Kayanai, look at this Shrian ship we got! Pretty great, hey?' Meanwhile Iran and Kayanai think they're being attacked and have lost their minds," she said, chuckling and wincing. "Ouch, laughing hurts."

"It was a poor decision on Waxman's part, yes." It was hard to tell from her voice whether the Waxen was annoyed or amused by this.

Day sighed and shifted painfully. "So, what did Kayanai think of Jevan's story?"

"He was … troubled. Yes, let's get back to Kayanai."

The Regent was en route back to Desigar space with the Shriean war-cruiser hidden safely in its hold. On its bridge the waxen were gathered listening to Jevan's story. As she finished, Kayanai shook his head, his face ashen.

"Ten thousand waxen dead… there are so few of us left." He lowered his head into his hands.

Iran was pacing, his face furious. "How come you didn't try to save anyone else?" He stopped and pointed at her. "I know why. Because you don't give a damn about anyone but yourself."

Jevan raised her chin and scowled at Iran. "The only reason I went out there was to find you! I went on that mission to try and save your hides, remember? I don't expect gratitude that I suffered all that just to come back to find you safe and sound, but I expect some acknowledgement of what I accomplished. Think of it, boys! We have their tech, and we know where they are. We can still win this war!"

Silence followed. Kayanai turned towards the bulkhead he was leaning on. Jevan could see he was fighting to keep calm. Waxman was looking at her with pride. Iran was looking at her horrified.

Finally, Iran spoke. "The war is over."

"Not till I say it is," said Waxman.

Kayanai turned around, slowly. He had managed to get his face under control, though his eyes were hollow pits of dread.

"If the fleet attacks Gengaru, the cease fire will end. The fleet will be destroyed. Then Cal will return, and he'll destroy us all. He made that clear. Is ten thousand of our lives not enough?"

Rage and disappointment rose in Jevan. "Cal!" she burst out, "Cal is one little man! You think he is stronger than you— stronger than us?"

Iran stepped forward. "You didn't see what we saw. Cal can do… anything."

Jevan leaned in and looked Iran straight in the eye. "You used to say that about us. Now all you do is whimper." She spat out the last word and turned away in disgust.

Iran's voice rose. "You don't know— "

Kayanai cut in. "Jevan. You know me, and I'm telling you, we should call back the fleet."

"It is my decision." Waxman's voice was not raised, but it commanded their attention. "I did not agree to any ceasefire. The fleet will reach Gengaru and they will attack. The Shrie Shrie think their speed and trickery make them stronger. They will find out they are wrong. Iran, Kayanai… show me your hearts. Show me there is victory there!" He let his voice ring out, then he added. "Or will we triumph without you?"

Kayanai was angry and afraid, but his face was stone. Waxman's words had pricked his pride. Finally, he raised his head and said, calmly. "I believe this is madness. I have made this clear, and you will not listen. But I will stand with you, as always."

Iran sighed and jerked his thumb towards Kayanai, "Yeah, what he said."

Waxman looked hard at them for a moment, then nodded. He turned to Jevan. "I wish to see the newest addition to our fleet."

"Come," answered Jevan. She turned on her heel and headed out the door to the narrow corridors off the bridge. She began leading Waxman down to the hold where the Shrie Shrie ship lay. As they walked, Waxman said, "Their loyalty is slipping." Jevan's lips narrowed with determination. "I'll talk to them."

"You will hold us together, as always. Well done, my dear."

Jevan managed to keep tears from pricking her eyes. The words filled her heart. To be given praise after all she'd done. She tried to avoid looking at the bloodstains on the corridor walls.

After some deep breaths, she asked, "What if I can't hold them together? To me it looks as if Kayanai is already coming apart. The way he fought on the beach. He wasn't himself; he was desperate."

"If they are going to break, we're going to need to know about it before it happens. Watch them." Jevan nodded. They stepped into a lift. When the door closed Waxman said, "When you have shown me the ship, I would like to see your other gift to me."

Jevan paused.

Waxman scrutinized her carefully. "Are you reluctant?"

Jevan glanced up, quickly, "No. The baby is in my chamber. She's in a life support cryosphere. I have a mech looking after her."

"But on the ship, you cared for her."

Jevan's chin went up. She knew what Waxman was hinting at. "I cared for her because I know her worth. In fact, I was just thinking that she could be even more valuable to us than first we thought. I think we can also use this baby to test Iran and Kayanai's loyalty."

Waxman's eyebrows raised slightly. "Interesting. I want to hear more. But still our priority must be to use her for my original purpose. All must happen exactly as planned."

The doors opened. They were now deep in the Regent's hold. Jevan led Waxman around the corner into a cargo space, and there hovering silently, he lowered his head and looked into her eyes intently. "Assure me you can do what is required. You'll be able to phase? Accurately?"

Jevan's eyes flashed defiantly and locked with his. "Are you questioning my ability? She stepped closer. If you're worried, I can't do what I say I can, why don't you try it yourself?"

Waxman reflected for a moment, then placed his heavy hand on her shoulder and answered, "I'm confident in your abilities, if you are confident. You will not fail me."

He let the full weight of his hand and his words rest on her, till he was sure she was calmed, then he turned away. "The return of Kolorov'son's ship must be as quiet as possible."

"Then the engineers and those manning our entry port must be sworn to secrecy."

"It's been done. The whole port side has been shut down "for repairs." Only those loyal to me are working and preparing our ships for victory. I assure you; they know their lives depend upon their discretion. I want to keep this from Jordi Tan especially, or he'll sneak to Kolorov."

"Sounds like he's becoming a problem." cut Jevan.

"He's an insect biting."

"Insects can be poisonous."

"I can swat him whenever I want."

"Let me know if you'd like me to take care of it."

Waxman treated her to one of his rare, slight smiles. "Thank you, Jevan. I appreciate your zeal. Rest your mind. I assure you, my dear, the future is ours."

CHAPTER SEVEN

As soon as Kolorov'son's ship was safely locked into Waxman's private docking space, Kayanai retreated once again to the bathing chamber. He hoped it would allow him to heave the weight off his mind long enough to be able to think properly, but each worry pressed on him like a layer of rock, and the water only added to the heaviness he felt.

"Think, Kayanai. There must be a solution. You must do something," he chided himself. He sighed. Concentration was impossible; all he wanted to do was shrink and hide.

Taking a deep breath, Kayanai sank down and held himself underwater. While he was submerged, something told him he was no longer alone in the room. He swam towards the entrance and surfaced at the edge of the pool.

Jevan stood leaning against the doorframe on the far side of the room, her form half lit by the pale light streaming in from the windows. He was struck by how small, even delicate she looked against the enormity of the chamber. He knew it was an illusion. She was nearly his height now, though he was still bulkier. She uncrossed her arms and moved towards him, moving with her usual cat-like confidence, though he sensed a slight uncertainty in the slowness of her pace. Kayanai's robe was on the other side of the pool. Scurrying over to grab it did not appeal to him, nor did staying in the pool while she talked down to him. Instead, he pulled himself out of the water in one easy motion and stood naked in front of her.

Jevan stopped. The only sound was the water dripping off his body. Kayanai could see her chest rising and falling quickly. She focused on watching the steam rising off him.

"The water must be quite warm today," she said, casually.

"What are you doing here?"

"Just wanting to see my old friend."

"You're seeing him."

The corners of her lips twitched.

"Indeed." Then her expression hardened. "Are you really my old friend though? The Kayanai I remember wouldn't have lost his head on that beach. He wouldn't have fired an atomic at close range against one small ship. That was a desperate act, Kayanai. I know the difference between being ready to die and wanting to die."

The words bit. There was a long silence as Kayanai turned from her and walked around the edge of the pool. He picked up his robe and wrapped it around himself, then avoided her eye by looking out the window.

"Those ships out there," he said, "They won't stand a chance if Kolorov'son's fleet makes it to Gengaru. The Shrie Shrie will return, and they will kill us all" He turned back to her. "I don't want to die, Jevan. I don't want any of us to die. Not like that."

"We're not going to die! The enemy is strong, but not as strong as us! Not if we stand together!" She looked at him, imploringly and stepped towards him. "My friend, my Kayanai knew his strength. He could do anything."

Kayanai trembled. His voice cracked. "Then I must no longer be your Kayanai."

There was a pause as they both tried to stop the tears stinging their eyes.

Jevan moved to him slowly, speaking tremulously. "All I went through I did because I wanted to bring you home. Now I've found you, but you're still lost. Please... come back to me."

She opened her arms, and Kayanai fell into them. His tears were hot on her shoulder. They held each other for a while, and she stroked his hair. Then slowly she moved her fingers down his head to his chin which she then gripped and pushed so she could look into his tear-stained face.

"Oh Kayanai," she murmured, shaking her head, disappointedly, "What happened to you?"

"Gengaru is what happened."

The voice from the door made Jevan and Kayanai move apart quickly. Kayanai turned away, wiping his face, and Jevan turned to face Iran, who was standing, arms crossed, his bulky shape outlined by the light from the open door behind him.

"Tell me," Said Jevan.

Iran walked in, his boots echoing loudly, and his white shirt gleaming in the dimness.

"I'll tell you about Gengaru," he said as he leaned on one of the thick metal columns that lined the room.

"We were blasted down the moment we flashed into Gengaru's sky. I don't even know what hit us. We all survived the crash, but when we climbed out of our wrecked ship, we found ourselves deep in a jungle. Gengaru's a nasty place, Jevan, full of creepy purple plants and large hungry creatures. And the mud… the mud was everywhere."

"Cal wanted to stay with the ship, but Ky and I both felt it was too obvious a target. So, we grabbed a few provisions and left Cal just sitting there in his driver's seat. Soon after the Shrie Shrie flew down and blasted the ship to smithereens. Bye bye, Cal—so we thought. That was the beginning of our long nightmare. Every day was worse than the last. We ate what we could find but found very little water. We soaked in mud to keep our growth in check. And we fought. We fought off the creatures who kept trying to eat us, and we hid from the Shrie Shrie who kept coming and coming no matter how many of them we dodged."

Iran had been telling the story to the smooth polished floor, but now he looked up at Jevan.

"The worst thing was that we couldn't really fight the Shrie Shrie. Anytime we came out into the open, their ships would fire down at us and turn the area around us into an inferno. All we could do was hide."

Iran called over to Kayanai, "How'd we live though all that, hey Ky?"

Kayanai had moved to the side of the pool and was staring at the water, unmoving. He didn't respond.

Iran looked at his friend, sadly. "How we kept going, thinking there was no way out, I'll never know." Iran looked back at Jevan and grimaced. "Well, actually, I guess we kind of did give up. At one point we decided to try to lure a ship low enough for us to jump from a tree on top of it to see if it would phase out with us, but we knew we were just going to get ourselves killed. Didn't matter. We just wanted it all to end. So, there we were, up in this tree, looking out through the branches, and we see this Shrie Shrie ship flying like we'd never seen before. It was amazing. The ship was darting and soaring like a living thing, like some crazy new species."

"No."

Startled, they looked at Kayanai.

He spoke slowly, as if speaking took effort. "There was never a creature that could fly like that… as if like graceful, deadly lightning."

Iran nodded. "Yeah, that was the other thing that got our attention. See, this Shrie Shrie ship was attacking the other ones. It was blowing them up in every direction, no matter how many came at it at once. It moved so fast that the other ships were exploding, and you couldn't even tell why. It was like the sky was on fire. And let me tell you, the rain from that fire storm was something fierce. But we didn't move. We couldn't stop watching. Then came the real miracle: through the smoke we could see the other ships weren't blowing up anymore, they were… flying together… like they were dancing. They moved as if they were one creature. It was… well, beautiful. And suddenly, the others were gone, and the one ship was just… there, hovering right in front of us. We were so stunned we just stood there with our jaws on the ground below. Then the hatch opened, and guess who was standing there smiling?"

"It was Cal. I wish you could have seen him, Jevan. It was like I'd never seen anyone alive before. It was almost like he glowed. When we saw him, we didn't shout or cheer the way we would have at one of us who'd blasted away so much of the enemy, 'cause, well, I guess because we could tell he wasn't one of us anymore. He stood there grinning, then asked us if we'd had enough of Gengaru. We just stood there like broken mechs, so he asked us if we wanted to go home. I guess we nodded or something because he waved his arm and said, 'Come on, then'. The ship moved close enough for us to jump in. I don't really remember any instrumentation, just that it was dark and smooth. There was a flash of light, and in the blink of an eye, we were home. We followed Cal out of the ship and onto the sandy plates of Desigar."

"Looking back, I don't know why we didn't ask him anything, but anyway, we didn't. He didn't speak to us until just before he left us. Cal turned to us, and I'll never forget it, he said, 'It's over for now. I hope next time I see you again, you'll be ready to die.'"

"As soon as he left, The Infidel went dark, and the Shrie Shrie vanished. So that's why we don't want to go back to Gengaru, Jevan. 'Cause our death is there— yours, mine, everybody's."

Unsettled, Jevan paced around the room, musing.

She turned to Iran and spoke. "Your story does make it sound like Cal caused the ceasefire. Waxman says there's no way to really know why the Shrie Shrie stopped their attack. He says they could attack again at any moment."

Iran shrugged. "That's true, technically. We've never communicated directly with the Shrie Shrie. We don't know why they stopped and there's no official ceasefire."

Kayanai looked at him and said sharply, "Cal made it happen. And he'll keep the ceasefire. Unless we break it. You know that Iran."

Jevan whirled to him furiously, "Neither of you know that. You don't know anything! All you have is guesswork and feelings. The Shrie Shrie could show up again at any time— Cal with them. Don't you see? Cal has switched sides! If he is as powerful as you say, all the more reason for us to go to Gengaru and destroy him!"

"How do you plan to do that, exactly? Convince him to kill himself?" said Kayanai. "You can't destroy him."

"He's a man and therefore vulnerable," she replied with pointed scorn. "We can defeat him. Waxman has a plan." Jevan looked at them hard. After a moment she said, "I will tell you, but so help me you'd better be worth my trust."

She took a deep breath and spoke putting as much of her considerable persuasiveness in her voice as she could.

"Waxman has been gathering an armada such as the galaxy has never seen before. Yes, the ten thousand waxen are gone, which is a great loss, but they were just supposed to be the beginning, anyway. Waxman has been collecting fleets of ships and first-class drivers from every planet under his influence since Kolorov'son left. Half of them are staying here and being docked on the side of The Station hidden from The Infidel. When the time is right, they will attack The Infidel and destroy it! The other half is being sent to Gengaru. He plans to attack the Shrie Shrie here and there at the same time. It's unlikely the Shrie Shrie will be able to withstand the armada, but even if they do, we'll eventually have new ships based on Shriean tech. When that happens, it'll be all over for sure! No planet could possibly stand up to such a force. We'll be unstoppable."

Silence followed her speech. She looked at them, hopefully, looking for a sign that they'd been convinced.

Iran finally said, "You think our engineers will be able to figure out their tech? You said yourself you have no idea how you can fly that thing, or how it came to be floating outside your scuttled ship."

Jevan hesitated, then said coolly, "I don't know how it works, but I don't know how a pilot's vest works either. I'm not an engineer. I'm sure they'll figure it out."

Again, Iran argued. "You'll need Kolorov's fleet. You know she's soured on Waxman, and she's already lost her son. She'll never agree to send any more ships to Gengaru after what happened to her son."

A sly smile appeared on the corner of Jevan's mouth. "Kolorov will agree to anything we ask of her. You see, I brought home more than just that Shriean ship. It turns out one of Kolorov'son's crew was pregnant with his child when they left for Gengaru. She gave birth on the journey. I brought back that child."

Iran processed the information slowly. Finally, he said, "You have Kolorov's grandchild?"

Jevan nodded. "You see, we hold all the cards. She turned to Kayanai. "You're very quiet, Kayanai. What do you think of the plan?"

Kayanai looked like he was barely listening. Again, he was watching the ships outside. He whispered, "The death of everything."

Jevan's patience ran out, and she yelled at him, "That's it? That's all you have to say? Coward! Do you fear death so much?"

Kayanai was silent.

She looked at Kayanai and Iran with her arms open, and though still angry, she nearly pleaded with them. "My brothers! How is it that you can hear this plan and not be filled with excitement?? You used to be eager for battle! Where is your pride?"

It was Kayanai's turn to lose patience. All the pressure inside him finally exploded free and he spat out, "My pride! We always speak of our pride! What do we have to be proud of? Our might? Our power? For what? What does it achieve? Peace and prosperity throughout the Alliance? You know that's a lie! All we've done is grow and grow our power till finally we found an enemy more powerful than us. Now the only thing standing in the way of us and them is Cal. And you and Waxman are bent on destroying him!"

The room was thick with shock. Kayanai had never said these things, even to Iran.

Jevan was a statue. Kayanai had no inkling of the inner struggle his words caused in her. Finally, Jevan spoke. "So," she said, her mouth twisting, "You've chosen Cal's side. You no longer want to be one of us."

Kayanai's rage dissipated as quickly as it came. He walked to her and looked deep into her eyes, which were full of hurt and disappointment. "No, I've not chosen that," he said, softly, but very firmly. "When the time comes, I'll fight. Though I feel no love of what we do anymore, I'm with you, Jevan. To the death."

Jevan knew he meant it. Slowly, her eyes softened. Then she nodded and walked to the door. When she reached it, she turned and said to Kayanai, "We're not going to die. I promise."

Jevan took all the strain and tension in the room with her as she left, but she took all the warmth and colour as well. The chamber now felt cold and dark.

"Damn," said Iran, after she was gone. "Notice she didn't include me in that final statement."

"I'm sure she meant all of us. I wish she wasn't wrong."

"Yeah, she's wrong, we're wrong, everything's wrong. I'm sick of it! We need to do something, Ky. "

"I know. We're going to. I just don't know what."

"Kayanai, the brave and mighty," Day scoffed. "He doesn't sound all that brave to me."

"You know nothing of true courage," The Waxen's voice was icy cold.

Day brow furrowed and her voice rose in protest, "I've been in battles. Once I—"

The Waxen cut in, "You've never battled the Shrie Shrie," she said bitingly. "You've never heard a warship coming in fast above you, the scream of their engines chilling your blood, knowing that when the sound stopped, many would be dead, perhaps even you. Then, if you survive the blast, you might catch a glimpse of one, like a terrifying insect with multiple spike legs beneath its body and long flat wings alongside its narrow cockpit before it, and you watch it change position faster than your eyes can follow and defy the laws of motion or watch it disappear completely, ready to kill again somewhere else. You've never seen warcruisers ejecting clouds of those deadly warships, each one capable of discharging an energy blast that can cut through the strongest of our ships. Kayanai and Iran faced those waking nightmares over and over, weaponless, helpless, trapped in a hostile jungle with no chance of escape. Most wouldn't have survived a sunset. They survived countless sunsets, and in the end, they escaped. It was only after their return that fear took hold of them. It's true that Iran seemed to fear only for his small life, but Kayanai feared annihilation, the end of everything he cared about. Could you overcome such a fear? Kayanai did, as you will hear. What do you know of courage compared to that?"

Day considered the Waxen's words, then answered, "I suppose courage does come easier to those who have nothing to lose. I know that from experience."

"True courage is being filled with dread and empty of hope but acting anyway. I no longer care for courage; it is a silly thing to strive for. Better to be beyond courage, to not need it. Now, stop making foolish interjections, and let me continue."

CHAPTER EIGHT

It was an underworld of endless night where no one ever seemed to sleep: Shade City. Anyone who'd ever visited that subterranean land beneath the plates of Desigar, knew that its dangers and its pleasures exceeded even its infamous reputation. Covered by a massive, inverted cone that opened at its centre just enough to fit a cargo cruiser through, it was originally built to protect Desigar's finest military and scientific minds from surface offenses, and eventually it became the home of the military's most secret and important experiments. It was deep within the bowels of this underground fortress that the waxen were born, and it was their revenge upon those that created them that brought about its ruination.

For a long time it sat empty, till eventually scavengers and vagabonds moved into the space and over time an anarchic city, run by both organized and disorganized crime, grew out of the ruins. Eventually the bustling metropolis became a favourite spot for soldiers on leave and Shade City was born. With layers upon layers of dark geometric shapes, and its glittering lights, and its vast forms of entertainment and violence, it was a beautiful, horrible place.

The power structure of Shade City was simple: if one was considered upper class, one was allowed to move among the levels higher up and closer to the rim, and as the levels dropped, so dropped the rank of the people living there. In the upper levels daylight found its way through the rim and offered some sense of brightness and freshness, which is why this is where the more opulent and wealthier of the crime class spent it's time entertaining high-ranking officers and pretending to be nobles.

When they tired of posing as sophisticates, they would amuse themselves in the next levels down, where it was still luxurious, but where the rich mixed freely with those who indulged any debaucherous whim.

The mid-levels were popular with common soldiers, as rougher sports and indulgences could be found there. As one moved lower, the dark piled on heavier and heavier, no matter how many glittering lights were lit, until it crushed down the hearts of those eking out their livings in the depths, never seeing daylight. The depths were brutal and dangerous. Even waxen needed to show caution there, and they were the only group who could visit any level of Shade City with impunity.

The boots of four waxen clanked loudly on the metal flooring as they strode confidently down a street on one of the lowest levels of the depths. The streets emptied quickly every time they turned a corner, and Kayanai could feel eyes watching them from every shadow. The Waxen too were watchful and wary despite their apparent nonchalance. Even the vendors, who normally accosted every passerby, gave them space, though they were at the ready in case the waxen were there as customers.

The giants arrived at a great slab of scarred wall. At a glance from Waxman, Gengai moved forward and pounded on it.

Gengai paused, then, intuition made him step back with the others. For a beat, nothing happened. Then, with a clang, the ground ahead of them suddenly became a gaping hole, as two folding doors dropped down and opened. They approached and peered in.

"That's one way of gaining an advantage over your customers," smirked Iran.

"Efficient," commented Waxman.

Kayanai stepped forward to enter the hole, but Waxman swung his pack from his back and blocked Kayanai with his arm in one smooth movement.

"Let me break your fall," he said, in a brief moment of camaraderie as he handed Kayanai his pack. Then Waxman turned to the hole and said, "Don't spill any." over his shoulder, and leaped into the darkness.

Dust swirled from the opening as they waited, listening.

Gengai raised his eyebrows and said, "He can't still be—."

Whump! Waxman's heavy landing shook the ground. From far below they could hear the barking of animals.

Kayanai gestured for Iran and Gengai's packs. Gengai passed his over, crouched down, looked in the hole, then looked up again.

"I'll go next. He can break my fall," said Gengai, then he put his legs over the side and slid into the hole.

"Hope he doesn't land on his face," said Iran.

"Wouldn't that be sad," grinned Kayanai. "I'll throw, you catch. I'll count to 5."

Iran's white shirt reflected the colourful lights of the street as he jumped.

After he heard Iran landing, Kayanai counted, then dropped one of the packs. He did this three more times, and as he did, he scanned the surrounding shadows and noted the number of faces watching him.

Finally, he leaped, and with a graceful twist, he grabbed the edge and hung for a moment. When he was sure he'd waited enough time, he let go and fell.

The drop was long enough for him to be able to see the dim light of the bottom rush towards him. At the moment of impact, he crouched and rolled, finding himself spinning down a pile of filth and bones.

Waxman reached down, put his hand under Kayanai's arm, and helped him up. As he did, Kayanai could see teeth marks in Waxman's arm, then noticed the corpse of a large, dog-like creature near the pile. Scanning the long, dimly lit room, he saw that there were more creatures tethered to six rough-looking individuals watching from a distance.

As Iran handed Kayanai his pack, he said, "Their teeth can't puncture, but they have a serious bite."

"They must—they left marks on Waxman," said Kayanai. He moved his attention to the people. "Our greeters looked as friendly as their pets." Iran smirked.

Waxman had walked over to the greeters and was now speaking quietly to one of them. He turned and gestured for the waxen to follow. The guards watched them leave through narrowed eyes.

They walked through metal doors and found themselves in an enormous sweatshop of material weavers and machinery. The small walkways were hard for Kayanai and Gengai to move through, and nearly impossibly cramped for Iran and Waxman. He couldn't help but be amused by the annoyance on their faces. "Smaller can be an advantage sometimes, I suppose," he mused, "and I'm definitely big enough to impress these people." The workers stared at them with dropped jaws.

A severe-looking woman approached them, flanked by mechs. She looked them up and down.

"Wax Adoor. To what do we owe this pleasure? We are not used to seeing you this deep. Normally, you give your orders to our associates on Level 12."

"We will speak to him alone," was Waxman's curt response.

The woman paused. She was not used to curtness. Still, she was wise enough to acquiesce.

"Come," she said, "You'll be more comfortable in his workroom."

She led them into a high ceilinged, furnished room, full of tools and gadgetry. Bent over his work, The Tailor sat, his soft arms and feathery fingers adeptly maneuvering small tools. His slight and slippery-looking frame was clothed in elegant, yet worn, garments.

He raised his thin, pinched face to them as they entered. He sat stock still for a moment. His face didn't change but Kayanai could see sweat break out on his forehead. He turned to the woman and said, "Leave us now please, my dear." The woman left, unhappily.

"I'm honoured by your business. Make yourselves at home. Whoever is first may sit here while I complete this final adjustment." They could see now that he was adjusting a complicated-looking vestment mech.

The furniture groaned as Waxman, Gengai, and Iran sat, while Kayanai moved to the brightly lit mech chair. As he sat, the chair lit up and hummed. An orb broke off and hovered in front of Kayanai, scanning his form.

Looking at the screen results of the scan, The Tailor said to Kayanai, "You're smaller than last time."

Turning to Waxman, he said, "No reprint. He'll need a full new cut."

"Then do it. You'll need to scan him too, he said pointing to Gengai."

The Tailor pressed several keys on the side of the chair and an apparatus clicked free next to Kayanai's arm and it spun and whirred towards his wrist. A needle emerged from the end and stopped poised at his wrist. The Tailor pressed another key, and the needle rammed through Kayanai's tough skin. The Tailor looked up nervously, but Kayanai's face was unchanged.

As his blood was sucked from him and began filling an adjoining metal basin, Kayanai breathed in deeply. The air was hot and stifling.

The Tailor turned to Waxman. "And a percentage of his blood is to be added to that which you've collected. For the vests and head-pieces..." He hesitated. You're sure of the sizing?

"I am. And of the number."

"Are you sure you have enough?"

Waxman signalled to Iran, who lifted the enormous packs one by one and placed them on a nearby worktable.

The Tailor walked over to the table. He tried to lift one of the packs to open it, but it was far too heavy. Iran smirked, lifted one, opened it, and slowly pulled out a clear bag which he placed on the table. The Tailor's eyes widened. The bag was twice as big as him, and was full to the brim with thick, purple Wax blood.

He fingered the bag wonderingly and said, "If it's as condensed as you say... yes, it will be enough to armor over a thousand regular soldiers."

He turned to Waxman and said, "I will not be able to do all the work myself, of course. I will need to give the job to my workers. Complete secrecy will be impossible."

"It is and will be possible. Why else would we have journeyed down to this dismal place? Use as many mechs as possible, and make sure they are reprogrammed. As for the workers, they know our power. And they have families, do they not? Make sure they do not speak of this. If there is any danger of it, make sure they never speak again. If I hear of word getting out, I will hold you responsible. I don't need to tell you what I will do if you fail me."

The blood drained from The Tailor's face as though he were strapped to his own machine. He shrank from Waxman's burning gaze and his head nodded jerkily.

A bleep from his machine snapped The Tailor out of his frightened daze. He slid back over to Kayanai and checked the readings.

"Complete," he said. "We got a surprising amount."

"Good." We want five shafts. All of us are volunteering today."

Iran stepped up and waved Kayanai out of the chair. "No need. You can get that much from me."

The Tailor raised his eyebrows at him. He answered, hesitantly, not wanting to contradict, "Removing that much blood from you will weaken you considerably. You'll be unable to walk."

"I'll be fine." He turned to Waxman. "I want to do my duty."

Waxman looked at him for a while, then a slight crinkle appeared at the corner of his eyes, and he nodded.

"Us waxen are masters at saying a lot without saying much," thought Kayanai. He couldn't tell whether Iran's wish to impress Waxman was personal or calculated.

Iran sat down and positioned his forearm. He reached down with his other arm and punched the appropriate buttons. The needle came out, punched through his skin, and Iran's blood began moving slowly through the tube. Iran looked at the needle, and flexed his arm, trying to make the blood flow faster. but though it seemed to move slightly quicker, it wasn't quick enough for Iran.

"Give me a knife," he said.

Gengai, wanting to place some of the attention himself, stepped forward, reached up to his vest and pulled out his knife with a flourish.

"Here. Use mine," he said, "I keep it incredibly sharp."

Iran looked at it, dismissively. "Thanks, but it won't be sharp enough for my skin. Kayanai?" He looked past Gengai at his friend.

As Kayanai stepped forward and handed Iran his knife, he only just managed not to smile at the twinkle in Iran's eye. They loved needling Gengai.

"My knife is made of jesicore and graphenona just as yours is!" said Gengai, hotly.

Iran passed the blade to the hand of his immobilized arm and reached so his free forearm was pressed against the blade. As he did so he said,"

Your blade is also forged from your first and only bleed. It will pierce your skin, but not ours, which is older, tougher."

Iran looked up and smiled at Gengai, "If you'd make yourself useful, grab something to catch the overflow."

Gengai scowled and crossed his arms as Iran strained his arm against the sharp tip and carefully sliced into his hard skin. The blood began pouring out, but The Tailor, heeding Iran's warning, had grabbed a metal basin and thrust it under the blood flow just in time.

All eyes watched in stillness as the blood poured freely from Iran, filling the vessel.

Into the silence, Waxman said, "Tailor." When the Tailor brought his unwilling eyes up to the giant's face, Waxman continued. "You will do your best work. The armor you forge will be worthy of these waxen."

The Tailor bobbed his head and murmured compliantly. Then looking down at the basin and seeing it was near overflowing, he looked around anxiously. "I need something to stop the blood. He is losing too much too fast."

Waxman reached down, deftly unwrapped a cloth from around his calf and handed it to The Tailor. The Tailor quickly wrapped it around Iran's arm, pressed some buttons on the side of his apparatus, and watched carefully as the needle slid out from Iran's arm. The Tailor then studied the adjoining screen.

"I'm afraid he might be quite weak for a while."

Iran's arm shot out and grabbed The Tailor by the front of his ruffled shirt, and pulled the man face down to his.

"Not me," Iran protested with a slight slur in his voice. "Iran Crowne is never weak." He smiled into the terrified face of the trembling man, then let him go.

The Tailor stumbled back mumbling apologies.

Putting his hand on each arm Iran lifted himself out of the chair. He did it slowly, but unwaveringly. He stood, but it was clear it took effort.

Gengai stepped forward. "I'm next."

"This one's on me," Iran said to him, breathing heavily. "Though the clothes will be on you," he chuckled, weakly.

"It's unnecessary," said The Tailor. "We have enough." It was clear he was looking forward to the waxen's departure. Then, obviously to please Iran, The Tailor said, "The contribution you made… It's remarkable."

"That's me," grinned Iran, "Remarkable." He then swung almost drunkenly towards Waxman. "Shall we?"

As they moved towards the door, Kayanai sidled up to Iran and walked next to him, ready to catch him if he fell.

Waxman turned back to The Tailor and asked. "Is there a faster way out of here than that hole we fell through?"

"I'll tell Mana to take you to my personal exit lift."

Waxman nodded, then gave The Tailor, one last hard look, and said slowly and deliberately, "Your best ever."

/ / /

The tall woman who'd greeted them, led them through a cramped hallway connected to the tailor's office to what appeared to be a blank wall.

"You're lucky," she said. "Normally, he and I are the only ones allowed to use this exit." She pressed a button and a door revealing a large comfortable rocket lift. "Good luck. It's a bit finicky." And with that she turned and clacked away.

Looking at the old, patched up machinery above the compartment, Iran said, "Might be faster to take the stairs."

Waxman glanced at it and said, "It can fit two of us at a time. Kayanai, you and Gengai head up first. Get some rest. You're going to need it."

Gengai turned to Kayanai. "Who needs rest? Not me. Care for a quick game of hand guards? See who's stronger?"

Kayanai managed to not roll his eyes. "No thanks, Gengai. Think I'll go wash off the stink of this place."

"Bathing again, hey?" Gengai smirked.

"Gengai, if you don't need rest, meet me on the transport deck. You can accompany me to the palace," ordered Waxman.

Gengai nodded and got in the lift. Kayanai hesitated and looked at Waxman and said, "It's going to be pretty crowded in there. How about I follow you two?"

Waxman deliberated then nodded, wryly. "Given your tempers and tendency to irritate each other there's less chance of the lift being damaged if you go separately. Go first, Gengai."

Gengai scowled, punched the controls, and shot off with a woosh and a worrying crackle of energy.

Iran, who'd been leaning against the wall, took an unsteady step towards Waxman, "You're the biggest. Why don't Kayanai and I—"

"You're with me," Waxman replied. He put his arm under Iran's to steady him. Iran looked at him in surprise. Supporting Iran, Waxman maneuvered them both towards the lift doors. There was a long, uncomfortable pause, then the noise told them the lift had returned.

The doors opened, and Waxman moved himself and Iran inside. When they were in, Waxman looked out at Kayanai and said, stone-faced, "Enjoy your bath."

The last thing Kayanai saw as the doors closed was Iran's face as he looked at Waxman. There was fear there.

When they were gone, Kayanai pressed the button, waited for a bit then began impatiently punching the control. After what seemed like a much longer time than before the lift capsule finally returned. Kayanai jumped in and pressed the top level button repeatedly, till the door swished shut and the machine shot up with a whoosh.

The lift was climbing with breathtaking speed. The machinery was new enough to be able to climb many floors in moments, but too old for proper inertial dampeners. Kayanai had to use a great deal of his strength just to steady himself. All was black outside, then, like the dawn sped up, the seemingly endless black became grey, then a lighter grey, then lighter and lighter till, till finally the lift slowed and stopped with a sickening lurch and the doors split open. Kayanai stepped out into the blinding light.

His ears were immediately assaulted by loud raucous music, yelling, and laughter. As his eyes adjusted, he could eventually make out brightly coloured dancers moving to the rhythm of a loudly playing band, and well-dressed and semi-dressed people draped over lavish furniture, locked in embraces, and ingesting consciousness adjusters in a variety of ways. He took this all in quickly, then began pushing through the crowd and scanning for the other Waxen. They were nowhere to be seen.

He was approached by a woman wearing little but her long black hair which was in many braids and wrapped around her in intricate patterns.

"Here's another one," she called over her shoulder to a blond woman behind her wearing a bright blue and yellow bodysuit.

The women came to either side of him and stroked his enormous arms "We would be honoured, Waxen, to help you find anything you desire," the blond woman called up to him.

"Surely, it's me you're looking for," laughed the black-haired woman, as she strained to reach his upper arm.

"Actually, I'm looking for my friends. Did you see where they went?"

The blond woman smiled craftily up at Kayanai. "We could..." she started to say.

Kayanai was in no mood to bargain. He leaned down and gave her his scariest scowl. "You can."

Her face sobered and she swallowed. "Ahem, yes... They went out to the balcony. Through there." She pointed to an arched doorway in the glass wall on the other side of the room.

"Thank you, ladies" Kayanai scowl changed to his most charming smile, then he pushed through the crowd sloughing off the women. People, at first turned to him irritated, but then when they saw him, they moved out of his way quickly. He ducked under the archway and found himself looking at a breathtaking view.

At the center of the decks of Shade City was an enormous chasm that revealed level upon level of brightly lit decks that gradually faded into the darkness below, a sight that made it seem as though someone had con-quered the stars and harnessed their radiance in orderly layers. Kayanai gazed down into this abyss through the transparent floor of an ornate balcony, one of many belonging to the renowned Den of Tika, a kind of crystal palace famous for its glittering beauty. Surrounding him were lav-ishly dressed guests, some drinking and talking coolly, some laughing and shrieking as they dared each other to look down. He took all this in before he spotted his friends towering above the crowd.

Waxman was standing with his foot up on the barrier that separated him from a fall to depths that were almost beyond comprehension. As Kayanai watched, frozen in shock, Waxman brought his other foot up and pushed himself upwards in an impossible leap that took him up, up and across the void. The crowd gasped. He seemed to hang in the air, and Kayanai held his breath.

As he fell, someone nearby said, "He's not going to make—-" and Waxman crashed into the other side just below the opposite barrier. Kayanai could see Waxman's hand reach out and clutch hard to a metal bar, then swing his other arm up and grab the base of the railing. Then, like a light-footed reptile, Waxman climbed swiftly up and over the barrier.

The crowd exploded into cheers and applause. Kayanai breathed out. He could see Waxman moving to the final rim of Shade city and escaping by the light of Desigar surface. And he was gone.

Kayanai walked forward and stood next to his friend. Iran's narrowed eyes were still on the spot where Waxman had disappeared, and his hands clenched the top of the barrier in frustration.

"He knew I couldn't follow him… that I couldn't make that jump," he said, softly.

"What did he say to you?"

Iran turned, leaned against the barrier and waved over a server with a tray of drinks. The server walked up, and Iran grabbed the largest glass off the tray. The server looked like he was going to say something but thought better of it and walked away.

Iran swigged the drink and said, "He said a hell of a lot, without saying a hell of a lot. He said he knew Kolorov'son's fleet still hasn't arrived at Gengaru."

"How can he know that?"

"He hinted that if the fleet had attacked Gengaru, we'd know because the Infidel would have woken up and started killing us again."

"That's no guarantee they haven't made it yet. Maybe they arrived and were instantly annihilated. Maybe the Infidel hasn't woken up because Cal—"

"I know, I know. That's what I said to him. As soon as I said Cal's name he leaned in hard and started grilling me about what I think Cal's going to do if we attack his favourite new planet."

"We don't know that he's still there."

"Come on, Kayanai. He told us we're dead if he sees us again. What do you think that means? He brought us here and wants us to stay put. Waxman keeps insisting that Cal is just one little man, but we know better. We saw what he can do. He'd kill us all."

Kayanai sighed. "Yeah, alright. I know.

"I wish Waxman knew it. He knows so much—he knows you and I want no part of this. That we'd stop him if we could. He's questioning our loyalty. Kayanai… I think we might be in danger."

Kayanai felt it too. It was the feeling of a caged animal surrounded by predators. He tried to shake off his dread.

"He wouldn't. Not us. Besides, there are so few of us left. He needs us."

Iran ran his hand through his thick hair, leaned heavily on the railing. "He kept going on about how much we owe him. He looked down into the abyss. "We do, you know. Owe him."

"What do we owe him for? For making us Waxen?" Kayanai shook his head. "He owns us. Slaves don't owe their masters."

"We're not slaves."

"Aren't we? You said it yourself, we're in danger. What would he do to us if we stopped doing what he wants."

"He did send Jevan to get us. They tried to save us."

"He sent Jevan to start a war. And they didn't save us. Cal did."

"It's tough though, you know? We've been loyal to him for so long. We can't just stop being Waxen."

"I know. But we can give our loyalty to something else now."

"What?"

"Ourselves."

CHAPTER NINE

Jordi Tan's bleary red eyes watched the golden tent cloth above him flap and dance in the fading sunlight. Sprawled across his throne, he raised a leg to catch some of the breeze coming in through the tent opening. The intricate lashing of his garment ties had unravelled during one of his outbreaks of dancing so when he moved his robe fell open revealing his groin. Silver light reflected off his bare flesh like a thousand tiny suns.

Eventually, the breeze let him in on the fact that he was exposing himself, but Tan didn't bother covering up.

"No one can gaze upon me long enough to get more than a glimpse anyway," he murmured to himself. "Let them try to get a good look!" he chuckled, drunkenly.

He glanced over to his usual entourage. A woman jumped forward to refill his glass. He looked past her, over to the elegantly dressed figures seated around him. One of them, a commander of the largest fleet from the outer planets, was standing and speaking to him. Tan was clearly barely listening, a fact that was adding to the commander's already considerable frustration.

"I feel like I'm repeating myself til I am blue in the face," the man said through gritted teeth.

"The orders to reconstruct 40% of the Stations docking bays all at once is preposterous. You've recalled every ship in the imperial fleet to come answer this great threat you speak of, and when they arrive, nearly half your main docking station is on lockdown! So, you have the ships land here, into this complete chaos, and insist on taking their precious cargo as gifts! Why? You owe us an explanation!"

Tan bobbed his head in the man's direction then scowled down his nose at him. "I owe you nothing. It's you who owe me! Your power comes from me and the waxen at my beck and call."

Just then one of Tan's aides ducked into the tent.

"Your eminence, Waxman's ship has just landed. He'll be arriving momentarily."

There was a pause while Tan's eye's widened and the council of commanders shot each other barely concealed smiles.

"Why am I just hearing this now??" shrieked Tan.

The aide backed out nervously, and there was silence as Tan took swigs from his glass and glared at the entrance, till finally, the tent's flaps were forcefully thrown back, and the massive form of Waxman ducked into the tent. He stepped forward and stared down at them, imperiously. There was another assault on the entrance as Kayanai and Iran crammed their way inside and stood behind Waxman. Despite the grandeur of the tent, the three giants filled the space.

"Here I am, Jordi. At your beck and call," rumbled Waxman, his lips curling slightly with contemptuous amusement.

Slowly, a murmur rose up among the commanders as they realized Waxman must have somehow been listening the whole time.

A commander stood and bravely raised her face to him.

"Perhaps you are already aware that many of us are displeased that the repairs to The Station are grounding most of our ships and leaving us vulnerable to attack. What say you, Wax Adoor? Do you agree with this decision?"

Waxman's eyes flicked to her briefly then settled back on Tan.

He replied emphatically, "I supported it from the beginning."

More murmuring. Many in the council were suspecting now where the order had really come from.

"But, Wax Adoor, with all the imperial fleets recalled and half the station down, most of our ships are grounded. Not to mention we have no means to resupply swiftly in the case of an attack."

Waxman broke eye contact with Jar Tan and directed the full force of his iron gaze to her.

"Are we not in peacetime, commander? Perhaps you know something I don't. Do you expect an attack?"

The commander hesitated, then burst out, "We want to know why we've been recalled here, leaving important colonization work for the Alliance, to sit here waiting with our pants down!"

Tan giggled. "You can have a lot of fun waiting with your pants down, my dear." he said, flapping his robe at her and causing more light to dance around the canvas walls. Everyone ignored him.

The commander tightened her lips and continued. "We all know this could merely be a brief ceasefire. The Infidel is quiet, but it's still sitting there, waiting."

"Which is why we must make preparations," replied Waxman.

"Prudent to repair the station now while it's quiet, rather than wait till it's active again.

The commander opened her mouth and shut it again. It was a good point and she knew it. She glanced around for support.

No one else spoke. She sank down in her chair, and Waxman turned his attention back to Tan.

Before Waxman could speak, Tan drawled, "So, back again so soon. Perhaps the festivities drew you? Tonight, I have planned a—"

"There is news," broke in Waxman.

All the ears in the room pricked up.

"We've received a comm from deep space. Jevan Khran will be returning to Desigar shortly."

Tan's mouth fell open, then contorted into a confused smile.

"Jevan? Coming here now? But she's been lost for ages. Everyone knows that!"

He turned, shouted at his entourage, "Why do I keep finding things out just before they happen!" then started patting ineffectually at his wild hair.

Another council member stood and addressed Waxman.

"What of the fleet? Any news of Kolorov'son? He had great stake as leader in large collections of planet alliances and had close ties to Kolorov.

"The fate of your ally, Kolorov'son and my ten thousand waxen is still unknown. What I know from the binary signals received is that Jevan's return is imminent. And she returns alone."

The council member sat. Silence covered the room.

Waxman broke the silence. "I believe celebrations are in order. We must welcome Khran's return. Jordi, this is your area of expertise."

Tan was musing to himself, then suddenly he sat up and pointed to a porter. "Mech! Bring me my plot blocks!"

The porter jumped forward and stood directly in front of Tan.

Then his chest panel opened top down and a display board covered in multicolored blocks made of hard light appeared.

"This news is just the little piece I was missing." Tan looked over the haphazardly stacked pieces and rubbed his hands with glee. He smashed at the pieces and giggled as the glowing blocks tumbled down. Then he beckoned to the council members and his entourage, his eyes bulging wildly.

"Come see! It's all here!" Jordi picked a handful to reassemble a tower of blocks. "See, I've done this many times. I know what I'm doing."

He began arranging some smaller blocks on the bottom, then stacked a couple on top carefully.

"And now the missing piece... See these little blocks here? Then you with your waxen and I came along." He placed two blocks much larger than the rest on. One of them was silver-colored.

"This one's me. It's the most important. Then, more came to the alliance and we grew and grew until..." Jordi picked up a long thin block and placed it like a lid on the top of the pile.

"The Wellspring Accord. It leveled the field, you see. And, funny, just when we thought we had it all sealed up—didn't we Waxman—the Shrie

Shrie showed up!" Jordi slammed a big block, larger than the waxen block, on top of the stack.

"Now we've got to pile on the ten thousand waxen," he stacked another, "Kolorov'son fleet," and another "the new armistices. Then—" Tan paused dramatically, "came Cal, with the ceasefire!"

He reached down below the wellspring flat block and carefully tapped free a small block and pulled it out safely without toppling the tower. Tan then raised the little block and pulled at it making it bigger and bigger till it exceeded even the Shrie Shrie block. Then he held it up over the tower and dropped it on top. The Tower swayed but held. Tan laughed and clapped his hands.

"Now watch!!" Another block materialized between his finger and thumb. The color glowed and reflected off his mirror-like skin. "This block is Jevan's return. Shall I make it big or small, Wax Adoor? Do I put it down here, below the Wellspring, or does she get a position higher up? If I put her up here, she might topple the tower…"

Tan's guests are all frozen. Most are dumbfounded or uncomfortable, though some of his followers are rapt, believing there must be a method to Tan's madness. They look at Waxman, waiting for his response.

Waxman's face was stone. "It's up to you, Emperor, Jar Tan of Desigar."

Jordi shrieked with joy, and with a flourish as if adding an embellishment to a grand dessert, he placed the piece representing Jevan on the top of the tower.

"Enough of this!" A man in a high-ranking military uniform stood up abruptly, shifting everyone's attention to him from the mad emperor.

"Wax Adoor, I'm Commander Hubo, leader of the third fleet, and I must ask you for some clarification. Why do you not use the same comm code system as the rest of us? You and your waxen are supposedly part of the imperial military and yet you hide things from us. Why? If the rest of us commanders were as well informed as you are, would that not benefit us all?"

In one fluid motion, Waxman took a step towards the commander and went down on one knee so they were eye to eye.

For a moment he said nothing, just watched Hubo's face grow paler and paler.

Finally, he spoke. "Our Imperial Lord, Jordi Tan has his reasons for deciding who knows what. If you want to question the good sense of his decision," Waxman gestured to Tan, "he's right there."

Hubo flicked his eyes from the giant granite face in front of him to the half-dressed Tan, gibbering and chuckling over his light blocks. He looked back at Waxman, then looked down.

Waxman put his enormous hand on Hubo's head and stood up. When the hand was removed, Commander Hubo, with shaking legs, plunked back down in his seat.

"Anyone else?" said Waxman, quietly, as he stepped back to his place in front of his waxen.

A chirrup from Tan's comm mech broke the heavy silence that followed Waxman's question.

"Jordi," said Waxman. "If you're finished with your blocks, I think this may be important."

"What now??" Tan shoved the blocks mech out of his way, stumbled back to his throne, and flopped heavily onto the soft cushions.

"I'm sure I'll need another drink for this." He gestured to the comm mech and a woman holding a large ornate jar. The woman jumped forward to fill Tan's glass while the mech positioned itself in front of the council and the emperor.

With a whirr and a click, the mech's head snapped back, and its mouth opened impossibly wide until the top of its jaw was nearly perpendicular to its base. A bright holographic image of a head took shape. A woman's head now sat where the mech's had been, her face distorted in anger, shouting though no sound could be heard.

Chief Commander Kolorov's head turned impatiently to someone outside the field view of the comms device and was clearly trying to resolve the tech issue from her end. As they waited Kayanai studied the comm mech's jaw upgrade. The lower jaw acted as a protective shield that was set to envelop the comm device in the case of an explosion or a system virus. This meant the mech could either protect the message, or the recipients of the message from being destroyed. Kayanai also noted how far back Jordi was pressed in his throne and how he looked at the mech warily. He'd once been injured in an assassination attempt when a rebellious planet had infiltrated his comm mech system. Kayanai shook his head slightly to avoid the memory. Jordi's retaliation on the rebels had not been pretty.

Finally, the signal issue was resolved and Kolorov turned back to continue. The leader of the greatest fleet in the Alliance, looked over Tan and the council with an uncharacteristically angry expression on her usually flinty face.

"Good. You're all here." Then her eyes settled on Waxman. "I've been informed that Jevan Khran is en route to Desigar. Please update."

Waxman was a statue, his eyes fixed on Kolorov's. Finally, just as Kolorov's mouth opened to say something, he spoke.

"We received a signal from deep space. We were unable to pinpoint its source. It was encoded with proper enigma protocol. When decoded, it contained the message that Khran is returning."

"And the fleet?" Kolorov's voice was still even, but there was an edge to it now.

"One line of code. That is why we're here. We need to prepare."

Kolorov's mouth trembled, and her eyes were angry. She swallowed, then said rigidly, "As interested as I am in these preparations, I first want to know why you've ordered a full recall of our fleets, while you've shut down half of The Station! It's pure lunacy!"

"We were just addressing this very issue. Commander Fol is the appointed person in charge of arranging the recalled fleet. She'll answer any questions you have." Waxman turned and gestured to Commander Fol who looked as if she'd eaten something that had disagreed with her.

Commander Fol stood up and addressed Kolorov.

"My apologies, Chief C-C-Commander," she stuttered. "If there's anything I can do to help accommodate—"

"There is something you can do, yes," cut in Kolorov, bitingly, "You can clear my fleet for direct access to the palace dock or I will be taking my fleet home."

Commander Fol barely had a chance to nod before the holograph blinked out, and the top of the mech's head whirred up and snapped back into place.

As the fleet leaders whose ships were currently in the palace dock stood up to protest angrily to Commander Fol, Tan jumped back down from his throne demanding his blocks again.

Waxman gestured to Kayanai and Iran and they ducked their way out of the tent. The tinkling sound of falling light blocks and the roar of yelling and mad laughter followed behind them.

Waxman, Kayanai, and Iran stood gazing at the umbilical cord that coiled up into the sky all the way to The Station. Gengai was there too, kicking the shimmering sand impatiently. In front of them a cargo cruiser was slowly coming down into loading position.

"Finally!" burst out Gengai, when the cruiser came to a rest. "I'm ready to get off this rock."

"Iran, Gengai, load this cruiser and take it up to The Station. Kayanai, you're with me. Gengai, I'm taking your Five Finger Fighter"

Waxman turned smartly, missing Gengai's expression. As Gengai fumed, Kayanai beamed at him.

"Thanks for lending us your fighter, Gengai," said Kayanai.

"You'd better not scratch it, Stubby," snarled Gengai, then he whipped around and began loading cases into the cargo cruiser.

Kayanai shared a grin with Iran and turned to go, but Iran's hand stopped him. Kayanai looked back and saw his friend's smile had dropped from his face. Iran pointed to the distinct tricoloured insignia on the side of the cruiser.

"It's the same marking as the other one," he said.

Kayanai remembered. In his mind, he could hear the soldier saying, "The cargo is intact. Of course, you probably guessed that from the fact that we're all still alive." He gripped Iran's shoulder.

"Be careful."

Iran nodded. Kayanai turned and climbed into the fighter.

Moments later he was looking out of the fighter's viewer at his friend loading the cruiser. He saw Iran pause and look up almost as if he knew Kayanai was watching, then Iran turned and continued his work.

"Something's in that cruiser," thought Kayanai, "something dangerous. Is that why Waxman chose Iran..?"

Jevan's voice cut into Kayanai's foreboding thoughts. "We're lucky the council hasn't overthrown that fool. What was all that with the building blocks? I couldn't quite see from my vantage point." She was at the helm, keying in the liftoff codes.

"You were watching?" said Kayanai, surprised.

"I watched from here. I wanted to see the reaction to the announcement of my return," answered Jevan.

"I always keep a spy mech on Jordi now. He's increasingly unstable which makes him potentially unreliable," Waxman replied, calmly.

"If he can't be trusted, why keep him?" Jevan swung her seat around and raised her shapely black eyebrows at Waxman.

"He's still a useful pawn. For now." Waxman lifted a finger, and Jevan swiveled back and began raising the ship into the air, slowly first, then swiftly up into the thick pink atmosphere.

"So, when's my party?" Jevan asked, her voice amused.

"When the lovely Khran of Desigar has returned, of course," replied Waxman, in a surprisingly accurate impression of Tan's voice. Jevan snorted with laughter.

Kayanai stared back and forth at Jevan and Waxman in disbelief. "They're enjoying this," he thought, with creeping horror. "It's like a game of strategy with them. Who will live and die doesn't matter. All that matters is that they win."

Kayanai used his voice. "What if Kolorov'son gets to Gengaru before us."

"Then he'll have to hold the tide till we show up and save the day." Waxman spoke as if he had practiced the response for just this moment.

"And Kolorov?"

"She'll be busy with the Infidel. By then everyone here will be focused on averting another attack."

Jevan grinned. "It's perfect."

Kayanai's insides churned. Their plan was so complicated, so contorted, he couldn't even follow it.

"Were they always like this?" he thought. "Was she?" He tried to think back to the days before the Shrie Shrie came. "Was I?"

Was there a time when he would have wanted this war?

As if he'd heard Kayanai's thoughts, Waxman turned to him suddenly and stared thoughtfully into his eyes.

"You'll have a short rest on the Station while I check the fleet ships for readiness. Before you and Iran must return to Shade City to pick up the armor, there will be time, Kayanai, for you to take another bath—if you want one." Waxman's eyes bore into him a moment longer, then he turned and let the words hang in the air.

Jevan glanced over her shoulder at Kayanai.

A bitterness began growing in Kayanai. He did want to bathe. He wanted to shrink till he disappeared. He was so sick of death.

But the bitterness rising in him was not despairing, it was angry.

That night, he did not bathe.

CHAPTER TEN

It was dawn on Desigar, but it was always night in Shade City. Darkness enveloped the cargo ship as the roof above them twisted shut, blocking off the morning light.

Kayanai and Iran were readying the cargo area for the new armor.

"What do you think Jevan and Waxman are doing while we do the grunt work?" asked Iran.

"Plotting. Complimenting each other for how scheming they are." Kayanai answered with a twisted smile.

They worked quietly for a bit, then Iran asked, casually, "So, did you get in a bath last night?"

Kayanai glared at him and was about to answer when the comm interrupted. "We've arrived," they heard Waxman say.

"Let's go," said Kayanai.

"Hope this doesn't take long. I hate this place," sighed Iran.

They headed out into Shade City, through the docking area and the breathtakingly large central hub, then the labyrinth of corridors that eventually led to a service lift large enough to fit them.

Down, down, down they went till finally they reached their destination: Floor -O52. The doors swished open and headed straight for The Tailor's factory. Kayanai was glad there was no need to go through the security procedure of their last visit. This time they were expected.

They rounded a corner and Waxman stopped short. In front of them, The Tailor's factory dominated the street. Also in front of them was a thin figure wearing a suit of Liquid Wax armor. Though tiny in comparison to the waxen, they stood tall and seemingly unafraid.

After considering the person for a moment, Waxman said,

"Tell me you are just verifying that armor's perfection. Remove it quickly, and you will live."

The figure removed the headpiece revealing the stern face of the woman who'd led them to The Tailor on their last visit. The woman's cold stare never left Waxman's face as she slowly shook her head. She began to speak, her clear strong voice echoing through the metal street.

"You waxen came from us, but now we are so beneath you, you can barely see us. We unaltered are sometimes useful—we can be fodder, or servants, or soldiers, or scapegoats—but mostly you ignore us. I was nothing to you. I only matter now because I'm wearing a suit of your blood. Clothed in part of you, you can finally see me."

The door of the shop burst open, and the tailor ran out towards the woman.

"Leanin! He reached out as if to grab her, but his hand froze in midair when he saw her face. She was still looking at Waxman with open defiance. And hatred.

"Go back to your shop, Danher."

"But why—?"

"Because I'm tired of these freakish, swaggering bullies, colonizing, controlling, murdering!"

"What the waxen did to your planet happened before the Wellspring Accord. Did Waxman himself not sign it and promise to protect the innocent, the families?"

Leanin finally broke her stare with Waxman and turned to the tailor.

"What about us, Danher? We don't live on a wellspring planet! All of us here deemed unworthy of procreation or protection, having our children in secret, knowing they could be killed indifferently, we're little more than slaves. And the billions on other non-wellspring planets, they, like us, mean nothing."

Waxman's voice cut in before the tailor could reply. "If you think that by putting on that armor, you can somehow become worthy of our attention, you are about to learn how very fleeting our notice of you will be."

Leanin turned back to Waxman. "You'll notice when my dagger pierces your cold heart," she spat, pulling a thin dagger from the weapons belt.

Waxman's eyebrows flickered with interest, perhaps even respect. "I see. You've made it from one of The Tailor's needles. Still, do you really think you can bring us down with that alone?"

"I am not alone."

She let out a sharp shout, and all round them the shadows moved. Within moments they were surrounded by fighters, all of whom were wearing the waxblood armor. Kayanai, Jevan, Iran and Gengai immediately split the street in quadrants and moved to cover one each.

Waxman, in the center of the four of them, stayed still and said, "Disable them all and get that armor back. And try not to get blood everywhere. I don't want the armor to stink." His voice sounded mildly irritated by the delay, but Kayanai could tell he was relishing the chance for combat.

Suddenly, there was a whirring sound and mechs came shooting out at them from every direction. They were collapsed into balls for maximum self-protection and lightning speed. As they approached the waxen, they burst outward, extending long arms to grab them. There were two for each of them.

"They're trying to shackle us so the others can attack us with their needle daggers." The thought passed through Kayanai's mind calmly as he watched them approach.

The mechs were fast, but Kayanai was faster. He extended his right leg and planted a kick that sent the first mech flying, then pivoted and leapt onto the second, feet first, crushing it to the ground. As he calculated the time to disable it before the first one came back at him, the mech beneath him clamped around his legs and heaved, throwing Kayanai off balance. As Kayanai rolled to the ground, he reached into the center of the mech and tore out its central system, disabling it. He then rolled back to his feet just in time to meet the return of the first mech. He caught it in midair, ripped it easily in half, then threw the pieces at the fighters approaching him. It gave him a moment to check how his other companions were getting on.

He saw the other mechs strewn about in pieces and his fellow waxen engaged now with the fighters. Iran was stepping on one fighter's neck and pulling off armor with one hand while punching anyone getting too close to him with the other. Gengai had two fighters in what looked like a bear hug, then he let go and they crashed to the ground. Kayanai was impressed. Constricting them was a clever method for following Waxman's order surprising for Gengai. Then he looked at Jevan, and his breath caught in his throat.

She was leaping from one soldier to the next, snapping their necks with such grace and efficiency that her movements seemed almost like dancing. She was so beautiful, it hurt.

His momentary distraction was broken by three needles glinting in his periphery. Three fighters brandishing their daggers were nearly on him. He broke down his opponents in size and potential skill, then responded accordingly. The first was a woman holding her dagger high and leaving her torso open, so he kicked her in the stomach so hard he knew he was putting her out of the fight. As he did so he turned so the second attacker's dagger would hit his side at an angle that only gave Kayanai a small scratch but caused the fighter's hand to smash into him with such force that the bones in the man's hand snapped. The man fell to his knees clutching his hand. The third fighter slowed his attack as he saw what happened to his companions and the look in his eyes hit Kayanai harder than anything else the fighters had come at him with. He was looking at Kayanai as one would look at a monster. With almost a sigh, Kayanai knocked the dagger from the terrified man's hand and grabbed him by the throat. While the fighter pulled at Kayanai's giant fist feebly, Kayanai stripped him of his armor and dropped the pieces on the ground with a thump. Then Kayanai heaved the nearly unconscious man away from him and grabbed the fighter with the crushed hand by the neck. He continued to strip the fighters this way till he had a substantial pile of armor, and his opponents were either down or fleeing and dropping the armor behind them.

When he looked up from his work, he saw that Iran and Gengai were finishing off the last of the fighters, and Jevan was carrying the woman, Leanin, to Waxman. Jevan plunked her down in front of Waxman, pinning the woman so she was unable to move despite her furious struggles.

She was screaming, "Go ahead, kill me! It's all you can do! You do nothing but destroy! It's you who are nothing!"

Waxman took her head in his hand and tilted her face up to meet his.

"Peace," he said. "I admire your courage. You will not die with your friends today." He reached down and took her hands in his.

"But you do need to be taught a lesson." He squeezed, and she screamed as he crushed her hands to pulp. "Don't start fights you can't finish," he announced to the street, over her moans.

Leanin collapsed, and from all around in the shadows and darkened corners of the street the sounds of voices shouting and wailing with grief and despair could be heard. But no one dared run to her aid.

Waxman stepped away from the sobbing woman and called out, "Tailor!" He paused. "I suggest you come to me now, Tailor! The alternative is that you will be found!"

A door opened down the street and Danher came out and walked quickly and reluctantly to Waxman. Waxman looked down at him and said, "Don't worry Tailor, I need those hands of yours. However, you do need to choose your staff more carefully in future." He reached down and picked up a fallen dagger. "Perhaps this will help you to remember—"

He slashed the needle dagger across Danher's face. For a moment the tailor stood there stunned as blood poured from his wound, then he moaned and shakily fumbled in his pocket for a cloth and pressed it against his face.

Waxman gestured to the surrounding destruction and said to him, "I want this armor cleaned and brought up to my ship on level 3 before midday." Then he turned and walked away saying, "Gengai, you stay and make sure it happens. Iran, Jevan, Kayanai—you're with me."

As they left the street, scared and desolate eyes followed them from every shadow.

"I really hate this place," said Iran.

/ / /

Kayanai was standing at attention on an elaborately decorated dais watching the light shift and dance in the clouds. His new armor, though form fitting and light, was uncomfortably warm in the hot sun, but he was far too disciplined to move—unlike the emperor. Next to him sat Jar Tan, squirming impatiently on his throne and watching the sky. On the other side of Tan was Gengai, also standing at attention. Behind Tan's throne, loomed Waxman, looking out at the scene below him with his arms crossed, like a watchful deity.

In front of them was a sea of landing pads most of which were occupied with the recalled fleet ships. The two directly in front, also lavishly decorated for the occasion, sat empty, waiting.

There were walkways connecting the platforms and Tan's ornamented dais and crammed in between all of them were throngs of people. News of the return of Jevan Khran had spread fast.

The crowds spoke in hushed tones, and it was strangely quiet. All were waiting to hear the familiar noise of incoming ships.

Then someone yelled, "Listen!" And there it was: a distant hum that grew exponentially louder until, suddenly, two ships rose over the palace. One was Iran's cruiser—an imposing sight—but it was the strange ship it accompanied that the people stared at. It was so badly damaged that it was hard to believe it could still fly.

As the ships landed, hands were thrown up to shield eyes and ears from the flying dust and the roaring engines. When the dust cleared, a puzzled murmur started up. The ship was a mystery; no one could identify the derelict husk in front of them.

A whoosh sound brought everyone's attention to the cruiser.

Iran Crowne walked down the exit ramp, his brilliant white shirt shining like a beacon. He stopped when he reached the platform, then turned his attention to the other ship.

There was a pause, then with a creak and a groan, the ruinous ship's ramp lowered, and out stepped Jevan Khran.

She stood in the entrance, a magnificent figure. Her towering, shapely form was framed in tight, royal ruby waxblood armor, and her hair was piled high and wrapped in a silvery dark cloth.

Cheers started up, but they died down when, ignoring the crowd, Jevan grabbed the side of the entry frame, swung herself up to a ridge on her left, and began scaling the hull of the ship. Then she swung herself up to a small outthrust, balanced upon it, reached up and unwound the shining cloth from her hair. Her long dark tresses fluttered behind her in the wind like a flag as she held the cloth high and called out in a ringing voice, "Behold. The great tomb of our most mighty and worthy of warriors!"

With those words she used the cloth to wipe the blackened and dirty hull to reveal the emblem of the Regent, the lost flagship of the Alliance fleet.

Shocked gasps were followed by silence, as the crowd realized that they were looking at all that was left of the mightiest ship in the Alliance. It was so scarred, and there was so little left, it was unrecognizable. Most upsetting was how little was left of the command levels, where the ship's captain, Kolorov'son, was once located.

Jevan's voice again rang out over the crowds, "Yes, it is a time for mourning, as I have returned to you, alone. But in my heart, I also celebrate. For long have I yearned for my feet to touch the sacred dust of Desigar, and here I am, back in the hallowed heart of our great empire, ready to protect you once again!

The masses erupted into thunderous applause and cheers.

Jevan waved, then launched herself off the side of the ship, soared in the air, and landed solidly on the metal platform with such a loud clank that it could be heard over the screaming crowds.

"Desigar!" She called over the noise. When the people quieted, she continued. "Though we have suffered a loss, be assured, my return is proof that no matter how much wax is spilt, wax will always rise, and wax will always triumph!"

There were more cheers.

"But we have unfinished work. Now is a time for vigilance, my friends. And any time the enemy may strike at us again. But know that we are ready for the task that now lies ahead. And that task is to unwaveringly, undeniably defeat our enemies!!"

The response from the crowd was deafening. Jevan raised her fists in the air, and Iran marched towards her across the connecting walkway, carrying a large staff. When he reached her, he handed her the staff, then together they walked down the central walkway, the people below them reaching towards them and shouting their names with ecstatic fervor.

As they approached the dais, Jar Tan rose from his throne and opened his arms wide and smiled even wider.

A guard stepped forward and yelled, "Your illustrious jar wants to speak! There will be silence." The crowd, familiar with their emperor's violent tendencies, quieted quickly.

Tan, half addressing Jevan, half the crowd, bellowed,

"Welcome home, my dear!" and as he did, he held his arms out to her as if to embrace her. In response, Jevan flourished the staff she held and presented it to him, arms outstretched, deftly forcing Tan to keep his distance but making it seem like a gesture of respect. Kayanai, just behind Tan, allowed himself a small smile. "She really is something," he thought.

"Jar Tan," said Jevan, "before I left, I was given this staff by my illustrious commander," she bowed her head to Waxman, who inclined his head back to her, "to assist me on my journey. It's crowned with a blade stronger than any other in existence and was forged with the blood of Wax Adoor himself. Now that I've returned, I present it to you."

Tan had jumped back in fear of the blade, but now stepped forward, his eyes shining with greed. He cackled and shrieked,

"A present! I do love a present! Let me see it!"

Jevan nodded to Tan and as she did, so she caught Kayanai's eye. She gave him a barely perceptible wink, then swung the staff high, spun it, and rammed it with all her considerable strength into the metal platform. She stepped back next to Kayanai and gestured to Tan as if to say, "go ahead and take it."

Tan took a moment to admire the silver base of the staff which was skillfully carved into the likeness of a fist, its fingers ringed with real jewels. He ran his hand over it, then planted his feet, grasped it and pulled. It didn't move. His brow furrowed, then he flashed a weak smile at the crowd before taking the staff firmly with both hands and pulling with all his might. His teeth were gritted, his knuckles white, his arms shaking—still the staff didn't budge. Finally, he released his arms and yowled in frustration. He staggered around, breathing heavily, till his eyes fell on Kayanai.

"You! You try and pull it out! I bet you can't!" Tan spat, furiously. "You used to be the strongest, but you've shrunk Kayanai. She'll be stronger than you are now." He pointed at Jevan, who looked at Kayanai with raised eyebrows. Clearly, she too wanted to see him try.

In response, Kayanai nodded at her, shrugged, and said, "I'm sure she is." Jevan's eyebrows went higher and looked pleased.

He focused on the staff and appraised it carefully, noting the angle it went in. Then he put his hand over the end and looked again at Jevan who was now watching him, speculatively. Her skepticism made his fist tighten and his face harden. He yanked, and there was a metallic scraping noise as he pulled the blade out with one fluid motion. As the audience clapped and hollered his name, Kayanai gave Jevan a wink.

She was smiling, her face grudgingly proud. Then he held the staff out to Tan, who grabbed it from him and swung it around, showing off for the crowd.

Tan yelled, "Let's start this part—"

He was interrupted by a roar of what sounded like thunder.

The sky darkened and filled with an approaching armada of ships. One of them, larger than the rest, lowered itself onto the empty platform adjacent to Iran's cruiser. It landed gracefully, and all that was heard was the hum of the other ships hanging in the air and the crowd murmuring till someone called out, "It's Kolorov!"

Excitement filled the air as the people realized they were witnessing the arrival of yet another famed personage. When the ramp began to lower the crowd was already calling the name of the illustrious leader of the empire's biggest fleet.

The atmosphere on the dais was less enthusiastic. The waxen and Tan were all aware of the anger this powerful woman was about to unleash on them.

Kolorov strode down the ramp and gazed out at her surroundings as if she'd just purchased the whole planet and was unimpressed with the state of it. She was weathered by battle and the stresses of her position, yet her energy and fitness belied her years. Her suit was perfectly cut and embellished with numerous adornments of honour and status, and her long grey hair was wound tight around her head. Behind her trailed a similarly adorned military entourage. Kolorov led them across the walkway to Tan's dais.

When she was standing in front of them, she became tiny next to the giants, yet she maintained her authority. She gave a thin-lipped gesture of politeness to Tan to show him proper courtesy, gave a long hard look at Jevan, then focused her attention on Wax Adoor.

"I have questions for you, Waxman," she said in her famous gravelly voice. "I know you don't like to come out behind the throne, but a proper greeting is in order, don't you think?"

It was more of a command than a question.

Waxman unfurled his arms and said, "I dislike unnecessary movement, but I agree that politeness is called for."

He came around the throne and gestured respectfully to Kolorov.

"Now," said Kolorov, sharply, "first, where is my fleet to touch down in this wretched landing area? My ships were given positions further back in which to land, and it will not do. If they can't be docked at The Station properly because of your outrageous shut down, you can at least assign my ships platforms adjacent to mine."

Tan, wanting some attention, interjected his simpering face and shouted, "Kolorov! Of course, your entourage deserves the best seats in the house! And be assured you'll never experience a more exciting celebration—"

"Yes, thank you, Jar Tan," Kolorov interrupted, "Please take care of it."

Tan turned and began shouting at his attendants, and Kolorov took a deep breath and looked up at Waxman even more intently. "Second, what is the status of the Regent and the rest of the fleet? I want your underling's report immediately."

"Khran has returned alone. She can tell you herself."

Kolorov turned sharply towards Jevan.

"Jevan Khran. Where is my son?"

The two women, both so different, yet equally powerful in their ways, stood looking at each other, and though she was younger, and far bigger and stronger, Jevan's eyes were the ones that wavered. She was not happy about deceiving this woman that she respected. But she could not tell Kolorov that Kolorov's son was still alive. If she knew he was still out there without his escort of ten thousand Waxen to protect him, Kolorov may send out her fleet to rescue him. That was not part of the plan. She had to stay here.

Jevan's eyes turned to the ruined flagship. "The Regent," she said, in a soft voice. "It's all that's left. I'm sorry."

Kolorov may have expected the news, but while gazing on the broken remains of her son's ship, her hands tightened into fists and her eyes filled with pain. When she looked back at Jevan, however, her eyes were dry and hard.

Before Kolorov could speak again, Jevan said, "I'm proud to have served with so great a man. He and I, we were close. I miss him."

Jevan allowed her voice to tremble and crack on her last words. It did the trick. Kolorov breathed in quickly, turned, and began marching briskly back to her ship. As she did, she yelled over her shoulder, tremulously, "I expect a full debrief sent at your soonest convenience!"

Jevan breathed a sigh of relief as she watched Kolorov stalk away. She had deceived Kolorov, but at least she hadn't had to bald face lie to her.

Jordi Tan jumped forward and yelled, "Enough somber talk! I want music, lights, and dancing! Begin the celebration!"

The sky burst into a symphony of exploding lights and colors, and a huge band behind the dais began to play a lively tune. Tan bobbed and weaved to the music unsteadily, showing how much he'd already had to drink. "To the palace!" he commanded, and he threw himself into his throne and snapped his fingers.

While servants lifted Tan's throne and began carrying him down and over to the ostentatious tent that he'd declared his new palace, the waxen turned to Waxman for orders.

"Let the soldiers have some fun," he said. "They're going to be working hard soon. But keep the peace. I have things to attend to."

Suddenly, Tan turned in his seat and hollered, "Wax Adoor!! Come here! I have news for you! A gift!"

Annoyed, Waxman turned and walked down to Tan, the others following.

When he reached the throne, Tan, lifted high, was able to throw his arm onto Waxman's shoulder. Waxman's eyes flickered to it in disgust, but otherwise he was unmoved, even when Tan bellowed into his ear. "My soldiers were spending some time in Shade City—you know, as soldiers do— and they came across a whole cargo of drivers! They ambushed and captured them for me, and now I'm giving them to you! Ha-ha! Isn't that a fabulous party gift?"

Waxman responded by pulling back and walking away, while saying, "I need elite drivers, not small planet dirt drivers entertained by Shade City."

Tan jumped up in his seat, causing his servants beneath him to groan, and called after him, "They are elite drivers! They were trying to avoid detection by hiding down in the shadow zone! But I'm happy you don't want them, Waxman —now I can use them for entertainment!" He shrieked with laughter and flopped back down on his throne.

"Onward!" he commanded his sweating servants.

Waxman, still walking ahead, turned to Gengai.

"Find those drivers and get them suited up and added to the others," he ordered. To Jevan, Iran and Kayanai, he said, "The rest of you, enjoy the party."

Then he left them, walking past the palace tent in the direction of his ship.

Jevan put her hands on her hips and smiled widely at the other three waxen.

"So, who's going to dance with me first?" She raised her eyebrows suggestively, then sashayed into the tent, laughing at them over her shoulder.

Kayanai grinned at Gengai.

"Not you, I guess. Too bad you've gotta work, Gengai!"

Gengai, mad at being left out, got into Kayanai's face,

"You know I'm getting pretty sick of you, Kayanai! I'm bigger, stronger, and younger and I could take you down like— "

"Whoa, whoa…" interjected Iran, pushing himself in front of Gengai, "I'm going to be spending enough time stopping meatheads from punching each other tonight; I don't want to have to start with you two."

His white shirt glowed in the lights like a flag of neutrality.

"C'mon Gengai. This party's going to be no fun anyway."

Gengai stopped glaring at Kayanai and looked at Iran. He calmed down.

"It's true. This party is going to be full of idiots—like you, Kayanai! I'll have more fun with those drivers anyway."

Gengai clapped Iran on the shoulder and left. Iran turned to see Kayanai, still amused, but looking at him questioningly.

"What do I owe for this service, O saviour?" asked Kayanai.

Iran leaned in and said, excitedly, "We needed him gone. This is our chance, Kayanai!"

He quieted his voice to a whisper, "We talked about Kolorov and how she could be the one to put the brakes on Waxman's plan, and how if Kolorov knew her granddaughter is here on Desigar, being kept from her by Waxman, she'd turn against him. We could make this happen right now! We could stop this war, Kayanai!"

Kayanai looked at his friend, wonderingly.

"You're thinking about going after the baby, tonight??" he whispered, hoarsely.

"It's the perfect opportunity! Gengai's busy, Waxman's not here… All you must do is keep Jevan busy—and given the way she looked at you just now, as long as you're with her, I'm sure she won't notice I'm gone!"

"But what if… wait, the way she looked at me? What do you mean?"

"Come on. You two - It's obvious from before you were waxen."

Kayanai paused for a moment with a surprised half-smile on his face, then he shook his head and said, "But wait, say you do manage to get in and take the baby without anyone noticing, then you still must get in to see Kolorov. How are you going to do that?"

"I'll improvise! Now get in there and keep Jevan busy. I'll be back in no time, you'll see."

"Wait Iran… us doing this… you realize what this means, right?"

Iran met his eyes and nodded. Waxman wanted to keep the baby for leverage to maintain the upper hand over Kolorov. By doing this they were going against Waxman—something a younger Kayanai would have found unimaginable, not only because it was disloyal, but also because it was profoundly dangerous. But Kayanai knew Iran was right; this was their chance.

"Good luck, my friend," he said to Iran, clasping his arm.

"Thanks, Kayanai."

Iran turned to go, then turned back and said, "And hey, if I don't come back. Don't go looking for me. No need for both of us to pay the price." And he was gone.

Kayanai took a deep breath, then ducked back into the tent.

CHAPTER ELEVEN

The lights, noise, and disorienting refreshments were making it difficult for Kayanai to gauge how long Iran had been gone; it seemed like forever.

"Maybe he's completed the mission already. Maybe he's just sitting in his ship right now. I could go check…"

It was a tempting thought, but Kayanai knew it was unlikely. Not to mention, he couldn't take the risk of Jevan wanting to come with him. Speaking of tempting…

It was hard to look away from her. At the moment, she was nodding and smiling charmingly at Council Member Yolan, despite the fact that Yolan was easily one of the most boring people alive. She glanced over at Kayanai and caught him staring at her. Her smile widened. Kayanai's face grew hot, and the tent suddenly felt unbearably stuffy.

"I need some air," he signaled to her. She nodded, and he squeezed past a loud group of Tan's entourage who were playing some messy game involving food and shrieking and pushed his way out of the tent.

It was a relief to be out of the noise and in the cool night air. Kayanai walked away from the tent, trying to push away his thoughts about Jevan. All night she'd been dancing, laughing, and blatantly flirting with him as if she had no care in the world, as if they weren't on the cusp of a war that would surely kill untold millions, including themselves. Cal and the Shrie

Shrie were sure to return the moment Kolorov'son's fleet attacked, and Iran's undertaking were sure to bring on Waxman's terrifying wrath, but those facts evaporated from his mind while Jevan was pressed against him and swaying to the music. She made him feel too much at once: admiration, affection, delight, desire, frustration, fury, disgust, sadness... It was too much.

He gazed up at the stars to calm his mind, but the atmosphere on Desigar caused the stars to streak and whirl; looking at them just made him feel even more unsteady. He was just considering heading back into the tent, when he heard his name whispered hoarsely.

"Kayanai!"

He turned, and there in the shadows next to the tent was Iran.

"What happened? Did you—"

Kayanai was silenced by Iran's iron grip pulling him into the shadows.

"Yes, I did," whispered Iran, pulling back the fabric of his white shirt. Inside, in a makeshift sling, snuggled into his hard chest, was a slumbering baby.

"You got it!" breathed Kayanai.

"Yeah," answered Iran, "but that's not all I got."

He reached down behind him and lifted the hulking remains of a busted mech.

"What the—? What's that? And why did you bring it here??"

"It was guarding the baby. I couldn't just leave it there. You know Waxman and Jevan; there's sure to be an internal recording device in it somewhere. They'd know it was me for sure. We have to bury it! You must help me, Kayanai. I can't do it with this little grub attached to me."

Kayanai swore under his breath, then said, "Okay. But we can't just bury a mech out in the open where anyone can see us. Let's go behind the council tent and shove it under there."

Iran nodded.

They moved in the shadows as silently and inconspicuously as two giants with a baby and a broken mech are capable, until they came to the council tent. They went behind it, then Kayanai knelt and began scooping sand out from the edge of the tent.

"Well, this is not how I expected my night would go," he muttered.

"Did you expect it to go more like, you and Jevan getting—"

"No." Kayanai paused, scowled at Iran, then went back to his digging and asked, "So what happened in there?"

Iran let out a hard breath and answered, "Well, let's just say it wasn't as easy as I expected. I thought I'd just sneak in there, swipe the kid, and sneak out again, but I ran into some trouble. Well, I didn't turn the lights on, 'cause I didn't want to announce my presence, right? So, first I have to make my way through that big, broken ship in the dark—not easy. Then, I finally find the room they were keeping her in, so I creep in, find the cryo unit, and I'm looking at the controls trying to figure out how to open it, and I hear that thing," Iran points the collapsed mech on the sand, "whirring behind me. So, I turn to grab it, and it zaps me! No questions asked, just gives me a zap! And Waxman cranks his mech's stunners extra, of course, so I gotta say, Ky, it bloody hurt. Now I'm mad, right? So, I reach out, grab the thing and just start smashing. Next thing I know, I'm standing there with a mech who's obviously Waxman's and obviously there to guard the baby, and it's now in a bunch of obvious pieces. - There's nothing I can do about it though, so I hurry back to open the cryo unit. I fiddle with the damn confusing thing for a while, pressing what seems to be the right keys, but nothing's happening. So there I am, punching stuff in randomly now like an idiot, sure at any moment Waxman's going to come in and catch me, and I start getting really damn mad at the piece of junk for not working, and, well… I punch it."

"Hell, Iran, you might have damaged it and hurt the baby!"

"Nah, I barely tapped it. And it turned out to be the right thing to do. See, the unit then figures it's in danger, so it beeps, and this chunk of the mech beeps back! So, I pick up the piece that beeped, hold it up against the control panel, and the thing opens!

Kayanai had to chuckle. "You're a lucky bastard, Iran."

"It's all brains, man. Anyway, there's the baby, still sleeping away, thankfully, and she's all wrapped up in this long fabric, so I wound it around me, put her in it, and there's the little bug all snug!"

He looked into his shirt and grinned at the little bundle.

"After that, I pick up all the bits of the mech, hightail it out of there, and now, here we are. You just about done with that digging?"

"I think so. Pass me the pieces."

Iran crouched down carefully, held the baby with one arm, and passed Kayanai the bits of the mech one by one, while Kayanai shoved them into the hole.

When all the pieces were in, Kayanai covered them, smoothed the top and pulled the tent fabric over top. "Alright. That's that," he breathed, relieved.

"Thanks, Ky. Now why don't you head back to the party and get back to keeping Jevan busy. I've got to get this kid to Kolorov."

Kayanai cocked his head, assessed Iran sceptically, and said,

"So, what's your plan to get into Kolorov's ship?"

Iran shrugged. "Won't be hard. I'll improvise."

Kayanai shook his head. "I'm coming with you," he said, firmly.

"You don't need—"

"You're going to need help getting in there. I'm in this too. C'mon. I can distract the guards."

Iran slowly smiled, nodded his head, and said, "Yeah, alright. It's a good idea."

They headed for the landing area, then made their way alongside the walkways to avoid being seen till they got to the platform that held Kolorov's ship. Then they peeked over the edge of the platform. Further down from them, a light spilled out of an open cargo hatch, and they could see workers and mechs moving large crates into the hold.

"They're restocking the ship," whispered Iran. "See, this is going to be easy."

Kayanai grimaced and whispered back, "What always happens when you say that?"

They waited and listened to two guards discuss how they would bring down a Waxen if they had to do it—a conversation that brought Iran and Kayanai dangerously close to being discovered by their laughter—till finally an opportunity presented itself when the loading crew took a break. Kayanai and Iran then crawled up, snuck behind the guards, and got behind a crate. Kayanai pointed to it and motioned to Iran that he should get into it. Iran gave Kayanai his best "you're crazy" look, but Kayanai just nodded emphatically. He motioned for Iran to stay put, then crept back to the side of the platform, silently lowered himself down, and moved to the other side of the guards where there were more crates waiting to be loaded. He grabbed the edge of a crate, paused, took a deep breath, then ripped the back of the crate off with a squeal of protesting metal. He was off and running before the side hit the ground with a thump.

From the edge of the platform, he could see the guards moving to investigate. He ran back to Iran who, thankfully, had figured out what Kayanai had meant and had already gotten the side of the crate open.

As Iran crept into the cramped crate, he looked out at Kayanai, and before he could speak, Kayanai whispered, "Good luck," and he shut Iran in.

Just in time too; the crew was coming out to see what the commotion was, and Kayanai barely had time to get away.

The guards had shut the open crate back up, shrugged their shoulders, and repositioned themselves by the entrance. The crew were back to loading supplies into the hold, and as Kayanai watched, two mechs lifted the crate that held Iran and the baby into Kolorov's ship.

Kayanai, from his hiding place, considered what to do next. He could go back to the party, but he couldn't shake the feeling that Iran might still need his help.

The workers were finished loading, and one of them called the guards over. The guards conferred with each other, then one walked over to find out what they wanted. The worker produced a couple of bottles and there was much laughing and slapping of backs. The second guard went over to join them, a little unsurely, and a little party began.

Kayanai made a snap decision. He straightened up, put on his best no-nonsense expression, and approached the group.

"What have we here?" he barked at them.

The guards jumped up and turned around, guiltily. Their eyes widened when they looked up and saw the fierce eyes of a Waxen peering down at them.

"I didn't realize Kolorov's ship was included in the celebrations," continued Kayanai.

"We were just—" one guard began.

"What are you—?" began the other.

Kayanai cut them off. "Looks like you're having a good time. I bet Kolorov herself would like to join you. She could guard her own ship while you enjoy yourselves. Why don't I go ask her?"

The worker who'd brought out the bottles, squeaked, "We were just finishing. We should get back inside."

One of the guards cleared his throat and said, "We were just telling them to stop fooling around and get going."

"Well then," said Kayanai to the workers, sharply, "you'd better get going then."

In a flash, the workers grabbed the bottles and disappeared up the ramp.

Kayanai then turned to the guards. "Get back to your posts and I won't have to mention this to Kolorov."

They immediately rushed to take their places. Then Kayanai walked up the ramp to enter the ship, smiling to himself. He knew the guards wouldn't come after him, nor would they mention the incident to anyone. All Kayanai had to do now was avoid being seen. Easier said than done given his size.

He was now in an enormous cargo hold filled with crates identical to the one Iran was in. The workers were all gone, and the lights were dim.

"Iran?" he said, softly.

Then came a sound so eerie and unfamiliar it caused the hairs on Kayanai's neck to rise. It took a moment for Kayanai to recognize what it was; it was the muffled sound of a baby crying.

He followed the sound until he came to the crate with the barely perceptible cuts on the edges. He stuck his knife in the sides and pried the crate open. The crying was suddenly very loud.

"Iran?" Kayanai called.

Iran pushed his way out of the crate, his face a mixture of profound vexation and relief.

"Ky, man, I've never been so happy to see anyone. How do we get this kid to shut up??"

Iran held open his shirt. Kayanai looked in at the furious little face, and a dim memory came to him from what seemed like many lifetimes ago.

"She's probably hungry. Put your finger in her mouth and bounce her around," said Kayanai.

Iran looked at him in surprise.

"Way, way back, I had a little sister." Kayanai said shortly.

"Just do it, or we'll be surrounded in no time."

Iran dubiously began rocking side to side and stuck his enormous finger in the tiny child's mouth. She immediately began sucking and blessed silence followed.

"Okay, let's go find Kolorov," said Kayanai.

They peered out into the corridor and saw no one. They counted themselves lucky in two ways: first it was late enough that only a skeleton crew was operating the ship, and second, they were in the cargo area and the lifts there were large enough for both of them. They found a lift and got inside.

Kayanai looked at the control display and said, "Which deck do you think she's on?"

"She'll be near the bridge. I'd say here," Iran, unthinkingly, pulled his finger from the baby's mouth and pointed to a spot on the display. Kayanai looked at him in horror, and they both waited for the screaming to begin again. Iran looked down and breathed a sigh of relief.

"She's asleep again," he said.

Kayanai punched in their destination, and the lift took off.

While they were waiting Iran said, "So, a sister hey? I thought you didn't have a family."

"By the time I became a Waxen, I didn't." Kayanai shrugged,

"I don't even remember their faces."

Suddenly they heard little gasping noises coming from Iran's shirt.

"Quick! Bounce her!" said Kayanai.

Iran began bobbing up and down.

"Finger!" demanded Kayanai.

Iran shoved his finger into the baby's mouth. The noises stopped.

Watching Iran, the corners of Kayanai's mouth turned up into a small smile.

"This is not funny," insisted Iran.

Kayanai's split into a grin. "You should see yourself."

Iran's mouth twitched as he bounced. "Hey man, this is a serious situation."

He looked at Kayanai, and they both started laughing.

The lift slowed and they sobered a bit.

"Seriously though," said Iran, his smile fading. "What am I supposed to do if there's trouble? I can't fight like this."

"That's why I'm here. I'll deal with any trouble. But let's do our best to avoid any."

The door to the lift opened and Kayanai peered around the corner. A woman was standing just outside the lift giving orders to a mech. As she turned around, Kayanai jumped back in and closed the doors. He waited a bit, then opened them again. The woman was gone, and the mech was interfacing with the ship's computer.

Kayanai stepped out and said to the mech, "I need the location of Kolorov's quarters."

The mech turned to Kayanai, assessed him and said, "You are not authorized to be here."

Kayanai moved like lightning. The mech was now pinned against the wall and unable to move.

"I still need the location," said Kayanai.

"I am loyal to Kolorov and will choose deactivation over disclosing her whereabouts to her enemy."

"I'm not her enemy. I'm here to give her something precious. Something she'll want more than anything."

The mech considered, then asked, "What is this thing?"

"Iran?"

Iran stepped out and opened his shirt.

"This is her granddaughter," said Kayanai.

The mech scanned the face of the baby and said, "There is a high probability that you are telling the truth."

"Then take us to Kolorov," demanded Kayanai. "Come with us, and if you see anything you don't like, you can raise the alarm."

"I could raise it now," said the mech.

"But you would be in a million pieces by the time anyone got here," said Kayanai.

The mech considered, then answered, "I believe that Kolorov will want to see you, and I am confident she can handle any trouble you cause her. Follow me."

"Take a quiet route," said Kayanai.

The mech set off down the corridor, and as they followed Iran murmured to Kayanai, "Seems our new friend here has a strong self-preservation program."

"Good thing—for him and us."

They continued down corridors, the mech stopping occasionally to avoid crewmembers, until finally they came to a large set of doors.

The mech pressed a panel next to the door and waited. Nothing happened.

"I don't believe she's in."

"Well, let's go in and wait for her," said Kayanai

"It's not my place to do so."

"It's not our place either, Scrapheap. Just open the door," growled Iran, impatiently.

The mech hesitated, then keyed in a code and the door opened.

Kayanai stepped into the spacious living quarters of the most powerful commander in the Alliance and was immediately impressed with its atmosphere of calm and order.

Iran went to sit down on a divan, when the mech said, hastily,

"It's not right that you should sit on her furniture."

Iran looked at the mech in disbelief, "I'll tell you what isn't right," he said as he approached the mech slowly, "us keeping you around when we don't need you anymore," and he shot his hand out, grabbed the mech with one hand, and pulled the mech's power unit from behind it's back with the other. The mech crumpled to the ground, and the baby started crying again.

"Iran!"

"What? It's fine! Totally fixable!" He stuck his finger in the baby's mouth and it sucked furiously.

Kayanai looked around and thought quickly. He dragged the mech behind a large plant and went over to the door leading to Kolorov's sleeping area.

"We don't know how Kolorov is going to react. For all we know she may try to lock us up or give us up to Waxman. We'll have an advantage if she doesn't know I'm here," he said. "I'll stay back here and come out if there's trouble."

"Good plan. I tell you though, there's going to be trouble if we don't get this kid some food. She's going to suck my thumb raw," replied Iran, who had now settled himself onto the divan.

There was a sound at the door, and Kayanai slipped into the adjoining room and peeked out just as the door slid open.

Kolorov stepped in, unbuttoned her jacket, hung it on a hook and turned around. Finding a giant lounging on one's furniture might startle most people, but Kolorov was made of stronger stuff than most. Iran may as well have been a cushion for the amount her face reacted.

"I should call for security, though I imagine if you were sent here to kill me, I'd be dead already. Tell me what you're doing here, Iran Crowne" she commanded, calmly, stepping forward so they were nearly face to face.

Iran suddenly realized he had no idea where to start.

"Your son…" he paused.

Kolorov swallowed heavily, but she kept her composure. Suddenly she moved, she took the chair from a nearby desk, placed it in front of Iran and sat down,

"You have my attention."

Iran sat up and took a deep breath. As he looked at Kolorov, he realized that he liked and respected this woman, and he was glad he could give her the news she so desperately wanted to hear.

"He's alive. He's still on his way to Gengaru. He may already be there."

Kolorov's hard face softened, and she closed her eyes. Tears came from the corners, but when she opened them again, the steely look was back.

"Why am I hearing this now? Like this?" She paused, her mind working. Suddenly, she looked at him sharply, "Waxman doesn't know you're here. Why does he want me to think my son is dead?"

"She's damn quick," thought Kayanai, from behind the door. "She deserves her reputation. Well, Iran. You might as well tell her everything."

Iran must have agreed, because he said, "Waxman doesn't want you to send your fleet to Gengaru to save your son, and he figures you might do this, given your son is now without his flagship, without his escort of ten thousand waxen, and is about to go up against the Shrie Shrie. See, Waxman wants your fleet for something here. We're not sure for what though."

Kolorov's eyes narrowed in silent anger.

"He's right," she said, icily, "You can be sure, I'll be ordering to send my fastest ships this very night. I know they won't reach my son for a long time, but at least as they approach, he'll be able to receive the message that they're coming, which might make a difference. I will keep the rest of the fleet with me, however. I have a feeling I'll be needing them here. Waxman will need to be very convincing about why he wants my fleet, or I'll be taking my ships back to The Wellspring."

The baby chose that moment to express her dissatisfaction with Iran's finger and let out a howl. Kayanai was glad he got to witness the Unmovable Kolorov react to that cry. She nearly jumped out of her chair.

"Iran Crowne! Is that a baby in your shirt?" she exclaimed in wonder.

"Uh, yeah! I was just getting to telling you about her."

He opened his shirt and showed Kolorov the baby's tiny angry face. Kolorov stared at the baby in confusion.

"Her? Who is she?"

"She's your granddaughter."

Kolorov froze, flabbergasted.

"I guess Kolorov's son met someone on the mission and, well, here she is! Jevan brought her back."

Tears now flowed freely from Kolorov's eyes. She reached for the baby and pulled her from Iran's shirt.

"My granddaughter," she said softly. She clutched the baby to her chest. Her wondrous expression shifted to cold anger.

"Tell me why Khran was keeping my granddaughter from me."

"Waxman figured she'd be a good bargaining tool. In case you didn't do what he wanted."

The anger in Kolorov's face would have frightened a weaker man than Iran.

"He's about to be very disappointed. I suggest you get off my ship now, Crowne. We'll be leaving shortly." She began walking towards the door.

"Yes, ma'am. Oh, so you know, there's a mech behind that plant there that'll need putting back together. Sorry."

She paused then turned and looked at him with something that approached affection.

"You can leave by the escape hatch from my bedroom. Thank you for giving me my granddaughter. I will not mention your visit to Waxman." Then she turned around and exited quickly.

"Let's go," said Kayanai from the doorway.

Iran ran over and they searched the bedroom till they found the hidden exit hatch.

Jevan stood looking out at the looming dark shapes of ships layering the monochrome purple landscape. The sounds of lazy music and murmurs of the last lingering revellers came from the still brightly lit palace tent behind her.

Kayanai had not returned, and she hadn't seen Iran all night. They were out there somewhere without her. Why without her? She briefly considered that they were off somewhere being "manly" where a woman would be unwelcome, but she quickly dismissed the idea. They weren't like that. Why then? Certainly, they were doing something she wouldn't like, or she would have been invited. What could they be doing?

Suddenly, the sweat on her brow felt cold.

"Would they? Would they dare—?" Jevan didn't even finish the thought. She slid quickly into the night, trying to move fast without being noticeably in a hurry. She climbed up to the battered Regent and slipped into a back hatch. Then she ran to the biomed chamber where the baby was being kept and slammed opened the door.

There was no mech to greet her. She moved to the cryo unit.

The red light glowed UNOCCUPIED.

Jevan reeled, placed her hands on the counter behind her and breathed heavily.

"They did it. They took the baby. They betrayed Waxman. They betrayed me," thought Jevan. Then came a worse thought. "I told them. I betrayed Waxman."

Fighting tears, she reached for her comm.

"Wax."

There was a long pause, then his voice filled the room.

"Here."

He didn't sound tired, though it was likely she'd woken him. He never sounded tired.

"The baby is gone."

"I'm coming."

While waiting for him, Jevan paced the room, trying to steel herself.

His anger, his disappointment would be unprecedented.

"How could they do this to him? How could they do this to me?" She would have to tell Waxman it was them… her boys… her friends… her Kayanai. She would have to give them up.

"What will he do to them?" she thought. "What will he do to me?" She shook her head. "I can't think that way. I must do my duty."

Jevan tried calming her mind by picturing what had taken place; that way at least she could explain to Waxman what had happened, competently.

"They would have come in and been approached by the mech. The mech… what did they do with the mech?"

She looked around, but saw no evidence of a fight, and saw no trace of the mech.

"Where's the mech?"

Her thought was interrupted by the sound of the door opening.

Jevan brought her eyes up to meet the hard glare of her leader, and in that moment, she had the thought that could save them all. Her agony dissipated and she was confident once more.

"What happened?" said Waxman.

She could tell Waxman was very, very angry, but he was, of course, calmly controlling it.

"I came in to check on things, and the baby was gone."

"Why?"

Jevan paused, then said, confused, "Why is the baby—?"

"Why did you come check on things?"

Fear began creeping back into Jevan, but she pushed it down.

"I had a feeling. She was alone. I just… wanted to make sure everything was okay." Let Waxman think it was an enigmatic maternal thing.

"Everything is not okay, evidently," growled Waxman. "Where is the baby?"

"I have a theory."

Waxman waited for her to continue.

"The mech is also gone. It belonged to Kolorov's son, given to me by him to care for the baby during the trip back to Desigar. As you know, some mechs are loyal not just to one person, but to whole families. I believe this mech's loyalty drive was activated when Kolorov arrived, and it contacted her, and brought her the baby."

Waxman considered her for a long time. Despite her calm exterior, a bead of sweat trickled down her hairline. She hoped he didn't see it.

"It seems a likely theory," he answered, finally. "We'll have to contact Kolorov and do damage control. You must convince her that you were going to tell her about her granddaughter but were waiting for an appropriate time."

Jevan nodded, letting her breath out slowly.

As they left the ship, a rumbling began. It started low, then grew to roar, and the ground began to shake. Then, as Jevan and Waxman watched, the entirety of Kolorov's fleet took off from the surface of Desigar and one by one shot off into the starry sky.

The silence that followed was deafening. Jevan couldn't take her eyes off the stars. Like a dormant volcano woken, she could feel the heat of Waxman's rage bubbling up next to her.

"Jevan," he said, surprisingly softly. "How much did that mech know about our plans?"

She forced her eyes to meet his. His eyes were like flames.

"Nothing. The mech knew nothing apart from that it was to care for the baby," she managed to answer evenly.

He leaned closer. Then he asked the question she'd been desperately hoping to avoid.

"Now, think carefully. Did anyone else know about the baby?"

Jevan breathed in slowly and was suddenly calm.

"No," she said. "No one else knew."

He held her eyes, then, he turned and stalked off towards his ship.

Over his shoulder he barked, "Call the others and get them aboard the Regent. We leave for Wellspring Solichia by dawn."

Jevan followed him, her soul feeling black and heavy. She'd chosen. There was no going back.

CHAPTER TWELVE

The sky was lightening along the horizon; dawn was not far away. Jevan was still standing next to the ruined Regent when the silhouettes of three waxen approached her.

"Jevan," said Kayanai, trying to sound normal. "How was the rest of the party? Sorry I disappeared like that, I was just tired."

Jevan stepped towards Kayanai till she was toe to toe with him. Her eyes drilled into his.

"Kolorov is gone. And so is the baby"

She watched him closely for a reaction. Kayanai forced himself to keep his eyes steady. He didn't want to lie to her. His unlikely saviour was Gengai.

"Baby?" said Gengai, irritably. "What baby?" He snapped his fingers annoyingly in Jevan's face. "Hey, I finally get to join the party and he calls us in about some baby? What's this about, Jevan? What's Waxman doing?"

Jevan nodded towards Waxman's silhouette in the distance.

"Ah," said Gengai. "He's walking. That means he's doing his thinking," he informed the others, knowingly.

Jevan rolled her eyes at him. "Thanks for the insight, Gengai."

"He's coming back," said Kayanai.

Waxman was stalking towards them.

"Good. Now we'll find out what's going on," said Gengai.

The others didn't share Gengai's enthusiasm for Waxman's approach. Kayanai could feel his stomach tightening, and Jevan quickly wiped another bead of sweat from her forehead.

When Waxman was standing in front of them, he stopped and surveyed them with complete authority. When he finally spoke, his voice was soft, yet commanding.

"Kolorov's fleet is a necessity. It must be retrieved. Kayanai, we will escort you to Wellspring Solichia where you will request a diplomatic meeting with Kolorov. You will tell her you have news of her son, and that you would like to discuss upcoming military operations. She will admit you, and when you are given the signal, you will assassinate her and take her fleet emblem vest."

Kayanai goggled at Waxman in disbelief, and Iran burst out,

"Assassinate Kolorov? And on a Wellspring planet? Wax, if we break the accord, we'll be instant enemies of the Alliance. Our ship will be detained, for sure, and they'll throw every bit of firepower they have at Kayanai. He's tough but he can't take on the security of an entire planet!"

Waxman considered Iran's words, then said to Kayanai, "It will be difficult, but we will get you out." He walked away again.

"This is crazy!" said Iran, hoarsely. "C'mon, Jevan, even you have to admit killing Kolorov goes too far."

"He means it, Kayanai," Jevan said, uncertainly, as her eyes followed Waxman pacing in the desert. "He'll get you out."

"No, he won't," said Iran. "Because Kayanai isn't going, I am."

"He picked me to go," said Kayanai.

"It makes more sense for me to go," Iran looked at Kayanai, pointedly.

"Why?" asked Jevan.

"Because…" Iran thought wildly. "Kayanai is Waxman's best soldier. Kolorov will suspect trouble. Besides, I look more like a diplomat, don't I?" he finished, triumphantly.

Gengai snorted, and Jevan looked sceptical, but they refrained from comment as they saw Waxman returning.

Iran greeted him with, "Waxman, I want to go instead. I'm the better choice for this mission."

Waxman considered briefly, then said, "If you are keener, then you are the better choice. You will not be attacked. We will not break the accord."

"But killing Kolorov—" started Kayanai.

"Hers will be one of many bodies," interrupted Waxman. "Her death will be a tragic accident."

Jevan broke in, confused. "How do we attack the palace without breaking the accord?"

"Docked at The Station is a Partisian water freighter called The Eventful. It's a terraforming ship with enough water inside it to drown a city. Gengai, I'm sending you to steal The Eventful. You will dump the ship's load on Kolorov's headquarters. Iran, it will be your job to ensure Kolorov drown and, most importantly, to secure the fleet vest."

Kayanai's blood ran cold. He'd been a part of countless attacks on many planets and against many people, but he'd never brought death and destruction to a wellspring. This was wrong.

"The Partisians will go after Gengai," warned Jevan.

"I'm counting on that," answered Waxman. "Gengai will be away fast enough to avoid capture, but he will be followed. Lead the Partisians into space jump, Gengai, but don't lose them. Bring their destroyers to Wellspring Solichia at the appointed time, and when they arrive, armed and angry, the planet's defense systems will engage them, not you. Once you're in position and I give the signal, release the water and jump ship— but leave no trace. We will all meet in front of Kolorov's headquarters. I will then inform the authorities about Kolorov's death and take command."

Silence followed. It was a clever, cruel, and dangerous plan.

Finally, Kayanai said. "At least let me go down with Iran in his cruiser. I'll wait outside the headquarters. That way I'm there if he needs backup."

Waxman nodded. "Agreed. Jevan, you can fly the Regent. Any other concerns?"

His wax men had many other concerns, but they knew protesting was pointless. Waxman knew it too, so he walked away after barely a pause.

Once he'd gone, Gengai broke the silence.

"What does all this have to do with a baby?" he said, turning to Kayanai.

"Kayanai doesn't know!" burst out Jevan, suddenly realizing her mistake. She thought fast then sidled up to Gengai. "Nobody knew about the baby except Waxman and me. I forgot because I was… upset." She put on her best doe-eyed expression, then continued. "The baby doesn't matter now. All that matters is that you and Iran make it out of there okay." She hugged the surprised Gengai while scowling over his shoulder at Iran and Kayanai. Then she hugged Iran, murmuring, "I hope you know what you're doing," and walked up the ramp to prepare the Regent for flight.

Gengai groaned, and said, "I can't believe I have to do this with no sleep. Still, it's going to be a great way to show off my skills."

He smirked and headed off in the direction of the tower.

Kayanai and Iran were left alone. Iran shook his head in disbelief. "Well, this is… not good," he said.

"Jevan knows," said Kayanai, softly.

"She doesn't. She might suspect, but she doesn't know."

Despite his horror, Kayanai suddenly felt less hopeless. "She covered for us. She's with us, Iran."

"Hey, even if she is on our side deep down, Jevan's not going to help us thwart Waxman's plan to kill Kolorov and start a war without him knowing. That is what we're going to do, right?"

Kayanai nodded. "Yeah. That's what we're going to do. If you don't get killed." Kayanai turned and headed up the ramp. Iran followed, shaking his head.

The tranquil image of Wellspring Solichia floated in the Regent's last remaining viewscreen, a pale green jewel in a sea of black. Many artworks were dedicated to Solichia's endless lakes and rolling hills, and its beauty was described in countless poems and songs. The sight of it, however, brought Jevan no peace.

Next to her sat Waxman, speaking over the ship's comm system to a diplomat at Kolorov's headquarters. Waxman signed off and touched his cheek. "Iran. Kolorov has agreed to meet with you after her midday meal. Once we reach low orbit, you'll take your cruiser down and wait for her to call you in. I specified the information would be personal so you should be alone but be prepared to deal with it if you're not."

In the bowels of the Regent, Kayanai was helping prepare Iran's light cruiser for ejection. He listened to Iran answer Waxman.

"Got it. I'll head out as soon as we're in position. See you at the rendezvous." Iran tapped his cheek and looked at Kayanai.

"Deal with it? How many bodies is Waxman expecting me to make? This keeps getting better and better."

"She'll see you alone if you insist." Kayanai lowered his voice despite being safely in Iran's ship. "Remember, you have to get Kolorov out, but you can't let her know what Waxman is planning. She'll want to stay and save her people, but if she does that, Waxman will be on to us."

"What if I can't convince her?"

"You have to."

Waxman's voice cut in over Iran's comm giving Kayanai a turn. "We're in position. Iran, don't let us down."

Iran tapped his vest and the ship's controls and the floor beneath them opened to reveal Soldicha's atmosphere. Another tap and they were plunging towards the planet's surface.

Back up in the Regent's secondary command station, Jevan watched the cruiser sink down till it was out of sight.

"Jevan," said Waxman, "After the water dissipates, you will bring us down in front of Kolorov's Headquarters. Then you will go into the Shrie Shrie warcruiser and prepare to phase into Desigar airspace between The Station and The Infidel. At that point, it will be all up to you."

Jevan nodded. She felt an odd anticipation about returning to the alien ship, the way one would feel about returning to a favorite hideaway, or an old sleep room. She knew flying it meant starting a war, but that too was familiar territory. The unease she felt was for her friends below, not for her own work ahead.

"They'd better pull this off," she thought, worriedly.

/ / /

Iran guided the cruiser over tall, translucent buildings nestled among lush, green forests until they came to the older, stone-walled structure that was the chief commander's headquarters. Then he lowered them down onto the adjacent landing platform to which they were assigned.

"So, you're going to wait here?" Iran asked Kayanai.

"I'd come in with you if I thought they'd let me in."

"I'm sure you're wishing you could come in and find out what it's like to have a small ocean dumped on you."

"Hey, given Gengai's aim, I'll probably find out anyway."

Iran chuckled. "See you soon, Ky." Then he lowered the ramp and left the cruiser.

Kayanai went up to the cruiser's cockpit and directed the viewscreen to the sky. Then he sat back and waited. "Good luck, buddy," he said softly.

From their position, Waxman and Jevan could see both Kolorov's armada floating above them, and with the viewer fully zoomed, Kolorov's headquarters below. Jevan hated waiting and was trying not to show impatience. Waxman sat like a stone, as usual.

Suddenly, there was a blinding flash and the water freighter appeared. The freighter's great bulk managed to veer around the Regent, then it blasted down through the atmosphere. Another flash and the Partisian destroyers were bearing down on The Regent.

Jevan smiled, "Nice driving, Gengai," she thought to herself.

She watched, fascinated, as the Partisians, suddenly finding themselves surrounded by the largest fleet in the Alliance, dissolved into confusion. Some of them braked off immediately, and some kept after Gengai intent on retrieving their freighter. Some of the fleet ships took off after the Partisians following Gengai.

Waxman grunted with satisfaction. "Excellent. He's leading them into position." He tapped his cheek. "Iran, status?"

Iran's strained voice came over the comm, "I need more time. Kolorov isn't here yet."

"Get her there! Insist!" Waxman barked.

"I'll signal you as soon as I'm ready."

Waxman tapped his cheek again. "Gengai, you're going to have to delay a little."

"Will do!" yelled back Gengai. He sounded like he was having a great time.

"At least someone's enjoying himself," thought Jevan.

Kayanai sat looking at the placid green Solichian sky for what felt like a very long time. His mind was wandering when he suddenly realized that a section of the sky was getting brighter. The light steadily increased, then out of the glow emerged a bulky freighter ship coming in fast. It was Gengai in The Eventful. Behind him, Kayanai could make out two small but dangerous looking Partisian destroyers, then behind those followed three fleet ships. Kayanai watched as Gengai led the other ships on a wild chase, impressive given the water freighter he was driving was definitely not built for complex maneuvers.

Still watching, fascinated, Kayanai tapped his cheek. "Hey Iran, better move!"

"I'm trying!" yelled Iran over the comm. Before he broke off Kayanai heard him say, "Kolorov, I'm telling you, you need to take your granddaughter now!" There was a long pause then Iran came back on. "Okay we're good. I'll be able to give the signal momentarily." He sounded profoundly relieved.

When Waxman felt Iran's signal on his cheek, he tapped for Gengai. "Get ready to take position and drop."

Time ticked by slowly till finally Iran's voice came on the comm.

"Ready."

"Gengai," said Waxman, "Now."

If the situation hadn't been so awful, Kayanai would have really enjoyed watching Gengai outfly the Partisian and fleet ships in the water freighter. The Partisians were smart enough not to use weapons on a wellspring planet, but this meant the only way they could stop Gengai was by blocking and trapping him. Their task was made all the more difficult by the fleet ships trying to detain them with pull shields. It was astonishing that Gengai was able to avoid capture, but he somehow kept slipping away from them.

This went on for a while, till Gengai positioned the freighter high above Kolorov's headquarters, then suddenly dropped the ship straight down, stopped and set it to drift.

The shadow of The Eventful engulfed the elegant old building.

Kayanai could picture its numerous inhabitants stopping their usual bustling along the headquarters long corridors and winding staircases to look up and wonder at the sudden darkness and the screams of guards. Kayanai realized that he was about to get wet if he didn't get to higher ground, so he jumped up and grabbed the side of the cruiser and scrambled up to the top. When he looked up again, he saw a slice appearing along the Eventful's base as if the ship were fatally injured, and as its bowels split open a torrent of water was released. The water became like a solid mass that seemed to hang in the air. and in that brief moment Kayanai could see the shadow of a giant posed above it, proud and triumphant, then the shadow dove, and the water came crashing down on Kolorov's headquarters, pummeling it with the force of a malevolent god.

The extensive building with its sprawling grounds was surrounded by a historic stone wall, and in a single moment the space within those walls had become a tumultuous sea, crashing over the sides, running into the streets, and swirling around the base of the cruiser. Kayanai could now hear the screaming and wailing of the people outside the walls and could see guards and citizens running forward to lower the stone gate to allow the water out.

Kayanai made a mighty leap down from the cruiser and ran towards the people about to lower the gate.

"Wait! You'll be swept away!" he yelled. He shoved some away from the gate and bellowed at the rest till they moved back. Then, steadying himself as best he could he reached up and flipped the release mechanism. The gate would have slammed down with the great force of the water pushing against it had Kayanai not reached up and strained against it. Using all his considerable might, he lowered the gate slowly and the water gushed overhead. It ran out into the street and wet all those nearby, but it didn't sweep anyone away. Kayanai stood there a long time, the water pouring over top of him, people shouting and clamoring to get inside and help those within the walls. Finally, the water slowed enough for people to climb up over the gate, and Kayanai was able to lower the gate to the ground.

When he was able to push through the gate into the front courtyard, he saw an appalling sight.

Bodies floated everywhere. The water was still up to most people's knees and the current was making it difficult for the emergency workers to get to those who were still alive and needed help.

Kayanai splashed his way towards the rendezvous point on the stairs at the front of the headquarters. When he was nearly there, he saw a small door be pushed open causing more water to gush out and join the rest. He recognized the wet white shirt clinging to the muscled torso of his friend before Iran ducked under the doorway and emerged from the building.

His face was grim, but when Iran caught sight of Kayanai a smile flitted across it, and he held up the fleet vest. Kayanai nodded. The two waxen met in silence and walked together until the edge of the building. Kayanai stopped for a moment and turned to Iran.

"You could have told Waxman you couldn't get it," he said, indicating the vest."

"I thought about it," answered Iran, "but that would have just brought down his wrath and done nothing but delay him. You know he always gets what he wants."

"He didn't get Kolorov's death."

Iran stood taller. "No, Kolorov got out with the kid. You know, before she left, she said, 'I won't give you away. I'll stay hidden. But I'll strike back one day. He just won't know it's me.' I believe her. Waxman just made himself a powerful enemy."

"If there was ever anyone whose word you can trust, it's Kolorov's."

They came around the corner of the building to the stairs and the front courtyard. The normally carefully tended, pristine foliage was wet and bedraggled, debris and bodies were strewn about, emergency response teams were rushing to and from, and security forces were pouring in and securing the area. At the top of the stairs stood Gengai, looking down at what he'd accomplished with his shoulders back and his hands on his hips. As Kayanai and Iran approached him, he turned and gave them a smug smile and a wink. He was clearly revoltingly proud of himself.

The remains of the Regent had landed outside the ornate front gates. In front of the gates stood Waxman and Jevan, speaking to the guards. The gates were thrown open and Waxman strode in to meet the security leads to discuss the situation.

Eventually, a crowd of people consisting of security officers, diplomats, comm mechs, survivors and citizens were gathered at the foot of the stairs, while Waxman climbed them to join Iran Kayanai and Gengai.

When he'd reached the top, Waxman said to Iran, "Vest," and held out his hand. Iran handed it over. "Well done."

To Gengai he said, "We're all saddened by this event. Adjust your face accordingly." Then he turned and looked out at the people below and began his speech.

"Citizens of Solichia, know that this tragedy is being investigated by your capable security forces, and that everything is being done to help the victims. My waxen and I are happy to offer any assistance we can, but first I must be the bearer of very sad news."

Waxman held up the vest and there was a gasp from the audience.

"Iran Crowne had gone to meet Chief Commander Kolorov to discuss with her the next movements of the central fleet and was nearby when the water hit. They were both taken by surprise when the water impacted, and he lost sight of her. I'm very sorry to say that by the time he located her, it was too late, the Chief Commander was gone. It is significant that her vest, this vest, was not on her person, but floating nearby, as if she'd removed it. I believe Kolorov knew that the command of the greatest fleet in the Alliance needed to be passed on, as she had just heard from my representative Crowne that danger may soon be returning to our section of the galaxy.

A comm mech was blinking at the foot of the stairs and taking in every word. Suddenly, it's head split and a holo of Solichia's political leader Vola's sleek head materialized above.

"Wax Adoor - Waxman. Your presence now is truly serendipitous. Apart from this outrageous and depraved attack on our wellspring capital, we have just had news of another tribulation to deal with; we are receiving reports that a Shrie Shrie ship has been spotted outside the Infidel. The fleet needs to be deployed immediately. The fleet emblem vest you hold will allow you to control our fleet. We would be most grateful if you would take command and confront our enemy."

Kayanai knew that if it wasn't for Waxman's extreme self-discipline, in that moment he would have exuded supreme satisfaction. Kayanai looked at Iran, and Iran mouthed "Jevan".

This was it. The war was beginning.

CHAPTER THIRTEEN

In the smooth, darkly luminescent cockpit of the Shrie Shrie warcruiser, Jevan Khran sat, legs crossed, mind calm. She felt strangely at home back in the alien ship, and strangely at peace for one who had just rekindled a violent war. All her deep worries about whether she would again be able to control the Shrie Shrie ship dissolved when she stepped into the cockpit and sat down.

She had only to will the ship to the chosen location and with the telltale vertical flash of Shrien phasing, she was there.

"I could go anywhere," she thought.

She shook it off, and changed the thought to, "I want to see The Station."

Suddenly it was right there before her, it's dark shape barely visible against the inky black surrounding it. There was no sign of the assault that would soon be directed towards her.

Jevan smiled unconcerned and changed the view to The Infidel looming behind her. She gazed at the alien station with fascination. It, too, was dark. No energy could be detected, yet through some unexplainable method, it maintained its impossible orbit around Desigar. She couldn't decide whether she wanted it to wake or not. Either way, she felt safe in her cocoon.

Iran and Kayanai were flashing through jump space towards the Station in Iran's cruiser and musing over Waxman's final words to them: "Go to the Station and prepare the ships on the operational side to launch an attack against The Infidel. Limit activity to the working side and leave the other side dark. All ships must be detached and ready on the opposite side of the Infidel by my time mark. You must be off that station at this time. You do not want to be on that station when the signal for the attack comes. Do you understand?"

In response they had nodded smartly, hiding their uncertainty. Now, moments from arriving at the Station, they tried to unravel their mysterious orders.

"The ships with the special marks on them all went to the side of the Station that's "under repair," said Iran.

"Perhaps they're components of a secret weapon that will be unleashed on the Infidel," replied Kayanai.

"If that's the case, why is it so important we be off the Station?"

"Maybe it's volatile."

"Too volatile for us? If it's a weapon, why isn't he having us stay and deploy it?"

Kayanai shook his head. "It doesn't make sense."

Iran snapped his fingers. "I'll tell you what does make sense—Waxman's going to blow up The Station!"

Kayanai looked sceptical. "We're about to make an attack on the Infidel, breaking the cease fire and rekindling the war with the Shrie Shrie, so Waxman's going to kick it off by blowing up our busiest, most important station? Even with half of it shut down and the fleet ships detached there will still be thousands of people on that station. How does blowing it up make sense?" he said drily.

"Waxman doesn't care about them or the Station, he only cares about defeating his enemies. If he detonates in the right places, the Station will be propelled down and it'll fall out of orbit— "

"Leaving a clear path for our ships to attack The Infidel," finished Kayanai, thoughtfully. "I don't know. It would give us a slight advantage, but I don't think…" Kayanai frowned, thinking furiously. "Unless…" He looked up, suddenly. "He's going to blame the explosion on the Shrie Shrie."

Iran nodded slowly. "He needs a reason to attack the Shrie Shrie with full force. If everyone believes they struck first, he'll have complete support to do whatever he wants."

"So, what do we do?"

"Find the explosives and deactivate them?"

Kayanai let out a whistling breath. "We won't have a lot of time."

Iran smiled, wryly. "Guess we'll have to move fast."

They came out of jump space, and as the cruiser approached the Station, Kayanai noticed something interesting.

"Wait. Slow down," he said. "Pan and scan the lower perimeter ships."

Iran did as he asked, and Kayanai leaned in looking carefully at the screen.

"See look," said Kayanai, "Notice every eight ships—"

"They all have that insignia!" exclaimed Iran. "He's spread them out around the Station."

Kayanai nodded. "Why go through the danger and effort of unloading the explosives if you can just put them at key points and blow the ships."

"We're not going to be able to get into each of those ships to deactivate those bombs in the amount of time we have."

"No, but we can get those ships away from the Station so there's no critical damage."

"We're going to have to make a visit to the Stationmaster."

Iran deftly swung the ship up and into a waiting docking opening, keyed in the code, and slammed in the locking coils far below with impressive speed.

"Nice," said Kayanai with appreciation. "Let's get to the control tower."

The Station was on high alert; the corridors were flashing red and were full of people racing to their ships and their posts. They were moving frustratingly slow till Iran began yelling for people to get out of the way. When a Waxen yells to move, people move.

"Where's the stationmaster?" demanded Kayanai as he burst into the room.

"I'm here," answered a handsome middle-aged man, his hair pulled back into stylish braids. "What's this about, waxen? There's been a Shrie Shrie sighting as you may have heard, so I'm rather busy organizing our fleet ships for deployment at the moment," he said, testily."

"Master Tullid, you must eject all ships sent by Waxman recently and push them out into space immediately," demanded Kayanai, putting as much authority in his voice as he could muster.

"Eject... which ships?" Tullid questioned in disbelief."

"I'll point out which ones," Iran said, stepping forward. "Who do I show?"

"Well, I work the port controls," said a woman, putting up her hand and looking at the stationmaster, uncertainly.

"Hold on. Why would I eject these ships? Waxman himself speci-fied that those ships had to remain in those precise locations," said Tullid, suspiciously.

"Orders change, Tullid," answered Kayanai, managing to keep voice controlled and measured. "Those ships are now a danger to this station. For the sake of everyone aboard, detach those ships, and eject them, NOW."

Tullid thought for a moment then turned to Iran and said, "Show Officer Arra which ships, but do not eject them until I say." He then went to a screen and began tapping at it quickly.

Iran and the woman, Arra, went through all the ships in the lower perimeter selecting those with the tricoloured markings while Kayanai breathed deeply and checked the time repeatedly.

Suddenly, Stationmaster Tullid turned to Arra and said, sharply, "Stop! I have contacted Waxman to confirm his orders and he has answered very firmly that those ships are not to be ejected." He snapped his fingers, "Security!" Two men came forward brandishing their weapons. "These waxen are acting against orders. Remove them from the control room immediately."

A drop of sweat slid down Kayanai's face. He knew. Waxman knew.

"Tullid. Tullid, listen," Iran started, moving towards the stationmas-ter. "Those ships are going to destroy this station. We are defying orders so that..."

"Weapons ready," ordered Tullid. The two security officers pointed their weapons at the waxen with obvious satisfaction and Iran stopped.

A beep sounded from Iran and Kayanai's comms, and Waxman's cold voice spoke softly in their ears only. "I have no choice now but to detonate early. I will begin the sequence on the side furthest from your ship. We're so close, Iran, Kayanai... Good luck."

Kayanai felt like there was ice in his stomach. He had very little time to process his feelings, however, as the two eager soldiers chose that moment to unleash a volley of blasts from their weapons at the waxen. It did them no lasting damage, but their fresh clothing was tarnished, and the shots caused them some pain. Iran grabbed one of the soldier's weapons and threw it at him in irritation, knocking the soldier off his feet.

The other soldier sneered and growled, "You'll pay for that, monster!"

But before the man could retaliate, an explosion shook the room.

"What was that?" yelled the stationmaster. "Report!"

"Message from Waxman. The Shrie Shrie are attacking," called the comms officer.

"Status of fleet ships," called Tullid.

"The last of the fleet ships are making way now, sir," answered a crew member. "Orders are coming in for them to group up and prepare for attack."

"Sir!" burst in Arra, excitedly. "The location of the blast was the lower dusk side. Sensors report that the blast may have originated from one of the ships on the upper perimeter. It's possible it came from one of the ships Crowne identified," she exclaimed, wide-eyed.

Another explosion. This one caused the floor to heave. Stationmaster Tullid caught his balance and made eye contact with Kayanai.

"We have no cause to lie," said Kayanai, looking at him steadily. Tullid held his eyes briefly then swung around and pointed to Arra saying, "Eject indicated ships from docking bays."

"Releasing connector coils," responded Arra.

"Tullid, you need to evacuate," warned Iran.

Another explosion. Lights flickered and debris flew as The Station rocked.

"Arra! Status!" bellowed Tullid.

"Ships released but not ejected! Controls not responding!" returned Arra.

"Kayanai!" called Iran, motioning to the door. Kayanai nodded and as they rushed from the control room, they heard Tullid yelling, "Abandon Ship!"

Iran and Kayanai tromped through the corridors towards their ship. Kayanai's smaller stature allowed him to navigate through the streams of people quicker, and at one point he had to stop and wait.

"Come on, monster!" He called back to Iran with a wan smile.

"How close are we to the cruiser at this point, do you think?" he yelled over the blaring alarm.

"Nearly there," Iran called back.

Suddenly, the ground beneath them pitched like the deck of a sinking ship, followed by a deafening boom, and corridor shield doors began slamming down around them.

"There must be a hull breach," yelled Iran. Kayanai crouched down, dug his mighty fingers under the door and heaved with all his might. It didn't budge. Kayanai was shocked.

Iran slapped his shoulder. "Here let the monster try!" Then Iran smashed his fist under the door, got his hands under and pulled.

Slowly but surely the door lifted till at one point it gave way and slammed up into the ceiling.

"I loosened it for you," shouted Kayanai jokingly, hiding the shame he felt.

The corridor they stepped into was badly damaged and a breach was causing the air to escape quickly. They filled their lungs as best they could and continued on till they were outside the bay area where the cruiser was kept. Kayanai hit the key panel with his palm. Nothing happened.

Iran tried the same technique as he'd used on the last door. It wouldn't budge.

Kayanai, realizing it opened from the side, dug his fingers into the edge and pulled to the right. Iran joined him and together they were able to open the door enough for Iran to get a purchase. He heaved against grinding metal till there was enough space for Kayanai to get through.

"Go!" shouted Iran. "I'll hold it!"

Kayanai pushed through, then turned to help Iran. And then it happened.

This blast was so close it momentarily deafened Kayanai. The next events occurred in what felt like silent slow motion. When Kayanai was finally able to lift his head to the door, he saw that it had mostly closed again, aside from Iran's arm which was still wedged in it, but Kayanai couldn't see on the other side; all he could see was smears of purple Wax blood. He lurched to the door and peered through. His heart stopped. The door must have slammed shut on Iran's arm, and the force of the explosion flung him back and tore the limb from his body. The blast had also turned the hull breach into a gaping tear that exposed the charred corridor to space; and gripping the edge of the hole with his remaining hand, was Iran.

Waxen are extraordinarily durable, but they aren't invincible. Iran's famed white shirt had been incinerated revealing melted wax flesh and scorch marks across his chest, and his hair had been burned away. Still, he was fighting with the last of his strength against the force of the escaping air trying to suck him to his death.

Kayanai pulled at the door, straining till he thought he would tear muscles from joints, but he couldn't move it. He beat against it desperately, calling Iran's name, then suddenly Iran looked up and their eyes met. At that moment, Iran's fingers slipped. And he was gone.

Kayanai clambered for his comm. "Iran! I'll come get you! Hold on!"

Silence at the other end. "He's still alive," he thought. "If I can get the ship out and find him…" But then a horrible realization struck him. Iran had been wearing the cruiser vest. Kayanai couldn't fly it.

"I can't save him. He's gone," he whispered.

He stood inert, too grief-stricken to move, when something happened to add to the unreality of the moment: he began to float. All around him boxes, tools, and other various items began swirling around him. The artificial gravity had failed.

"The Station is falling out of orbit," he thought, listlessly. It didn't seem to matter.

Then out of the chaotic roar surrounding him, he heard a sound that slowly brought him out of his trance-like state. It was a voice, shouting. Kayanai looked towards the sound and saw someone floating in the middle of the bay, twisting to avoid the flying debris. Suddenly Kayanai felt a rush of energy. The man was wearing a driver vest.

Kayanai took in the view and thought fast. Behind the driver were three cruisers, all spun off their mounts, but still engaged by their magnet locks. One of them had black and gold stripes that matched the driver's vest. Kayanai's objective was clear.

He grabbed a metal case floating next to him and threw it as hard as he could. The act propelled him backwards till he could reach the wall. Then he kicked off and spun his way through the air till he neared the driver, and at the last moment threw his arms open and grabbed the man, shielding him from projectiles and protecting him as they slammed into the side of the black and gold cruiser.

Kayanai gripped the side of the cruiser with one hand and with the other slapped open the driver's helmet so he could see his face. A pair of large eyes, made larger by fear, stared back at Kayanai.

"This is your ship, I take it," said Kayanai, loudly.

The driver bobbed his head.

"Good. We're getting out here," said Kayanai, firmly. "Grab onto the back of my belt and don't let go."

The head bobbed again and Kayanai turned. When he was sure the driver had a good hold on his belt he reached up and hand over hand pulled them both up the side of the cruiser.

When he reached the cockpit hatch he said," Get in, start it up, and open the cargo hatch."

The driver looked momentarily confused, but after he released the hatch and pulled himself in, he looked back with clear eyes. Kayanai wouldn't fit.

"Go fast," ordered Kayanai. "And don't try to leave without me."

Kayanai crawled down the side of the cruiser, his head whirling from the chaos surrounding him. The cruiser started up. Kayanai made it to the hatch and waited, wondering whether trusting this driver was going to be his final, fatal decision.

The hatch opened. He leaped in and began pulling himself down the corridor, hoping he'd be able to maintain his bearings and keep moving in the right direction. He finally found the cockpit and squeezed himself into the small space next to the driver.

The bay doors were open and all the objects in the room were being sucked up into space.

"What are you waiting for? Go!" yelled Kayanai.

"How can I do this?" yelled the driver in a voice high with fear. "The Station is falling out of orbit. Even if I make it out of the bay doors, we're going to be smashed by all the debris out there!"

"Use your full thrusters, and don't let us get hit! You're a driver, aren't you?"

"But—"

"Do it!"

The driver grabbed the helm stick, punched the release, engaged the thrusters, and they burst out of the falling station.

If the zero gravity inside the station was disorienting, it was nothing compared to the swirling nightmare outside of it. The driver was dodging and spinning to avoid the pieces of the destroyed station which were burning as they entered Desigar's atmosphere, and all Kayanai could see were flashes of glowing orange chunks of metal against the glowing orange planet, and flashes of black space. Despite his fears, the driver was now hyper focused and was so far managing to keep them alive. But Kayanai knew it couldn't last.

"Dive!" yelled Kayanai. "Fast and steep!"

"We'll burn up!" retorts the driver.

"Not if we angle it right! We've got to get out of the debris field!"

The driver just shook his head. Something smashed into their right side and a warning buzz and red light came on. The driver fought to keep control.

"Dive!" barked Kayanai. "I'll help!" Kayanai pushed his massive bulk as far into the front of the cockpit as he could and reached for the stick. He wrapped his huge hand around the driver's and said, "We'll do it together. One, two, three!"

They dived. They were now plummeting to the planet's surface like a shooting star.

"Full power!" yelled Kayanai.

"We're going to die!" screamed the driver.

"We will if you don't do what I say!"

They went even faster. The ship was glowing red, and the cockpit's temperature was now dangerously hot.

Suddenly, there was an impact and the ship headed into a spin. Kayanai held tight to the stick and the driver's hand, but the driver was flung around in his seat and slammed hard against the left side. Kayanai glanced at him and was able to make out that the intense G-force had caused his companion to lose consciousness. He pushed off the driver's hand and turned his attention back to wrestling with the controls and stopping the spin. He tried to think back to when he'd once heard Gengai brag about how he'd gotten out of a similar situation.

"I just lowered the angle of attack and turned into the spin. Easy."

"Well, let's just see how easy this is," thought Kayanai. He adjusted the stick and punched a control and, amazingly, the world outside stopped whirling and they began to dive once again. All he could see outside were orange and pink swirling clouds, but the sensors indicated they would be making contact with the surface alarmingly soon.

"I need to pull up now or we'll be pulverized when we hit the ground," thought Kayanai. He fought to raise the stick, but it wouldn't budge. "Not working. I'll have to reverse thrust, but if I do it wrong, we'll be back in a spin. Here goes…"

Kayanai handled the thrusters with care and gave them a light tap. He was immediately snapped back into his tiny mock chair as the ship went from lightning speed to merely the speed of sound. Thankfully they'd decelerated enough for Kayanai to gain control of the ship and begin to slow their descent to a less deadly speed.

At that moment, Kayanai's comm beeped. It was Jevan!

"Kayanai, I have opened my tracker. Meet me at my location."

"Well, now I know what target area to aim for," thought Kayanai. "The questions are—where are we?—and can we make it to where Jevan is?"

Kayanai punched in her location and gave a sharp laugh of disbelief. She was in close range! He adjusted their trajectory and aimed the ship to come down near enough where she'd see where they'd land, but not so close that she'd be in danger if they crashed and exploded.

Kayanai could now see the ground rushing up beneath them and disturbingly fast. He focused all his energy on getting their angle of descent just right and slowing the ship without causing it to spin till a light flashed telling him to start the landing sequence. They were still coming in fast.

"Come on, come on," muttered Kayanai.

The horizon line disappeared. The ground was closer… closer…

"Here… we… go!"

There was a thunderous crash, and Kayanai was thrown against the ceiling of the ship. Things went dark.

Then Kayanai found himself opening his eyes and rolling over feeling quite battered and bruised. He sat up, and elation rushed through him. He'd done it! He was alive! He laughed out loud and began to cough. The cockpit was full of smoke. He jumped up and smashed open the above hatch to clear the air, then he went over to check on his companion.

The driver was still safely locked into his seat. His lips parted in a moan, he moved his head to the right and the left, and finally his eyes fluttered open. He looked bewildered, then blinked and focused on the giant smiling face in front of him. His eyes widened in shock.

"It's you… we're not dead?" he breathed, surprised.

Kayanai grinned, smacked the driver's chest and pointed to him with a long finger.

"Aha!" he said, triumphantly.

"Aha?" repeated the man, dazedly.

"Told you we'd be fine! Now let's get out of this thing." He was eager to find Jevan. But suddenly the thought of seeing her made his face fall. He had much to tell her.

CHAPTER FOURTEEN

There was something profoundly satisfying to Jevan as she waited for Kolorov's mighty fleet all alone in her ship. She was unconcerned, at least for her own safety. She knew that at the right moment she'd phase away, and Waxman would bring the force of the fleet against his real target: the Infidel.

"Are you going to wake?" she asked the gleaming alien shape looming behind her, "Will your ships appear in the skies of our planets once more? This time, will you kill us all?"

"No," she answered herself, huskily. "We have to win."

"Well done, Jevan," came Waxman's voice over the comm, jolting her out of her reverie. "Phase two."

Jevan closed her eyes and when she opened them, the stars were gone, and outside there was nothing but black.

"You're looking pretty dark, Shade City," she said softly to herself. It took only a moment for her to decide. She jumped up and headed out into the darkness." Waxman said to phase into the spot the Tailor arranged for us, and that I was to stay with the ship and wait for him. Well, I think as long as I stay in Shade City, that's close enough to staying with the ship," Jevan mused, defiantly. She felt broody and volatile and her racing mind needed distracting. Luckily, she knew a place with excellent distractions.

Soon she found herself gliding up the curved staircase of Zadenta's, her body already swaying to the pulsing, hypnotic rhythms, and her senses filling with the sumptuous smells and evocative imagery designed to be both soothing, stimulating and provocative. Even the air was luxurious; the warm, balmy breeze caressed Jevan as she walked, and she breathed deep it's heavy scent and sighed with pleasure.

Sinking deep into the enormous red cushioned booth reserved especially for giant guests like a waxen, Jevan watched the dancers for a while then idly chose an attendant and waved him over.

The attendant, flush pleasure at being chosen, gestured submissively and said, hoarsely, "Wax Khran, thank you for the honor of allowing me to— "

"Bring me a feast table. Sapphire."

The attendant gestured again and rushed off to prepare her table. Jevan watched him admiringly as he walked away, then stretched her arms, put her hands behind her head and gazed at the intricate carvings on the ceiling for a while.

Gradually, aberrant sounds began intruding on her reverie. Far away underneath the music she could hear yelling and clamoring, and though the floor she could feel the rumble of running feet. Soon uneasy murmurings of other guests can be heard as well. She considered getting up to investigate, but then saw her attendant leading her table to her spot and decided against it. Her eyes shone with anticipation as her meal was set before her and the table mechs locked into place.

Zadenta's feasts were a wonder. Jevan's favorite, Sapphire, involved curling ceramic masterpieces laden with delicately arranged sweet fresh plants and aged animal fluids, a collection of thinly sliced cooked meat with spicy sauces, small roasted winged tokens each on beds of crisp edibles, and a multitude of tiny, fluted glasses filled with drinks carefully chosen to pair with every flavor. It was an outrageous, celebratory meal, and one she'd never before eaten alone.

"This meal may be my last," thought Jevan, numbly, as she looked at her feast. She shook her head and smiled, wryly, murmuring to herself, "Eat up, warrior. You need fuel for battle."

She was ripping a leg from one of the tokens, when there was a commotion at the entrance. Scared voices speaking quickly were followed by numerous people fleeing to the exit and abandoning their meals. Jevan raised her eyebrows with interest, but she kept eating, wiping the meat juices from her mouth.

Suddenly, she paused. There was something behind her. She felt it the way one feels the heat of a fire on one's back, but it wasn't heat she felt. Jevan wanted to turn around. Her heart began to pound. The feeling travelled around her body till it was in front of her. Taking a deep breath, she looked up.

What she saw was just a normal man, young and unkept, with a mane of shaggy dark blond hair that curled at the collar of his old, faded driver uniform. He was even smaller in stature than most men, and yet, strangely Jevan's heart still raced with something akin to fear. She met his eyes and a charming, crooked smile spread over his face. Her eyes widened as she recognized him; It was Cal.

"It's you!" he said in a warm voice that expressed pleasant surprise. Cal slid his trim compact body into the booth next to her, stretched one arm behind her, and sparkled at her with his smiling brown eyes. She blinked with confusion.

How could Cal be here? Why is he greeting me this way? And… how is he so big? Cal was not a Waxen, and yet somehow his head was level with hers, and he was looking straight into her eyes. Jevan wanted to question him but found it difficult to speak.

Cal continued, "I sensed you once before, but you disappeared again, and I was having such a great time with the Shrie Shrie that I forgot about you. But then it happened again! This time your light was like a beacon, bright and calling me. So, I followed it, and here I am!" He finished his bewildering speech with a gesture as wide as his smile, then he casually reached over with his free hand, popped a cube of food into his mouth, and chewed, musing happily, "Hmm, I forgot about eating. This is delicious."

Jevan finally found her voice. "What light? What are you…" her voice trailed away.

Cal's head seemed suddenly to be… glowing somehow. She stared at the halo in awe as it flickered like fire, shifting in color and intensity. Then Cal raised his hand to put another bite into his mouth, and Jevan realized the light was emanating from his hands as well. She reached out involuntarily to touch his hand, and she gasped; around her hand glowed the same impossible light.

Cal nodded knowingly, then closed his hand intimately around hers. The glow intensified. For a moment, the room disappeared and Jevan was dancing among the stars, flitting here and there, romping in a way she hadn't since she was a child, playing with her siblings. Then Jevan was blinking. What had happened? It was like she'd been remembering something, but the memory wasn't hers. She'd been an only child. Her eyes focused and she found herself looking deep into Cal's eyes.

"Ah, not yet. You're on your way, Jevan," Cal said, softly. Then he gave her a crooked smile. "But you're not quite there. Still, you've impressed me. You could be as perfect as that ship of yours, you know. Mine is here, just outside." He chuckled. "The people here weren't expecting me to arrive unannounced. I should have made a reservation." He leaned closer and tightened his grip on her hand, looking at her as if he wanted to dive into her through her eyes.

Jevan could feel how much Cal wanted her to smile, and how much he wanted her to understand. His eyes, his hands… it was like she was sinking into him, feeling what he was feeling. Was she losing her mind?

She jerked her hand free, recoiled, and gasped, "What are you doing to me?"

"Nothing," Cal laughed. "You're doing this Jevan. I can't take the credit. You're doing it all on your own! You're so near to understanding, but you're holding back." Cal cocked his head and considered her, then said, decisively. "Your ship—that's the way in for you. Go back to your ship and come find me. I can show you places in the skies, the stars and down into the dirt." Cal gestured making arc-like movements that left a trailing glow through the air. "We'll play and battle and be what we are. You're like me, Jevan…"

Jevan felt a pull deep within her. She wanted to join Cal, to share in his excitement, to understand, but there was something between them that she couldn't cross. It was a blazing wall of anger, and at its core, icy fear.

She shook her head violently, stood up, and scowling down at him she spat through trembling lips, "I am nothing like you, traitor! Why have you come to me?"

It was Cal's turn to look confused. "Traitor?" He stood up and stepped towards her. "Jevan—"

"Your hunger for power made you betray us and take sides with the enemy," she interrupted, furiously. "You and your Shrie Shrie are finished. The Infidel is being destroyed as we speak, and as soon as Waxman is done turning it into space debris, we're going to lay waste to your precious Gengaru."

"You and Waxman?" said Cal, softly.

"And Iran and Kayanai. And Kolorov'son's fleet. We're all ready to fight you!"

"The Infidel…" Cal said. The joy and animation in his face had drained away, and he was now looking at Jevan, coldly. "There is no need," he said, softly. "You are all firing into the dark, still. I saved you. But you don't want to be saved." Cal pressed his lips together. "You've let me down. Kayanai too. Your mind has been opened, and yet you still desire the death of your imagined enemy."

"The Shrie Shrie is my enemy, and, yes, I desire their eradication," Jevan replied, then biting off each word, she said, "more than anything."

Cal stepped towards her. "And I am your enemy?"

"You're a traitor."

"You desire my death?"

Now she faltered. Struggling to meet his eyes she said, "I… Traitors deserve death."

Cal's face was a mask of contempt. "I have as much to fear from you as you do from the Shrie Shrie."

Jevan scoffed. "The Shrie Shrie laid waste to the Desigar systems and threatens the whole Alliance." She leaned in closer, fearless of the gun at Cal's side. "And I could kill you now with ease." Jevan's eyes flashed menacingly, but Cal just looked at her calmly. Slowly the fire went out of her eyes, and she blinked, confused. Of course, I could kill him, she thought, emphatically. But deep inside she knew it wasn't true.

Cal sighed. "Disappointing… Thank you, Jevan, for reminding me that I, too, am flawed. It appears my hopes have been misplaced. The slave Jevan will get the blood she desires, and the free Jevan will remain imprisoned" With this, Cal turned towards the door.

Jevan called out, "Where are you going?"

Cal turned back and met her eyes. "To your Gengaru," he said.

"Looking forward to seeing you and your friends again, Jevan. Don't make me wait."

As he walked out, Jevan yelled loudly enough to startle the people nearby. "We'll be coming for you, Cal! You and your Shrie Shrie!"

Cal called over his shoulder, "Yes! I want you to come for me!"

Then he was out of sight.

It took some time for Jevan to realize that she was just standing by her table, breathing heavily. Around her attendants twittered like tiny, winged beasts, warning her of a Shrie Shrie attack. She waved them away, then sat, and slowly began to eat.

As she did, Jevan watched the aura around her hand as it quivered and danced, and she pondered. What is a traitor, really?

CHAPTER FIFTEEN

"Yeah, of course she was wondering that. Sounds like Jevan didn't do right by anyone." The drugs in Day's system were causing her outpost drawl to thicken.

Her pain had receded to somewhere far enough away from her consciousness that she could now lie on the floor, look at the ceiling, and lose herself in the story.

"Jevan didn't "do right", as you say, by her true self, so she couldn't be truly loyal to anyone." The Waxen's voice seemed to be drifting somewhere above Day's head. She could hear sadness in it.

The voice continued. "I always found it particularly fitting that while she was eating her feast, Jevan's dear friend Iran was dying alone in space. I wonder, if she'd known, would things have happened differently?" the Waxen mused, quietly.

"Hey, back to the story. What happened next? Kayanai had gotten a message from Jevan. Did he go meet her in Shade City?" asked Day.

"No. Jevan had tired of her food and the noise of the pandemonium outside. As you can imagine, the arrival and disappearance of Cal's Shrie Shrie warship in the concourse outside of Zadenta's caused quite the state of panic. There were masses of people screaming and trying to evacuate and armed soldiers stomping and waving their weapons around, feigning eagerness to take on the Shrie Shrie should they return."

Day grinned to herself. "Jevan should have made her ship appear. She could have saved herself a trip and given those soldiers the thrill of their lives."

Suddenly a sound Day hadn't heard before filled the air; it was the Waxen's throaty laughter. It was a lovely sound.

"She did!" laughed the voice. "Jevan stood there thinking the same thing as you, and suddenly, there was her ship. Half those brave soldiers ran away, and the other half shot uselessly at the ship, then took to shouting at it when that didn't work. Through the chaos Jevan calmly walked up, opened the hatch, waved to the shocked crowd, and disappeared."

They both laughed.

"Aren't we having fun now?" Mano's voice floated over to her from somewhere in the room. "What did you give her, Waxen?"

"Mano, it's okay. I feel a lot better, really!" said Day. "Hey Mano, do you remember back home when the elders would fight about whether or not the waxen were in cahoots with the Shrie Shrie?"

"Yes, I remember. One the stories involved tales of Waxen phasing in and out of Shade City."

"They must have been talking about Jevan! That's amazing! Hey waxen, where did Jevan go after Shade City? Wasn't she supposed to wait there for Waxman?"

"She was, yes. But given she could phase to him instantaneously whenever he wanted, she felt she could safely break orders and take a walk to clear her head. So, she phased into the desert between Shade City and Tan's tent palace, and that's what she did—she walked."

Day closed her eyes and in her mind's eye, travelled to the vast emptiness and endless sparkling sand of the Desigar desert.

The desert night was cool and quiet as Jevan walked slowly, watching her feet sink in the shallow sand. Behind her she felt the looming, yet comforting, presence of her warcruiser floating effortlessly, trailing her like a loyal pet. Her face, turned up to the sky, was being bathed in the dazzling light of a hundred falling stars. In this moment, her unsettling encounter with Cal took on an almost mystical quality, and she wondered if she were dreaming.

Then her eyes became focused on a particularly bright burning star, and she woke to the cold reality that she was watching the death of the Station as it collapsed and tumbled out of the sky.

"Kayanai," she whispered.

Lifting her hand to her cheek, she called out, "Kayanai!" She waited, but there was no answer. "Follow my tracker and meet me at my location." Still nothing.

Her hand caught her eye as she slowly lowered it. She held it out in front of her and stared at it wonderingly. The flickering aura outlining her body was still there. Cal was right; something was happening to her, something she didn't understand.

Jevan sank down slowly and sat on the sand.

I missed my chance, she thought despondently. Cal was trying to tell me something, share something... but I couldn't... I wouldn't listen. Now he's gone. She lay back on the cold ground. The sky was dark again and the burning specks were now few and far between.

Suddenly, a burst of light in the sky caused her to raise her hand to her eyes defensively though the explosion was much too far away to touch her. It was the Infidel.

"You've got your war, Waxman," whispered Jevan. No sense of satisfaction came with those words.

She sat up and hugged herself with her long limbs for warmth, and she looked out at the horizon to the lights of Tan's palace.

Dawn was coming and the coloured, garish lights looked lame and feeble against the rising sun.

Jevan looked at the palace with distaste. Its extravagances held no attraction for her. She preferred the dark and danger of Shade City to the pomp and ceremony of Tan's court. At least Shade City didn't pretend to be better than it was. All the palace had was layers of wealth covering layers of hypocrisy, and layers of elegance covering layers of fear, layers upon layers upon layers...

The beep from her comm made her jump.

"Jevan. The Infidel is destroyed. Iran is dead. Find Kayanai and phase to your quarters at the palace. I'll meet you there. We are ready to make the jump to Gengaru. "

Waxman's heavy voice hung in the air while Jevan sat frozen.

Iran dead? Impossible. She knew all too well how waxen could die, but not Iran. Her mind whirled like the stars above her. Cold and loneliness seeped into her bones till her heart felt like ice.

When the whistling, rushing noise of a ship coming in fast pricked her ears, she didn't even move. It crashed down close enough to create a storm of sand and wind that nearly knocked her back. Jevan blinked as if she were just waking up.

Kayanai, she thought, fearfully, and she jumped up and ran to check the wreckage. As she reached the small fighter, the top hatch burst open, and smoke poured out. Kayanai's handsome head emerged and scanned the surroundings till his eyes fell on Jevan standing back lit against the rising sun. He smiled and gazed at her for a moment, happy and relieved, then he climbed out and leaped down onto the sand in front of her.

They looked at each other, conflicting emotions dancing across their faces, then they moved together and embraced, her face buried in his chest and his in her hair. As they clung together, Jevan could feel relief, guilt, and aching sadness welling up in her, and she couldn't tell if it was her feelings or Kayanai's, just as she couldn't tell whether the tears on her face were his or her own. Gradually, the ache they were feeling changed and a warmth grew between them. Their lips were drawn together…

"EHAAHH!"

The noise behind them broke them apart and Jevan found herself looking dazedly at a small wide-eyed man wearing a driver's vest. He was poking his head out of the hatch and pointing at the Shrie Shrie ship.

"How can you… we need to get… there's a Shrie Shrie!" The man could hardly speak from fear.

Jevan raised her eyebrows at Kayanai.

"Aha," said Kayanai, "he's with me. It's okay!" he called up to the driver, "That ship doesn't belong to the Shrie Shrie. It's ours!"

The man looked doubtful.

"Really! It's okay! Come down, and we'll show you."

As the man slowly came out, shaking with fear, Jevan touched Kayanai's shoulder gently. "Iran," she said, softly.

Kayanai was facing the man, so Jevan couldn't see his face change, but she could feel his muscles stiffen.

"I… I'll tell you. Not yet." Kayanai stepped away from her and called up to the man. "Come down here!"

The man eventually made it to the ground, but no amount of coaxing would get him closer. In the end Kayanai lost patience and just picked him up and carried him inside the alien vessel. Jevan sat down, closed her eyes, and with a flash of light they were inside the palace.

They came out of the ship into Jevan's spacious palatial quarters. Filling about half the room, the sleek black Shrie Shrie tech contrasted jarringly with the opulent softness of its surroundings.

The little man looked around, eyes like saucers and jaw dropped, till finally he turned and bowed to Jevan and Kayanai, gazing up at them with awe.

To Kayanai he said, "I owe you my life and my name, great Kayanai." Then he turned to Jevan. "Where I am from, we tell a story of a woman who can bend light to her will. She is the mother of all wisdom. I believe you are she, and I pledge myself to you."

Jevan was shaking the sparkling sand from her hair during his speech, and when he finished, she smiled at him wryly. "Well," she said, "if you really want to do something for us you can go find refreshment for the great Kayanai and a broom to clean the sand out of my ship."

The man nodded eagerly and scampered out the door.

"I like your new friend," said Jevan, moving to sit next to Kayanai who had sunk his tired body into a large plush couch. His face was sad.

"Jevan," he began. "I have to tell you…"

At that moment, the door opened, and Waxman stood in the doorway. He took in the room quickly then froze his gaze on Kayanai. Waxman slowly stepped in, watching Kayanai as a predator stalks its prey.

Kayanai stood up. He opened his mouth to speak, but before he could, Waxman struck. The massive fist hit Kayanai with the force of a missile causing the air to burst from Kayanai's chest and sending him flying across the room. He smashed against the rigid hull of the warcruiser and collapsed to the floor.

Kayanai lay there, trying to breathe, pain coursing through his body.

Will he kill me? he wondered. Normally in a fight, Kayanai would have gotten up and counter-attacked by now, but he didn't want to fight Waxman. He deserved what he had coming to him. Waxman was over him now, reaching down, grabbing him by the shirt.

"Why are you doing this?? Wax! Stop!" Kayanai could hear Jevan yelling frantically.

Her voice seemed to come from far away. Waxman lifted Kayanai off the ground, then smashed him in the face knocking him back down to the floor.

"Please…!" cried Jevan. Then she stopped and took her hand away from Waxman's shoulder as it hit her that Kayanai must have done something horrible to bring this on. Iran, she thought. Kayanai what did you do?

Waxman stepped back and scowled down at Kayanai. Jevan had her hand on Waxman's arm and was looking wildly back and forth at them, her face white with shock.

"Iran. Your lack of loyalty caused his death." A tear trickled down Waxman's face. It was strange to see him cry.

"What are you talking about, Waxman?" gasped Jevan. She stepped back and looked down at Kayanai.

"I should kill you," growled Waxman.

Kayanai's eyes were still locked with Waxman's. He was not afraid. He felt only sadness now. His friend was gone. Jevan would soon know he'd betrayed her. And Waxman, whom he'd followed for so long, could no longer be his leader and mentor. Everyone he loved was lost from him. Tears and blood stung his eyes. He closed them.

"But I have lost enough already," he heard Waxman say softly.

Kayanai felt Waxman's strong arms wrap around him, and he was lifted gently off the ground. When he opened his eyes again, he found that Waxman had carried him to the couch and was laying him carefully down.

Waxman looked at Jevan whose face was still frozen in shock. "Get him cleaned up and rested. I want to leave for Gengaru as soon as possible." He looked back down at Kayanai.

"You will fight by my side as you always have. You will not betray me again." Waxman held his eyes for a moment, then turned and stalked out. Kayanai lowered his head. He was going back to Gengaru.

CHAPTER SIXTEEN

Crammed inside the dark flattened sphere of the command room of Jevan's warcruiser, Kayanai felt they'd been swallowed by a biomechanic monster.

He, Waxman and Gengai stood pressed against the warm smooth walls around Jevan who stood in the centre, her eyes fixed on the floor in front of her. Suddenly, the room brightened and took on a pink hue as the black floor disappeared and became the swirling clouds of Desigar.

Gengai yelped and pressed his limbs flat against the wall to avoid falling. Even Waxman had jumped involuntarily and breathed in sharply. Kayanai felt strangely calm. He looked down at the planet that was his home more than any other with indifference.

For Jevan though, the familiar sight of Desigar's warm coloured clouds and sparkling metal plates filled her with a surprising sentiment.

"Saying goodbye?" Kayanai asked her.

"No," she answered coldly. "I'll be back." She looked up at Waxman, who'd regained his calm after the first shock of phasing and was now looking down at her with such tenderness and pride that her throat tightened. They shared a moment of satisfaction, then Waxman nodded, and Jevan closed her eyes.

This time as they phased Kayanai could see a glow around Jevan that pulsed once, then was swallowed up by the light of an alien sun pouring in from beneath her feet. Even Waxman's jaw was dropped as they gazed down at the planet below.

Large areas of blue interspersed with patches of dark purple on the planet's surface were partially obscured by thick white and yellow clouds. Its strange beauty filled three of the waxen with mixed emotions, but for Kayanai the view brought only dread.

"We're in orbit," said Jevan, and she looked at Waxman expectantly.

After a pause he said, "Any sign of Kolorov'son's fleet?

At the end of his sentence, a man's head materialized in front of Jevan, causing everyone but her to jump back in astonishment. It looked exactly like a comm mech holo, except that it floated disembodied, and the facial features were remarkably sharp and detailed. Surprise then pleased relief registered on the man's face, for it belonged to Kolorov'son, commander of the greatest attack fleet in the empire.

The hardships of the long journey were etched on the commander's face, but his eyes were clear and alert.

"Khran," he said, warmly. "Welcome to Gengaru."

"Kolorov'son," Jevan answered with a smile. "You made it. I hope you haven't been waiting long."

"Long enough. A less patient man may have gotten a bit restless, but luckily, I am a patient man," he answered, smiling with the charm of a natural leader, "and besides, we've had quite the spectacle to keep us occupied."

Waxman broke in. "Thank you, Kolorov'son. Please explain what you mean by 'spectacle.'"

Kolorov'son inclined his head, respectfully. "Good to see you, Wax Adoor. We've been monitoring the planet from a safe distance behind a nearby moon, and during this time we've been witness to many remarkable battles between a singular Shrie Shrie ship versus squadron after squadron of others. Every morning the one ship would take position in the sky, then the others would attack. Both sides would be phasing in and out and shifting positions faster than you can blink, but the one ship would always win, finding ways to bring the others down in the most stunningly creative ways. I've never seen anything like it. Then yesterday, it all stopped."

"Yesterday," said Jevan softly.

"No ships, no battles… our scanners couldn't pick up a single trace of them. Not even on the surface of the planet,"

Gengai burst in, "They knew we were coming! The cowards took off when they figured out who they were going to have to deal with!" he exclaimed, smugly.

"Impossible", said Waxman. "Even Kolorov'son didn't know we were coming."

"Cal," broke in Jevan, hollowly. She turned to Waxman. "I didn't get a chance to tell you…" Jevan broke off abruptly, then continued. "He knows," she said, tightly, her chest constricting. "Cal knows we're here."

Her companions followed her gaze out to the planet below. For a moment they all stood frozen, waiting for clouds of ships to appear and attack without warning.

Then Waxman broke the silence with a brittle voice.

"Commander, get the fleet to our location and prepare to engage with the enemy." Kolorov'son nodded and his image blinked out.

"But wait, surely that was Cal fighting against the Shrie Shrie," said Kayanai. Shouldn't we— " With a scowl, Waxman cut in and said to Jevan. "Where is he?"

Suddenly, the wall in front of them disappeared and was replaced by the dark of space, and in the centre of it, a single Shrie Shrie warship floated motionless.

Jevan too was motionless, as she stared, spellbound.

"Well done," said Waxman to her softly. Jevan couldn't answer him. She hadn't done anything. It was Cal. Cal wanted her to see him.

She could feel him in that ship. It was as though he was reaching across the space between them and gripping her hand the way he had in Shade City.

Do as I do. The words appeared in her mind, and with lightning speed Cal's ship burst towards them letting forth a volley of energy beams that would have sliced them to pieces had Jevan not phased them swiftly away. They reappeared on the other side of the planet.

There was silence again. Now, thought Jevan. They'll attack us now while we're away from the fleet. But still no Shrie Shrie appeared.

"Where is he?" snapped Waxman.

"I got us out of range," said Jevan, breathlessly.

"Bring us back and engage the enemy."

"I…" Jevan faltered.

Seeing her distress, Waxman's voice softened.

"Jevan," he said. "Remember the beach. I know you can do this. Now…," his voice sharpened. "Bring us back and attack that ship. Do it!"

The view in front of them was suddenly a whirlwind of stars and glaring red light, as Jevan phased, spun them and fired on where she knew Cal's ship would be. He phased and the beams shot out harmlessly into empty space. She found him again, but this time he was busy with a new target.

"Look," she said, changing the view so the others could see.

Cal was attacking Kolorov'son's fleet, firing at the ships seemingly at random, dodging around them and almost lazily taking pot shots at the ships' underbellies. The fleet ships were trying to coordinate a counterattack and sending wave after wave of atomics, but every missile burst where Cal had been and not where he was.

"He's targeting their engines…" said Gengai. His hands kept opening and closing convulsively as he watched Cal with naked, furious envy.

"He's disabling them," said Waxman, fascinated.

Suddenly, Kolorov'son's ship broke formation, and seemed to be bolting away. Cal moved to pursue, and Kolorov'son's ship cut engines and sent out a flurry of atomics that burst out in every direction. It was a desperate move and must have used up every atomic the ship had. Cal phased away just in time, but it was a near thing. When Cal phased back in, he blasted Kolorov'son's ship with devastating intensity.

"Jevan!" barked Waxman.

A strange feeling had been blossoming inside her as she watched Cal battle the fleet. An exhilaration that she didn't understand and wasn't quite hers but was nevertheless causing her to lick her lips with anticipation. At Wax's voice, she phased and attacked Cal with an eagerness that would have surprised her if she hadn't been so entirely focused on her goal. She found that her body had melted away and her ship was now an extension of herself. Her only other awareness was Cal's ship which felt as though it was tethered to her heart. She flashed into being right behind him and fired a beam of energy that would have sliced through him had he not made a quick half twist then burst away. At that moment, Kolorov'son, who'd brought his ship up beside them, began firing at Cal as well. Cal phased.

Jevan smiled.

Somehow, she knew Cal had been forced into phasing and hadn't liked it. She was about to reach out with her mind and find him, when her breath caught in her throat. With a blinding flash, thousands of Shrie Shire ships appeared in space, surrounding her ship and the fleet. A split second of eerie silence followed, then all the waxen's voices filled the small space at once.

"Incoming!"

"They're everywhere!"

"Get us out of here! Jevan phase!"

The last voice was Kayanai's, and she listened to it, phasing them to just outside the range of the ships.

The Shrie Shrie looked like a cloud of insects when they looked out through the viewer, and in the center of the swarm they could Kolorov'son's tiny, wounded ship beginning to plummet towards the planet.

Then just as suddenly, every Shrie Shrie ship disappeared again. All except one. It floated menacingly in front of them.

"What... ?" said Gengai, shaken. "Where'd they all go?" he asked, leaning to look at the side of the viewer.

Jevan's eyes narrowed, and a ferocious half smile twisted her face. "It's just Cal. He's messing with us."

"Just messing... Jevan, there's nothing just about what just happened," said Kayanai. Those were Shrie Shrie! We're going to get—"

"Jevan," interrupted Waxman. "Find Cal."

She needed no prompting. Finding Cal was exactly what she wanted to do. In her mind's eye she could see Cal shooting down into Gengaru's atmosphere. Yes, let's take this to the skies, thought Jevan with relish, and phased them directly next to Cal into thick yellow clouds lit gloriously by the sunshine. They soared side by side for a moment, slicing their black ships through puffs of gossamer gold, then Cal phased his ship, so it was coming straight towards them and fired a volley of direct hits.

Jevan could feel the energy crackle on the surface causing certain systems to overheat and others to compensate. There was no permanent damage, but Jevan knew the ship wouldn't be able to take an extended attack from those rockets.

Well, I'd better not let you do that again, she thought, her lips curved in a smile, her eyes feverous.

She was unaware of the reactions of her companions as the shots hit their ship—Gengai's involuntary flinch, Waxman's voice as he called out orders, or Kayanai's arm on her shoulder. Their experience of the battle was very different from hers as the view outside was so fast and jumbled that despite the ship's astonishing inertia blockers (they felt no movement at all), the constantly changing scenes in front of them tricked their brains into feeling every twist and turn.

Gengai, an experienced driver, showed no sign of disorientation, he just seemed both frustrated and exhilarated. Waxman was flicking his eyes back and forth from the view and Jevan's face, his expression unreadable, and Kayanai, unable to help and dizzied by the view, spent most of the time watching Jevan.

She was mesmerizing. Her body was outlined in a flickering light as though she were aflame, and her rapturous, fevered expression filled him with wonder.

Outside, the thick yellow clouds parted and revealed an electric blue ocean. Far ahead, Jevan could see a purple landmass. Cal was still in front, leading her in a swirling dance as he avoided her blasts with easy grace. He dropped low over the ocean causing the waves to ruffle up into a long tail of water.

Jevan shot through the spray turning the beads to flashing emeralds. Cal let loose a volley of rockets, then jumped to the side and let out another, then another. Jevan found herself dodging the shower of rockets effortlessly, her awareness of each one complete. Joy was coursing through her veins, and she felt as if it was coursing through her ship as well.

My turn, she thought and let loose a multitude of rockets, just as they were coming up to a range of towering grey and purple mountains. Cal zipped up one of the mountainsides and the rockets burst underneath him causing rocks and foliage to rain down on Jevan. Then he phased and popped up behind her. She twisted till they were flying backwards and fired another volley as they reached the mountaintop. She whooped as the rockets burst just behind his ship when in a flash Cal phased again, and this time she lost him.

Jevan froze the ship. As they floated at the peak of the mountain, she reached out and felt nothing. The emptiness left by Cal's disappearance drained her joy.

"Jevan," came Waxman's voice as though it were far away. "Be ready. This could be a trap. The Shrie Shrie could return at any moment."

But all was silence.

He's out there somewhere. Jevan took a deep breath, closed her eyes and concentrated hard.

There he is. He was north… far north.

Suddenly, the view out front changed from purple mountains to a world carved of ice and snow. She brought the ship down onto a cliff of blue ice overlooking a stunning vista, a valley of pure white marred by a streak of black at the centre; it was Cal's warship.

"There," said Waxman, huskily. "Hit it with all you've got."

Jevan hesitated. The game was over, and the exhilaration was gone. Something had changed.

"Jevan!" barked Waxman

She shook herself.

He'll phase away, she thought and unleashed a massive column of orange yellow light directly at Cal's ship.

It didn't phase. It glowed and trembled.

"Smash it!" roared Waxman.

The snow around the ship was melting and glistening and the valley glowed orange as Jevan gritted her teeth and increased the power.

"SMASH IT!"

She let loose a volley of fire beams and the detonations caused the ground to shake and ice and snow to tumble down from the valley cliffs.

Finally, through her tears Jevan could see glowing cracks in the warship. She kept pouring on the energy blast till it glowed so bright that the other waxen had to avert their eyes, and the warship erupted into a blinding ball of fire.

With a whoomph a cloud rose in the air and chunks of the ship blew apart and rained down, peppering the snow. Then the walls of the valley cracked and crumbled, and a massive avalanche buried the charred remains of Cal's ship till only bits of black popped up though the pristine white. Jevan looked at it, and it was as though the snow had blanketed her heart as well.

"Hahah!" cried Waxman, breaking the silence. He slapped Jevan on the back and growled with pleasure. "You impressed me, my dear. Now, take us down. I want to be sure the job is done."

The four waxen walked out into an eerily silent world. Waxman had pulled a handheld sensor from his vest and was scanning the ground for signs of life. Gengai was kicking the torn black chunks of metal sticking out of the ground, moodily. The funeral atmosphere had affected even him.

Kayanai just stood and stared at the ground. Cal was gone. He should have been relieved. Here he was, back on Gengaru, the place of his night-mares, and he had returned triumphant. The Shrie Shrie had disappeared, and Cal, whose retribution he'd feared for so long was just... gone. The threat was over. He could rest. He could recover. And yet right then Kayanai felt as near despair as the last time he'd been on Gengaru, and he had no idea why. Maybe it was because Iran wasn't there. No, it's not just losing Iran, he thought. I feel like I've lost everything. Tears stinging his eyes broke him out of his daze. He blinked, and the tears were gone. He exhaled icy air and felt cold and empty.

Jevan didn't hold her tears back, though she made sure they were silent and kept them to herself. Her eyes were focused blearily on the steam rising from the crash site and floating in the air.

"Nothing," said Waxman. The scanners aren't picking up any kind of life. It's done!" He looked at the others, his proud face beaming with self-satisfaction. "Turns out he was just one little man after all." His words were met with silence.

Waxman, unphased by their lack of enthusiasm, went on. "Let's get back to the ship. Jevan, check the fleet's status, then return us to Desigar."

Jevan didn't move. The steam she was watching had begun to thicken and curl oddly. Then it began to glow, softly. Soon faint colors began to flicker, and the glow got stronger and Jevan's heart gave a leap.

Waxman, seeing her face, narrowed his eyes. "What do you see?"

Jevan paused, then turned a blank face to him. "Nothing."

"Are you sure?"

Jevan shrugged. "I thought I saw something. It was just a trick of the light."

She walked past him towards her ship. Waxman watched her for a moment then began walking and motioned the others to follow.

As Kayanai walked woodenly back to the ship, he thought, It's over. But it wasn't over.

CHAPTER SEVENTEEN

"Was it Cal?? What did she see?" Her guest had fallen into a reverie, making Day impatient. "Hey, finish the story before I die here."

The Waxen stirred as though she was waking. "Jevan believed it was Cal, and she felt sure that Cal wanted Waxman to think he was dead, so she said nothing. The idea that he was still out there alive and could return to her at any time became a burning obsession, one that would stay with her for a long time.

"At first when they returned to Desigar, Waxman's pride ballooned. He believed that with Cal and the Shrie Shrie gone, and with Jevan and her powerful ship at his side, all resistance to his will was, and he would rule unopposed. But when he spoke to her of this, Jevan avoided his eyes. How could she tell him that she'd moved beyond wanting to keep order and quell rebellions for him? Jevan had a new purpose. Deep down in her heart she believed Cal would return to her and explain how and why she was so… changed. Waxman must have sensed this shift in her; he stopped speaking to her about their future and began watching her from the corner of his eyes.

Jevan had become powerful in a way that Waxman wasn't able to understand, and he viewed anything he didn't understand and couldn't control as a potential threat. He must have been so torn about what to do with her. Then one day, a fit of rage brought a brilliant solution.

When they returned to Desigar, Jar Tan insisted on yet another massive party to celebrate the end of the war. During a rambling speech to the masses, Tan took credit for the destruction of the Infidel and the removal of the Shrie Shrie threat. Waxman, who was standing behind him on stage, couldn't bear it any longer. He was so bursting with pride in himself and contempt and hatred for Tan that, in front of everyone, he snatched Tan by the throat, slammed him to the ground, and unleashed an assault of punches so swift and violent that Tan wasn't even able to cry out. Each punch drove Tan further into the metal beneath him until his exo skin crumpled and dented. Finally, Tan was dead.

Waxman stood slowly, and looked down to admire his handiwork, but the cracked skin of the corpse shone so brilliantly that even Waxman had to turn his face away. His eyes focused instead on the shocked and frozen crowd of people around him, and, as always, he thought as quickly as he acted. He stood in front of the amplifier and told the people that he'd just received intel proving that Tan had been behind the attack on Wellspring Solichia. There was a gasp, but as Waxman went on to remind them of Tan's depravity and instability it was clear that the audience did not doubt him. He continued assuring the audience that Tan was not responsible for the victory against the Shrie Shrie, and that instead they should be thanking the brave soldiers of Kolorov'son's fleet and the greatest hero of the war, Jevan Khran. When he spoke her name, he stood back and gestured to Jevan. Until that moment she had been barely listening and staring off into the distance, and then suddenly the crowd in front of her was roaring her name.

"Waxman took Jevan's arm, had her step forward, then turned to the people and said, "The death of the mad emperor leaves us with an empty throne. Who shall take his place?" Then he raised Jevan's hand into the air and the crowd went wild."

"So that's how Jevan Khran became emperor!" exclaimed Day.

"It was a masterstroke. In one fell swoop, Waxman solved three problems at once: He established a scapegoat to take the blame for the breaking of the Wellspring Accord, he rid himself of the irritating Jar Tan, and he found the perfect way to maintain Jevan's usefulness while setting her free."

"What a guy," Day growled. "You sound like you admire him."

"It's hard not to admire genius."

"Yeah, but it's also hard to admire a mass murdering egomaniac."

The Waxen shrugged. "If I allowed myself to care about the deaths of others, how could I function? But you should have seen where Waxman put that Staff of Tan's as the final word."

Day shook her head and answered wryly, "Regular people care about others and function all the time. It is possible to do."

"Even I know that!" chimed in Mano from the corner.

"Caring for others has only brought me dissatisfaction," answered the Waxen, crisply.

"Is that why you haven't bothered mentioning what happened to Kolorov'son's fleet after Gengaru?"

"Oh, the fleet was fine. Most of them limped back to Desigar eventually—except Kolorov'son's ship. The damage it sustained caused it to crash land on Gengaru. Search parties were sent down to rescue survivors, but they were never completely accounted for. Jevan considered going back to find out what happened to them, but she never did. She was too busy."

"Busy! My education is pretty spotty—I didn't even know it was Waxman who killed Jar Tan—but I have, of course, heard of Emperor Khran and what I was told was that she's never done anything! I've heard she just sits by herself in her underground palace and occasionally gets carted out for special functions and celebrations and stuff. What was she busy doing?"

"Meditating. Reading. Writing. Waiting… Cal knew something, understood something, that she didn't, and she wanted to know what it was. Try as she might, she couldn't figure it out on her own. So, she emptied out Shade City, built an underground fortress and filled it with plants from Gengaru. Zadenta's became a veritable jungle."

As Day gazed up at the ceiling, she had a moment of insight.

"She was waiting for Cal," she said softly.

The Waxen nodded. "Somehow Jevan thought if she were in the places she'd connected to him, somehow it would bring him to her." She shrugged. "It didn't work."

"He never came back?"

There was a long pause as the Waxen too studied the ceiling.

Then she took a swig from her bottle and said, "It's complicated."

"I like complicated."

"Then I will tell you."

/ / /

Jevan, sitting at her desk, was a flash of white among the lush purple trees and bushes. Wearing a white robe and sitting at a desk made from pale Gengaru wood, she was watching her brush intently as it made thin beautiful black strokes on the page when the leaves next to her trembled.

Never taking her eyes off the trees, she swiftly and calmly rolled up the parchment, put it in a large wooden tube which she then brandished, and took a defensive pose. Suddenly, she relaxed.

"Are you here to get some clothes?" she asked, mildly.

In front of her was a monstrous, muscular, headless form, the top of which being covered by the large leaves of a tree. The figure ducked down, and Kayanai's head appeared as he pushed his massive bulk through the thick foliage.

"Kayanai," she said, appraising him with eyebrows raised. "You've grown again." Her voice rang out into the vast space around them. The tall violet trees came only halfway to the dark, domed roof above them.

"Empress," he said, greeting her with the hint of his old charming smile. "You're looking well yourself."

Kayanai didn't look well. Though he was still handsome, his enormous body looked inflated and disproportionate. He must have outgrown Waxman by now, Jevan thought in wonderment.

Kayanai looked around and said, "It's still strange being here and remembering this was once the bustling upper levels of Shade City. It's so peaceful now."

"Peacefulness is easy to achieve when there's no one around." Jevan put down the tube, leaned on her desk, and crossed her arms. "I suppose you're here to bring me to the big race."

The big race was, of course, The Crowne Couloir. As everyone knows, Waxman began the race as a way to hone the skills of his great driver fleet.

What people don't know is that he created the fleet not only to replace the army of waxen he lost on the disastrous mission to Gengaru, but also because deep down he still feared the return of Cal.

Cal's power was something that Waxman wanted to either harness or destroy, but it was also something that he didn't understand. All he knew was that Cal was the greatest driver the galaxy had ever seen. So, he amassed a force of skilled drivers, through promises of power and wealth, through coercion, and eventually by force till they became valued as a type of currency.

Many people became rich selling drivers to Waxman. But with no enemy to fight, aside from the occasional rebellious planets, Waxman thought of an ingenious way to keep his drivers busy, propel them to stardom, hone their skills, weed out the weak, and, most importantly, increase his power.

"I have the pleasure of being your escort, yes." Kayanai smiled down at her, somewhat awkwardly. She was easily three heads shorter than him now.

Jevan and Kayanai gazed at each other for a moment. They had drifted apart. Her position and obsession had become a barrier, and for Kayanai, it had hurt to lose her almost as much as when he'd lost Iran.

Look at him, thought Jevan as her eyes trailed over his rippling muscles. He must be bathing the absolute minimum and pushing the boundaries of what is safe at that size. Why, Kayanai? Have you buried those old feelings of dissatisfaction and numbed yourself to your job? Is it because I've left you with only Gengai and Waxman and you're letting them define who you are? She felt a pang of guilt at that, but it faded quickly. It's a shame. At one point, I would have been proud of you for this.

But now, I liked you better before. "

He said it was because it allowed him to do his job to the best of his ability, but, truthfully, it stemmed from his feelings of helplessness over the death of Iran. He never wanted to feel that small and helpless again.

Jevan looked up at Kayanai and said, with a loud sigh, "So, Waxman's accumulated the best drivers in the galaxy, he's created the fastest, most talented, deadliest fleet, ever assembled, and he's still not satisfied. When's he going to give up? He'll never find another Cal."

Kayanai shrugged. "When are you going to give up?" he answered, pointedly.

Jevan's eyes flickered down, then she walked behind her desk and grabbed a vest off the chair. She fingered the waxblood cloth, thoughtfully. She hadn't felt like a Waxen in a long time.

Waxman's obsession with his fleet of drivers was matched by the citizens of the Alliance's obsession with the Crowne Couloir.

It was the biggest, most watched event in the galaxy. Watching the finest drivers execute jaw-dropping maneuvers while avoiding the Alliance's deadliest planetary defense systems was so captivating even Jevan could get caught up in the excitement.

Jevan looked up from the vest and said to Kayanai, "I'd rather not leave now. I'm in the middle of something. Does Waxman really need me?"

"If you left your comm on more often you would have expected this. And you'd also know why he needs you for this race."

She leaned against the desk and crossed her arms. "I'm listening."

"Gengai is winning all the races these days. You should see him. He's been bathing like crazy so he can fit into all the latest ships. He's tiny."

"It must please you to be so much bigger than him." Jevan said it mildly, but Kayanai caught her scorn. She was surprised to see him shrug ruefully.

"I'm not really what I seem Jevan," he said, softly. "I…" he shook his head. "Anyway, it doesn't matter."

Jevan raised an eyebrow. Perhaps there was still more to Kayanai than being Waxman's lackey. But he was right. It didn't matter. All that mattered was her purpose.

Kayanai continued. "Races are becoming less popular because Gengai always wins, so Waxman was thinking of taking him out of the competition. Gengai was not happy about this, as you can imagine. Then suddenly, Waxman graciously changed his mind."

"Doesn't sound like Waxman. What does this have to do with me?"

"Waxman wants to show that Gengai can lose, and he wants to shoot some new life into the Crowne Couloir. After Gengai inevitably beats everyone in all the races, there's going to be a surprise race… one that's going to be the talk of the empire: Gengai vs Jar Khran."

Despite herself, Jevan's hands twitched at the idea of seeing some action, but she answered cautiously. "I'm not a driver."

"I've flown in that Shrie Shrie ship with you. In that ship, you could beat him."

"In my ship he wouldn't stand a chance. Does Gengai know about this?"

"Nope."

"Now that sounds like Waxen," Jevan paused at the glint in Kayanai's eye. "The thought of me beating Gengai amuses you, doesn't you?"

"A little."

For a moment it felt like old times with Kayanai smiling broadly at her, and Jevan shaking her head at him, her lips twitching.

"Hey," protested Kayanai, "I gotta take my amusements when I can." His smile turned sad, and Jevan felt a momentary pang of sorrow for him, but she turned away and gazed at her quiet forest and the dark dome far above them as she contemplated Waxman's plan. It had been a long time since she'd really flown her ship. Waxman still requested the occasional quick trip from her when he needed to be somewhere fast, but she'd lost interest in using it for herself. She had realized long ago that the Shrie Shrie ships were not the key to Cal's power—obvious, since he'd allowed his to be destroyed—so she felt very little excitement during the quick phases she'd made for Waxman.

But the idea of being one with her ship the way she had so long ago, that intrigued her.

"Okay, I'm in." Jevan put on the vest she was holding. "Let's go."

Planet Amazi was an average sized planet almost entirely covered in water with only a few scattered archipelagos. With so little land to colonize and a tiny population, Amazi had been a planet of small importance and ignored by the Alliance until the discovery of the priceless mineral lydock-ite deep within its oceans. Suddenly the planet's citizens were inundated with new colonists looking to become rich. They built artificial islands and enormous machinery to extract the lydockite. Though it did bring them wealth, the people of Amazi were not pleased with the upheaval this brought to their lives as they suddenly found they were no longer in control of their own planet. Unrest grew, until it became a place of violence and endless strife.

The unrest was the reason the system of this troubled planet was the carefully chosen location for the Alliance's most prestigious event, the famous Alpha Fleet Race. The enormous racecourse spanned the distances between Amazi and the numerous other planets and moons in its system, and its size allowed for the many hundreds of ships competing for the grand title of Alpha Driver. To watch the race, spectators had to be onboard the great Khran Stadium, a floating arena the size of a large city, that picked spectators off the surface, and brought them to the planet's low orbit, where they would sit and watch and celebrate every race in luxurious style. Meanwhile, while ordinary citizens were being distracted by the race, the Alliance's enemies, the insurgents, would get a visit from Waxman's army, which was being overseen by Waxman's best and biggest.

Well, someone's gotta do it, mused Kayanai as he looked out at Jevan's ship's viewer at the vast sea of ships outside. The event designers had truly outdone themselves this time. The ships chosen to greet Jar Khran's arrival were arranged carefully by shape and colour to represent her insignia, and they were firing their weapons in carefully timed bursts to create a truly spectacular light show.

"Not bad, don't you think?" he said, turning to Jevan who was still sitting cross-legged in the center of her ship. Her eyes were closed, and she looked peaceful and beautiful. Kayanai felt a momentary tug at his heart, like the twinge of an old wound. He shook it off.

"Hey, wake up. You're missing it," said Kayanai.

Jevan opened her eyes, glanced at Kayanai, his head propped up on his arms and his huge body sprawling across the floor, then she turned her attention to the costly, carefully practiced display outside, made for the single purpose of impressing her, the great Jar Khran, Khran of Desigar.

She raised an eyebrow, her expression a mixture of faint interest and slight disgust. He hadn't made a joke or felt inclined to laugh in a long time. The endless emptiness and violence of his day-to-day existence and the constant discomfort of his size meant he was rarely in a good enough mood for levity. It felt good to be around Jevan though.

He cleared his throat and said to her, "You know, Waxman doesn't get this kind of greeting. You're much more loved than he is."

"Waxman doesn't want love. He wants obedience." She grimaced at him. "Besides, they don't love me, they love this ship."

"They love both. Your people are going to go insane with joy when they see you race."

Jevan sighed. "Do you think it's over?" she asked, jerking her head towards the viewer.

"I think so. We should get to the stadium. You need to take your rightful place on your fancy viewing throne, and I need to get to work."

Jevan looked out at the shining planet below them. "Another rebellion," she murmured.

Kayanai shrugged. "I was told it's a mild insurgence. Meaning it's probably a nightmare down there." It was his turn to sigh.

"Well, Empress, will you take us into port?"

"Yes, I suppose we'd better get down there."

Even to Jevan and Kayanai, who'd seen many of these events, the view as they approached the Stadium was an impressive sight. It was a long flat ovoid filled with millions of spectators, a seething mass underneath a transparent dome that separated the crowd from the freezing vacuum of space above. In the centre, ships from all over the galaxy were heading into the receiving docks and above, hovering over the elite viewing area, racing ships of every possible shape and style surrounded the structure like a multi-coloured halo.

The ten-flanking elegant and ornate escort ships, there not only to provide security, but also to provide the appropriate splendour for the arrival of Jar Khran, Emperor of Desigar, pulled ahead and lined up indicating the way to her place of honour. Jevan executed a smooth and skillful turn, backing her ship into place with impressive precision and as she did, she saw the mass of ships that had been following her like disciples.

"Time to greet your adoring fans," said Kayanai.

"I suppose so," she said, standing up and moving to the hatch. She paused, feeling momentarily reluctant. The event's outrageous excessiveness and the endless jostling for position reminded her of palace life when Tan was emperor, and though it was a diverting change from her quiet life and she often got caught up in the excitement of the race, she also found it all somewhat distasteful. However, she couldn't disappoint her people, and most of all, she couldn't disappoint Waxman. She took a deep breath and opened the hatch.

The noise that hit her was almost tangible. Jevan looked out at the millions of people who were cheering and screaming her name and felt a rush of adrenaline. She broke into a smile and waved. It was hard not to enjoy being so adored. Below her a platform was being raised up to meet her. She stepped onto the platform, lavishly decorated in flowers and vines, then felt it shudder under her feet as Kayanai joined her.

Kayanai looked out at the crowd and felt very little. Though this was the biggest race yet, these events were commonplace to him now. He didn't really enjoy them much. Seeing Jevan was the only bright part of what was for him a dark affair.

As they began their descent Jevan looked down and caught sight of the top of a smooth dark head far below. Waxman. It had been many orbits since she'd seen him. He looked up and bestowed on her one of his rare smiles. As usual, his pleasure at seeing her gave her a mixture of pride and unease.

She smiled back.

When the platform was level with Waxman's, he stepped forward and ceremoniously handed her the silver blade staff, the one she had once given to Jordi Tan. Jevan bowed, grasped it then swished it through the air, twirled it and brought it to her side. The audience went wild. Waxman took her hand and led her to her throne which she sank into and looked out to the viewers which spanned the entire circumference of the dome.

Though she had the place of honour, there wasn't a bad seat in the Stadium; you could see the action from anywhere.

"Looks like we've missed the opening ceremonies. Where are we in the first race? Anyone die yet?" she asked Waxman who sat next to her in his less ornate but equally comfortable chair.

The Crowne Couloir was a collection of races, each day involving the drivers navigating through increasingly difficult defense systems. The first races weren't about being the fastest, they were about staying alive and making it to the next race. Speed only mattered in the last race as the first to finish and touch down was crowned the winner.

"We've lost about 15%. It's nearly over. There are only a handful of ships left to cross the finish line." Waxman turned and looked up at Kayanai who was standing behind and to the side of him. "You're late," he said.

Kayanai shrugged. "We had catching up to do," he said, mildly.

Jevan glanced at Waxman to see if he'd react to this, but his face was impassive as usual. She thought it was interesting how their relationship had changed. Kayanai still followed Waxman's orders but seemed now to do it out of habit. He seemed to enjoy making it clear he no longer saw himself as Waxman's underling. There was even at times a hint of disrespect. Beneath their stoic expressions, Jevan could sense complicated feelings of anger, mistrust, and affection. Their relationship seemed fraught with danger. She pushed the thought from her mind— Waxman and Kayanai's problems were no longer hers, and there was nothing she could do anyway. The booming voices of the announcers brought her attention back to her surroundings.

"Well citizens, we sure have had our full share of excitement this race, haven't we? And just because most of the fleet have crossed the finish line—"

"Most, but not all." cut in the other announcer, cheerfully.

"Yes, a few of them were in far too many pieces to complete the round," chuckled the other. He continued, "Anyway, just because most drivers have finished doesn't mean the excitement is over. We still have two more ships approaching the end, ready to fight their way through the core of the Amazi home defense. These ships have already had numerous close shaves and have been declared bad tickets by betting folks. Let's see if they can beat the odds and make it through!"

All eyes were focused on the viewers that stretched along the bottom of the dome. Every screen showed the two final ships from numerous angles as they entered the final hot zone, the deadliest part of the track. One driver is in a large, coppery ship with vast engines and conspicuous weaponry, the other drives a sleek and shiny silver fighter.

Suddenly, some of the screens change to show a giant attack ship, famously named "The Garage" closing in on the other two ships. The viewers switched to the cameras inside the ships, showing the exhausted faces of the drivers which showed no awareness of the threat behind them; The Garage was black and had sensor blockers making it extremely difficult to spot. The audience leaned forward in anticipation.

When the blast came, it took the larger ship by surprise, knocking it off course and causing it serious damage. It returned fire, but the shots went wide. Then, The Garage let loose a barrage of torpedo blasts that eventually blew the driver's ship apart, causing a blinding explosion that was spread across every viewer. The crowd went wild.

The angle changed, and the camera mechs were now following the small silver ship as it dropped down in the planet Amazi's atmosphere.

"Looks like Driver Tokai is hoping the clouds will give him coverage and will make The Garage easier to spot," said one announcer.

"A good strategy," commented the other.

"We'll see. He'll now have to contend with the planet's automatic defense system, and he still has to get to us here at the finish line, and remember, we're on the other side of the planet!"

The last driver found a stable altitude and burned his engines at full blast to make the finish line still a long, long distance out. But he wasn't fast enough to blast past the net of defense mechs closing in around him.

Suddenly, the driver dove, down, down, then, splash, he hit the ocean and a vast fountain of water and foam burst upwards nearly dousing the trailing camera mech.

"WHOA!" yelled the announcers, over the screaming crowd.

"What happened?? Did he misjudge a dive?"

"I think it was pure exhaustion."

"Well, one thing's for certain. He's not coming up again. Which means… Race one is OVER!"

The stadium exploded. Pyrotechnics and music came blasting from all sides and people were jumping up out of their seats. Some were dancing and some were heading for the clubs and private party rooms.

Jevan stood up.

"Time for a drink," she said and headed inside. Kayanai stayed behind. A page had come up to Waxman and was whispering in his ear. Waxman's brow rose and his eyes widened momentarily, an expression which was equivalent to someone else's yell of astonishment. Kayanai was intrigued.

When Waxman stood up and strode away purposefully, Kayanai followed. They went into the Elite Chamber, a palatial room where lavishly dressed guests were already revelling in the festivities. Jevan was already surrounded by admirers, drink in hand. She looked up sharply when she saw Waxman enter and went over to join him and Kayanai.

"What is it?" she asked.

Waxman ignored her, grabbed a comms mech, and headed to a back chamber where it was quieter. Kayanai and Jevan shared a glance and followed.

As they entered the room, they saw the face of Bai Slinto, Head of Admissions, floating above the shoulders of the mech.

"It's definitely Shriean tech," the woman was saying.

"And the driver?"

"Very young. A girl. 'Jet' was the only name given."

"And she wants to join now."

"Yes. It's not against the rules for her to join, if she agrees to take a penalty, but given her ship, I thought I should check in with you first."

"You were right to do so." Waxman paused, then continued.

"Her penalty will be this: She will not start until the first pole position passes the Garage and handlers of the next stage."

Slinto's eyebrows raised. "She will be at an extreme disadvantage," she answered, then at Waxman's expression she stammered quickly, "B--but you know that, of course."

"Have the announcers interview her. I want to see her. And her ship."

He turned around and the mech's head snapped back into place. Waxman strode between Jevan and Kayanai saying,

"Let's have a look at this new driver."

Jevan followed him back out to the gala room, her mind in turmoil. A girl with a Shriean ship… she thought. Intriguing. But I'm not sure I like the sound of it.

They stood in front of the gala room's viewer wall and waited.

They could barely hear the announcers over the din, but they could hear them saying something about a new driver.

Suddenly, there she was.

"Quiet!" barked Waxman.

The room stopped and stared at Waxman, then followed his gaze to the viewers. There on the screens were multiple images of a wisp of a girl with long blue hair that fell in waves about her shoulders wearing a grey uniform with high collars. Behind her floated a shiny black Shriean warship, deadly-looking and perhaps even as close to stature as Jevan's warcruiser.

"Well, said Kayanai softly. "This will be interesting."

Something strange was happening inside him as he looked at the girl. It was as though his heart was lifting somehow. Not because she was beautiful, which she was, but because of something about her face, her smile. She looked free, happy, and somehow familiar.

The room was now full of curious chatter and shocked murmurs. Kayanai turned to Jevan and was struck by her expression. He couldn't read it. Fear? Longing?

"We need to meet her," Jevan said in a strained voice.

"Indeed," said Waxman, his face granite and impassive.

"Invite her to join you tonight. Find out all you can."

"We should get to her before the reporters do," said Kayanai.

At the word, "we" Jevan's lips tightened. She did not want Kayanai there while she questioned this girl, because she didn't want Kayanai knowing her suspicions.

She's connected to him, I know it, she thought feverishly. Her lips formed his name. Cal.

CHAPTER EIGHTEEN

Deep inside the diamond belly of the Blue Star lounge sat Jet, her dark driver suit contrasting sharply with the dazzling crystal decor and her hair glowing in the blue lights. Alone on a seat made for three, she sipped her drink quietly while around her, other drivers danced to pumping music, loudly and raucously celebrating surviving the day. A young man smiling widely and breathing heavily plopped himself down next to her. Jet gazed at her drink and ignored him. The man continued to smile at her but seemed at a loss for words.

Finally, he burst out "I love your hair."

She looked at him under her lashes and said nothing. Eventually, she turned her lovely face away from him and sipped from her glass impassively. The man opened his mouth as if to say something, paused awkwardly, then stood up and moved away quickly as if he hoped no one had seen the exchange.

Someone had. From a private room next door, Jevan watched a surveillance mech screen with an amused smile.

"Are we going to go meet this girl or what?" asked Kayanai. He was standing behind her hunched over, barely fitting inside the room and shifting his weight back and forth impatiently, wondering why they were wasting time. Jevan said nothing. The girl was more likely to show her true nature now than in the presence of the Jar of Desigar, but she didn't say this to Kayanai. She was irritated by his presence and wished he would just go and attend to the business he needed to deal with below and leave Jet to her.

When Kayanai was about to burst with impatience, Jevan finally said to the mech, "Observation complete. You can recall your recorder." Then she walked briskly to the door, opened it, and headed out into the cavernous Blue Star lounge without waiting for Kayanai.

The crowd parted as she entered, the people cramming back to give her the regulation personal space required for a jar.

Jevan ignored the fawning comments and admiring looks of the drivers and focused her attention solely on her goal.

Jevan's view of Jet's face was warped by a large glass the girl held as she drank the last few drops of her drink. When Jet placed it down in front of her, she found the Jar of Desigar towering over her, and a large percentage of the people in the vicinity staring at her intently.

Jet showed no sign of alarm and instead looked at Jevan curiously as if she were being presented with an interesting specimen.

Not the reaction to my presence of your typical young woman thought Jevan as she sank gracefully onto the seat next to Jet.

The girl seemed even tinier next to the Waxen whose long limbs and flowing robes took up the rest of the lounge seat.

Jevan studied her carefully. There it was: a flicker glow along the edge of Jet's outline. As Jevan focused on it, it grew brighter until the girl was entirely surrounded in a luminous, multi-coloured aura, the same as Jevan's. The same as Cal's.

As the two women gazed at each other as if they were the only two people in the room, the crowd watching them suddenly dispersed like prey in the presence of a predator.

Kayanai was lumbering his huge form over to Jevan and Jet, scowling at anyone in his way. Despite the large size of the lounge, he'd had difficulty maneuvering his way into the room and his irritation at being left to follow behind was exacerbated by the fact that now he'd managed to make it over to the two women, there was no room for him to sit. He was forced to stand behind the love seat awkwardly, leaning on it to hear what Jevan and Jet were saying.

Jet had started the conversation with, "You seem important around here." Jevan twitched an eyebrow in mild disbelief and answered,

"Most people recognize the person with the highest title in the Alliance."

A smile broke out on Jet's face making her look carefree and even younger. She shrugged lightly and replied, "Where I'm from, jars hold little importance—even the Jar of Desigar."

"So now you know who I am."

"I know who you are."

A jolt ran through Jevan as Jet's bright glowing blue eyes delved deep into her own.

"Of course, I know," continued Jet, lightly, blinking and breaking the spell, "Far-flung from all the politics of the Alliance as I've been, even I know that the Jar of Desigar is the most illustrious title there is."

"And where are you from?" asked Jevan pointedly, leaning in and watching the girl's face carefully.

"You don't know it," said Jet, dismissively, her eyes glancing up to Kayanai looming above them.

"Hi," said Kayanai, glad of the opening. He'd missed most of the conversation due to the music blaring from all corners of the decagon lounge and he was longing to talk to this girl who seemed so much more alive than anyone else in the room. To Kayanai's disappointment, Jet had already turned away from him and was asking Jevan a question.

"Do you fear for your life so much that you require a guard that size?" she asked Jevan.

Jevan smiled. "He's not my guard. As for fearing for my life, I honestly can't remember the last time I did." This was not entirely true, but it had been a very long time since Jevan had felt afraid of anything. She gestured to Kayanai. "Does he make you uncomfortable? We could take a walk somewhere if you prefer."

"He doesn't make me nervous. But I would be happy to get out of here," replied Jet.

"Well then, I'll gladly take you to somewhere a little more exciting," Jevan stood up, put her hand on Kayanai's arm and said in his ear, "How about we give her a tour of the combat ready deck?"

Kayanai's eyes narrowed, and he hesitated. "I have work to do down there. Why—?"

"I think she'll find it interesting. And I think I'll find her reaction interesting. It will tell me more about her. You'll need to take the cargo lift. I'll see you down there."

Kayanai looked as if he were about to argue with her, but Jevan had already linked arms with Jet and was leading her swiftly through the lounge and out into the hall to the lift area.

They entered a lift and Jevan keyed in an area on the lowest deck. Then she placed one hand under Jet's chin, placed her other hand on the girl's small, slim shoulder, and stared down into Jet's face intently. "So, my dear, how is it you have a Shriean warship?"

Jet met Jevan's intense gaze, her blue eyes as cool and deep as the waters on the planet below. The light surrounding them both intensified, the colors dancing wildly. Jet paused, then answered, softly, "My ship is mine the way your ship is yours. Our ships are instruments of our will, born out of suffering. Surely, you didn't think you were the only one."

Jevan's hand travelled from Jet's chin to her cheek. "I have felt alone for a long time, but I wasn't always. I'm looking for someone. I need to know if he—"

A cacophony of loud shouts and whirring mechs cut Jevan off as the doors sprang open and garish lights flooded the lift. Jet gently released herself from Jevan's grasp and walked out into a large echoey launch area filled with soldiers readying military ships, filling some with weapons and emptying others of battered, blood-splattered men and women wearing pale blue uniforms.

Jevan watched Jet's reaction carefully as the rebel prisoners from the planet below were hustled through a door where they'd be held for questioning.

Jevan put her arm around Jet's shoulder and led her further in, pointing down at the disorienting transparent floor and explaining how the ships dropping down to the planet below were airships bringing weapons to the troops on the ground.

"Amazi was chosen as host planet for the Crowne Couloir when news of their uprising reached Waxman. Now the citizens who care only for their own wealth and enjoyment sit up here safely enjoying the race while the rebels below are crushed. Come see."

They came to an area with display maps, monitors, and an enormous screen showing mech footage of the fighting on the ground. One moment it showed a blast of energy beaming down from the sky and obliterating a multistory building, the next it showed a firefight on a beach, and the next it showed rebels throwing themselves overboard from the deck of an enormous naval ship. A group of officers were standing in front of the screen apparently flicking through to find the footage they were looking for.

Nearby, a group of soldiers were apparently on break and making the most of their free time by playing strategy games and ingesting various mind-altering libations. They joked and laughed while images of carnage flickered behind them.

Jet looked at them with distaste then turned to Jevan, "This is what you call more exciting?" she asked with eyebrows raised.

Before Jevan could answer, a voice echoed into the area over a loudspeaker: "All personnel at attention immediately. Reserves suit up. Prepare the Maiden for deployment."

Kayanai had arrived and was now towering intimidatingly down at a group of soldiers playing a game who threw down their pieces in irritation, then seeing that Kayanai was watching, they jumped up from their seats and raced over to a large black disc mounted on a labour mech. Two keyed in operation codes while the other two opened a deployment hatch. The large black disc whirred to life and the mech maneuvered over to the hatch. Once it was locked into position, the disc was lowered into the floor. It stopped with a clank, and two of the soldiers nodded to each other and hit the release. The soldiers watched the object move out into space, then they walked back to their table, sat down and looked up at the screens.

"That weapon," said Jet. "It looks like—"

"Shrie Shrie technology?" Jevan finished for her.

Jet nodded.

"That's because it is in a way. The tech used to build it was gleaned from my ship. It's the greatest weapon we have. Watch."

Jevan pointed to the screens. One showed a group of soldiers outside an enormous complex being fired upon by mounted defense weapons, and the other showed the progress of The Maiden moving towards the planet. The soldiers were firing towards the complex to no avail, but then one of them snapped together a large rifle and aimed. The Maiden stopped, then let forth an orange beam of energy as wide as itself. Soon the other screen showed the beam of energy shooting out of the sky and into the energy shield protecting the complex. It burned through the shield in moments then poured into the front of the complex first making it glow red hot, then blasting it to bits. The soldiers on screen gave a cheer, then they moved forward, the rifle raised and ready to strike again.

Jevan leaned in and said in Jet's ear, "The Maiden fires from orbit, but the target is chosen by the soldiers on the ground. This way the target can be changed quickly."

"Why not give an aiming rifle to each officer?" asked Jet, her eyes still fixed on the screen.

Jevan inwardly smiled with satisfaction. Just what Cal would ask, she thought. "I believe they're working on doing just that. The tech is still quite new," she answered.

Suddenly, a soldier scuttled over to Kayanai and called up to him. "Sir, the reports coming in show the same results as the last two Maiden strikes: target buildings destroyed but very little sign of casualties. It's as if the rebels know the strikes are coming before they happen."

Jevan noticed that Kayanai's face froze at that, which she knew was usually a sign of his having a strong emotional reaction. Interesting, she thought.

Then Kayanai glowered down at the soldier and snapped, "You choose to suggest the enemy has insider information rather than accept that our intelligence is slow? Clearly the buildings are empty as the rebels have moved on. I need to know where the rebels will be, not where they have already been. See to it."

Jevan considered him, thoughtfully. I can read you Kayanai. That soldier's report worried you. What are you hiding?

Suddenly, Jet stepped forward, looked up at Kayanai, and said matter of factly, "You're helping them." Kayanai looked down at her startled, and a flash of fear flitted across his face.

Then Jet broke into a broad, dazzling smile. "There's certainly more to you than meets the eye, isn't there, Kayanai?" As she spoke, Jet reached out her tiny hand and placed it on his wrist. Kayanai's face softened immediately, and the tiny young woman and the giant shared a long look that was as intimate as it was unfathomable.

Watching them Jevan experienced a range of emotions. First, came shock with the realization that Jet was right; Kayanai's reaction made it clear that he was the reason the rebels were never where the Maiden struck. He must be working both sides, thought Jevan, wonderingly, for Waxman and for the rebels. He must be trying to do what he thinks is right without breaking his loyalty. A rush of old feelings for Kayanai that she thought were long gone washed over her. Kayanai, I thought you'd been swallowed by Waxman's will, but you're more you than ever. But the smile that tugged on her lips dropped away when she saw the glow. Where Jet's hand met Kayanai's wrist, a light danced. It was the same light she'd seen on Cal, on herself, and on Jet earlier. That's the glow of those who command Shrie Shrie tech. Like when Cal touched me. Why is it here, now, when they are touching? What does it mean?

Then, Jet stepped back and whirled around to face Jevan, her hair fanning around her shoulders as if in slow motion, and the moment was over.

"Is this why you brought me here?" Jet asked Jevan. "For Kayanai?" Her face was bright with curiosity.

It was not at all why she had brought Jet there. After a strange flash of confusion and something like jealousy, Jevan composed her mind and calmly replied, "I brought you here because I thought it might like to see the hidden reason why you and the other drivers are here to race. Is it below you?" She gestured to the cavernous room full of soldiers, some of whom were now staring openly at their exchange. "Don't you find all this interesting?"

"I'm not interested in this petty fighting." Jet locked eyes with her and stepped forward. "And Jevan, you're no more interested in this than I am. Nor is Kayanai though he is stuck with it. So why bring me here?"

The young woman's confidence and insight grated Jevan's nerves— she was used to having the upper hand and this tiny girl refused to be intimidated!

Jevan stepped even closer to make the most of her height and peered down at Jet and said quietly, "You sure know a lot for someone so very young. Tell me, who are you Jet, really?"

The girl gazed up placidly and answered, "I am myself and only myself. You could be the same," she said over her shoulder to Kayanai who was staring at her like a man entranced. He suddenly snapped out of it and turned to the soldiers watching them.

"Attend to your duties!" he said to them, sternly. Then with a glance of regret towards the two women, he walked away purposefully.

Jet turned back to Jevan. "But you are not ready, neither of you. If you were, you would not ask that question."

"Because I'd already know the answer?"

"You are the answer."

Frustrated, Jevan balled her fists and just shook her head, confused. Then she snapped, "Right! Well, there's no point in me hanging around here listening to you talk in riddles!" Slightly ashamed of her loss of control, she took a deep breath, and when she spoke again, her voice was even, "and no point in you hanging around here if it doesn't interest you."

Then Jevan made a quick about turn and began walking off towards the lift. "Come along," she commanded Jet over her shoulder. She got in the lift, turned around and saw with satisfaction that Jet was following her order. As Jet entered the lift, Jevan's eyes met Kayanai's across the room. Even at a distance she could feel the intensity of his gaze. His hand raised up and seemed to be pointing at her. Was he accusing her?

Then his hand opened as if to say, what are you going to do?

What am I going to do, thought Jevan, as the lift door snapped shut. She could feel the glow of the girl's energy as they rode up in silence. Who are you, Jet? Are you Cal? The question quivered on Jevan's lips, but she kept silent. She won't tell me anything, and besides, does it matter? Whether

Cal or just like Cal, Jevan suspected this girl had knowledge and abilities beyond Jevan's. Beyond Waxman's too. What am I going to do? Not tell Waxman my suspicions, that's for sure. Jevan shook herself free of her thoughts and looked down at Jet.

"Tomorrow's going to be a big day," she said. "Think you'll be ready for it?"

Jet nodded. "I'm always ready."

"I'm sure you are," said Jevan. But am I?

CHAPTER NINETEEN

"The ships are firing up and you can feel the energy crackling in the air, can't you?"

"I sure can! I don't know about you all, but I'm ready for race number two!" The roar of over a million citizens washed over the two announcers in their broadcast booth high above the crowd.

Below them on the elite platform, Jevan sat twirling her fingers around and around the long metal chain of her necklace. Behind her stood Kayanai, his blank expression hiding his surly mood and exhaustion.

He had been up all night battling insurgents on the planet below and was still irritated with Jevan for avoiding him the night before. Next to Jevan was Waxman, leaning forward in his chair in anticipation. Every so often he would tap on one of the numerous circular comms on the side of his face to give an order or request information. Jevan ignored the giant screens flashing images of the racers and their ships, and instead looked up through the transparent dome. Glittering in the black of space she could see a cluster of lights she knew were thousands of ships all with drivers preparing to dance with death among the stars for her amusement. She cared for none of them, but one. She was looking at the far end of the group away from the starting line. Jet would be there, waiting to join after everyone had made it past the first obstacle. This race would be harder for her than for anyone else.

Jevan gave up the impossible task of spotting the Shriean ship and focused instead on the nearest celestial body, the moon Tinus. It's swirling orange atmosphere was hypnotic and helped calm her nerves.

The Stadium had been maneuvered away from Amazi and placed near the uninhabited neighbouring planet Kolpa and its surrounding moons. Filling the space surrounding the planet and moons were fighter ships and mech stops sitting in waiting for the arrival of the racing ships. Everywhere in between were camera drones whirring around capturing all the preparations and beaming the images over to The Stadium's massive screens.

The two announcers continued commenting, the first saying,

"There's a 38% death rate projected for the first leg of this race."

The other announcer whistled and said, "That's quite the jump from yesterday's race. I guess it was deemed too easy. Sounds like we're in for a whole lot of action!"

"That's for sure. I don't think this crowd is going to be disappointed. Are you folks ready for a bloodbath?" The crowd roared again. A light burst from the starting platform signalling the start of the race. "They're off!" cried the announcers.

In unison thousands of ships fired their engines and billions of spectators from across the galaxy watched the tiny points of lights with ghoulish glee waiting to see which ships would be picked off first. The winning drivers from the previous leg had the dubious privilege of starting out the race in the lead; being out front meant they had a better chance of being first, but it also meant they had a better chance of being killed.

The course the ships were travelling down was a narrow one. It crossed the orbits of the two moons of the planet Nateus, moved around the planet itself, then across the system and ended at its planetary neighbor Legoma. The first challenges were to make it past the moons, each of which were equipped with first class defense systems. Rocket platforms on the moon's surfaces were armed with atomic rockets, and ten Handlers, incredibly powerful destroyer ships, waited in the first moon's orbit ready to defend the Garage, a giant refuelling station. The Garage offered respite to racers if they wanted to re arm, fuel up, or needed emergency repairs. It was always interesting to see who decided to risk the danger of stopping for extra fuel and gear.

Genjai held back his own ship and let some other drivers take the lead as the front pack approached the first moon, Tinus. His fighter veered away from the group just as the Handlers launched a volley of atomics into the fray. The spectators waited with bated breath for the atomics to detonate, then cheered wildly as they exploded and took out scores of ships and the death toll screens lit up with the names and stats of lost drivers. When one of the screens showed Gengai's position, part of the crowd began to chant, "Gengai! Gengai!" They loved him not just for being the best driver in the fleet, but also for his daring and showmanship as he often gambled his time to strike opponents rather than just outmaneuver them.

True to form, Gengai dove towards the first moon behind the Handlers catching their attention and drawing their fire. He got so close to the moon's surface, blasts of dust erupted behind him as the Handlers missed their target. Then he buzzed past one of the moon's rocket platforms triggering a massive launch of rockets. As he soared up and away, other racers, trying to follow his lead, drove right into the oncoming assault.

The screens at the Stadium lit up as the blast engulfed tens of ships. The delighted crowd cheered again and called his name.

Jevan smiled wryly and glanced at Waxman. His face was neutral as usual, but she could tell he was enjoying himself.

Gengai's pageantry, though risky, was good for business. Then she looked back to the other screens, scouring them for a glimpse of alien tech. She found one showing the final pack of drivers preparing to leave the starting platform. There amongst them was the pointed, threatening profile of Jet's warship.

Jet, thought Jevan, are you scared? Because she entered the race late, Jet would be last off the platform. Though it was called a "time penalty", losing time wasn't the big concern. The big worry for a late driver was being a lone target, easy for the primed destroyers and rockets to pick off. The other ships had burst away, and the starting platform was now empty but for Jet's hovering warship and one other ship surrounded by technicians working frantically to fix some sort of issue. Many eyes were on the Shriean ship, wondering how the girl in the alien tech would fare.

Finally, the signal for Jet to launch was given, and as soon as it lit up about her, she blazed away with such speed that the audience gave a gasp, the announcers bellowed excitedly, and the bettors and takers began yelling at each other and waving currency in the air. A camera mech zoomed in on the ship's two glowing engines then backed off to show the menacing-looking warship scream silently across the darkness towards the first challenge. It looked very tiny as the two destroyers turned to face it. The Handlers stopped, and suddenly the space in front of Jet's ship was filled with rockets. As the distance to impact closed, Jet's course did not waiver.

At the moment of detonation, her ship seemed to jump forward as if it were moving faster in time and the rockets slower, but it didn't seem to be enough; the atomics detonated, and Jet's ship disappeared within the blast after blast of light and particles.

"Well, that was quick. It seems the little girl in the big, bad Shriean ship was no match for..." the first announcer's voice faded away. The camera mechs had found the warship and was now following its progress towards The Garage. "I don't believe it! She made it!" the announcers yelled.

An enormous rumbling came from the crowd as shouts of surprise, admiration, and speculation rose up from the millions watching.

"Jet in the Shriean ship survives while at the same time so many promising drivers are being blown away by the first moon defenses. Check out the carnage on screen 8, everyone! That's the highest death toll we've seen yet!" crowed the second announcer.

The spectators obediently switched their focus to the screens showing a massive cloud of dust and debris being lit up by the explosion of rockets. A number in the corner of the screen was rising steadily to show how many ships were being lost. Another blood lusty roar rose up, then changed to cheers as on another screen Genjai shot out in front, leading the pack towards the giant refueling station, The Garage.

"Gengai's got a sizeable lead now! He handled the Handlers no problem. Let's see if he can get by the Garage," said the first announcer.

Jevan ignored the screens showing Gengai's progress and instead focused on the one that showed Jet's ship dancing close to the first moon, effortlessly avoiding the rockets from the surface, flipping and twisting along the deadly course like a child skipping down a street.

Jevan's heart pounded faster, and she leaned forward in her seat. Excitement was surging in her chest so intensely; she bit her lip to keep from whooping with joy. She wanted nothing more than to call her ship to her and join Jet in her frolic through space. With a jolt, she was snapped back to reality by Waxman's voice as he called to Gengai over his comm.

"Gengai, the Shriean ship is faster than yours. The girl is making quick gains. Keep on alert. She is not to pass you."

"She won't," responded Gengai. "The little one won't make it past the Garage. I'll make sure of it."

Jevan was now biting her lip so hard, were she not a waxen, her mouth would have been full of blood. Come on, Jet, she thought. As if in response to Jevan's thought, the Shriean ship changed its flight route from something that looked almost haphazard to something far more direct. Jet joined the mass of ships clumped together for cover and began weaving her way artfully through them. It soon became clear that she was heading for Gengai.

As Jet streamed towards him, Gengai was entering the defense radius of The Garage and being attacked by a cloud of attack mechs. As they swarmed, he put his ship into a spin and the carefully designed spikes on its hull cut the mechs to pieces. He continued in his spin till he made it through the mechs, then he shot forward to avoid rockets coming from the surface of The Garage. It was masterfully done, and the spectators showed their appreciation.

"Do you think Gengai will risk stopping at the Garage?" asked the first announcer.

"It's not a matter of risk with Gengai," answered the second. He's got a big fuel tank, and he never seems to need rest. If his ship doesn't need repairs, I don't see Gengai breaking his momentum."

"Maybe he has a tech issue then. He's moving awfully close to the Garage. See look! He's slowing down."

Gengai had slowed to the point that the ships closest to him were catching up. Another volley of rockets came from the Garage which Gengai dodged at just the right time for them to fly past him and into the ships trailing him. He shot away from the explosion and took a sharp turn around the tip of the Garage and came out the other side with an even bigger lead. But it was short lived.

The cheering of the crowd turned to gasps as Jet burst through the burning wreckage of ships and plummeted towards the Garage. It was as if she were aiming for Gengai and ignoring the fact that there was a large station the size of a city between them—a well-armoured station that was firing atomics right at her.

"What is she— ?" The announcer's voice petered out when the first line of atomics exploded just behind Jet, and she continued to blast straight at The Garage. The bombardment of atomics continued and the billions of spectators around the galaxy all held their breath as Jet's ship reached The Garage till suddenly a massive ball of orange fire blossomed in the centre of the great refueling station.

"WHOA!" exclaimed both the announcers. "Driver Jet appears to have committed suicide by ramming her ship into The Garage."

"Why'd she do it, do you think?"

"Well—" The first announcer was cut off by screams from the crowd. One of the screens was showing something impossible: Jet's ship, still intact, on the other side of the damaged station, closing in on Gengai.

"I'm afraid we can't report exactly what we just saw here, folks," said the first announcer. "But from the reports coming in says that the damage to The Garage was actually caused by their own atomics, and that the Shriean ship seemed to disappear just before it reached them."

While the announcers began a discussion about how phasing should be disallowed though it wasn't currently against the rules, Waxman tapped his cheek and said quietly, "The girl is coming up fast behind you. Your new objective is not to win the race. It is to stop her at all costs. Whatever it takes, Gengai."

Jet's ship was right behind him now. He waited till she was the distance he wanted, then he put his ship into its deadly spin and shot backwards straight at Jet. At his speed and trajectory, he should have made impact, but instead Jet's ship slid aside impossibly fast leaving him spinning into empty space. Then Jet did something even more astonishing. Rather than keeping on course and taking the lead, she turned, caught up with Gengai, and put her own ship into a spin, copying him perfectly. Then when he brought his ship out of the spin and aimed his ship towards her, he found she'd done the exact same thing and was flying past him so closely it seemed they would make contact for sure. He turned to find her again and this time he found her flying exactly parallel to him and matching his every move. Gengai began firing at Jet's ship wildly, but nothing landed.

The crowd watching was a mass of uproarious confusion. Some were incensed by this mocking treatment of their beloved favourite, some were laughing wildly, and others were loving it and cheering and chanting Jet's name. Jevan's eyes were glued to the screen, but she could feel anger radiating from Waxman as he tapped comm after comm, ordering every possible ship to converge on Jet's location and every possible weapon to be trained on her ship.

If he's mad, I can only imagine what Gengai looks like right now, thought Jevan.

She couldn't help enjoying seeing swaggering Gengai being teased so outrageously by Jet and fought to keep from smiling.

Again, she felt that enormous longing to be up there, part of the chase.

"Gengai, lead her to the far side of Oa!" barked Waxman.

Gengai stopped firing at Jet and turned sharply towards the second moon. Jet kept with him, then shot forward close enough to the moon's surface to trigger a volley of rockets.

She then pulled up in a flash and angled her ship towards the nearby planet Nateos. As she approached, more rockets were discharged from the planet's orbiting defense station and began racing towards her. Behind her, Gengai was coming at her, still firing though not yet in range, while at the same time rockets from Oa were tracking her, and in front of her she had rockets approaching from the defense station and behind them, a fleet of fighter ships were now on their way.

"This is it, everyone," said an announcer, huskily. "She's not getting out of this one." No one was paying any attention showing the destruction of other ships by the Handlers and The Garage. All eyes were fixed on Jet's ship.

As the threats converged it became obvious what was going to happen. Gengai realized it and was able to pull away in time, but the lead fighter ships weren't so lucky.

Jet's ship disappeared in a flash and the atomics smashed into each other and erupted into such massive circular blooms of brilliance that the explosions whited out the screens momentarily.

The noise in the stadium was a wall of sound, Jevan ignored it. She rose to her feet, scouring the screens for Jet's reappearance. Waxman too was searching the screen. Then he glanced at Jevan, and in that moment his eyes burned so hotly that she could still feel the heat of it as he looked away.

He suspects.

He's also thinking of Cal.

Jevan pushed the thought from her mind. It didn't matter what Waxman thought. All that mattered was that if Jet wasn't Cal, she was someone, something, like him. He won't catch her. I know he won't.

Some screens were momentarily black after losing their camera feed, until other feeds were switched over. Images of burning fighter ships covered most screens, the others were flipping through images as the screen controllers searched for Jet and Gengai. When the cameras found them, they showed Gengai racing to catch up to Jet who was now blasting through the space between the two moons.

Suddenly, Jet stopped and floated in space, the ship's nose turned towards the distant pile of burning ships as though she were stopping to admire the damage she'd caused. The stadium quieted as the spectators watched with bated breath. Gengai drew closer and closer. Before he was even in range, he began firing. Still, the Shrie Shrie ship sat motionless. Then, just as Gengai's ship was nearly upon her, Jet's ship blasted away impossibly fast, and shot like a shooting star directly at the moon, Oa.

Gengai had only time to point his fighter in her direction before she reached the moon. When she did, something astonishing happened; a bright shaft of light surrounded Jet's ship, and she flew straight into Oa.

For a moment nothing happened, then from the centre of the moon a light grew, causing glowing cracks to form and spread, till suddenly the moon cracked in two and burst apart in a cloud of dust and flying rocks and metals.

The crowd was silent. The closer cameras had been blown away by the shockwave, and the only screens anyone was looking at were those showing the unbelievable sight of two sides of a moon drifting slowly away from each other.

Finally, the crowd began to murmur. There was some triumphant hollering from the more inebriated, but most of the chatter was fearful. The people knew they had just witnessed a display of power beyond their understanding.

Jevan barely heard the noise over the sound of the blood thundering in her temples. She knew what she was looking at was impossible, the kind of impossible she'd only seen once before. Out of the corner of her eye she could see Waxman's hand gripping his chair.

"Enough," said Waxman. He tapped his cheek. "Gengai. If you catch sight of her, relay her position to me." Then he said, still looking at the screen, "Jevan. Your ship,"

He suspects too, Jevan thought for certain this time. He's thinking of Cal.

"I'll go after her," she said, standing up.

Waxman rose from his seat also. "Take me to her," he ordered, Jevan paused. She wanted to go after Jet alone. Can I say no to him? Can I? The thought hung in her mind for an endless moment.

"Jevan," Waxman said, sharply.

She jerked into action. "Come on then," Jevan snapped as she moved swiftly along the walkway to the inner hallway. She reached the entrance to the metal staircase that led to where her ship was docked and used her handprint to enter. She didn't wait to hold the door for him, and it nearly slammed behind her. As she descended, the noise of multiple boots pounded on the staircase behind her, and she realized that Kayanai was following too.

Fine, she thought. It doesn't matter. What matters is that I find her.

Upon reaching the bottom and opening the door, she could already feel it humming. Her ship was there, floating and ready, waiting for her. She reached up and ran her hand along its surface marvelling at its silky smoothness. Then the hatch opened, she entered its warm halls, made her way to the center, and sank to the floor cross-legged. She closed the hatch just as Kayanai's heel passed through the entrance, then she closed her eyes and focused.

"Do you have a fix on her?"

Jevan opened her eyes and saw Waxman and Kayanai pressing their enormous bodies against the wall, with Kayanai almost bent double. It amused her briefly to see them both fitting themselves into a space that was not built for them. They gripped the walls as the ship shook and the ship's viewer materialized in front of them and displayed what looked like enormous asteroids floating in space.

"Uh, maybe bringing us to the site of a recently destroyed moon was not a good idea," said Kayanai, pointing to a particularly large chunk of moon that was heading right for them.

"I need to pick up her trail," said Jevan, softly. She closed her eyes again. She reached out with her whole self, trying to sense Jet's energy. There, she thought. It was like there was a heat trail, a path of flickering warm colours leading off in one direction.

"Jevan…" said Kayanai, warningly.

"We're fine," she said scornfully. They were in no danger from the rock hurtling towards them. She would never endanger her ship.

The light from the viewer glowed a cool blue as they were suddenly in orbit around the water planet, Amazi.

"She's on the planet," said Waxman, looking to Jevan for confirmation.

"Yes," whispered Jevan. "Jet is down there." She closed her eyes again. "There," she said after a pause.

"Where's there?" asked Kayanai

"Take us there, Jevan," ordered Waxman

A flash and the viewer was engulfed in blue. Jevan jumped up and headed straight for the hatch, her companions following her with equal haste.

The hatch opened and she was momentarily blinded by the light outside. When Jevan's eyes adjusted, she found herself standing on the surface of a sheet of pale blue ice dusted with white snow. Next to her, the ocean, a disorienting similar white and blue colour as the ground, lapped near the base of her ship. They had phased onto the surface of an enormous iceberg. The ice spread far out in front of her, and there was no sign of life. Then Jevan saw it—the black shape of a Shrie Shrie warship, far off in the distance, and next to it was a tiny flame. It's her! thought Jevan, eagerly. Jet and her ship were on the other side of the ice, just visible.

Jevan strained forward, wanting to run, but a vice-like hand gripped her arm, stopping her in her tracks. She looked back and saw Waxman's eyes fixed on Jet's ship; his face hardened into an expression of cruel satisfaction.

"Kayanai".

Kayanai had stepped out and was shielding his eyes from the glare of white, trying to focus on what his companions were looking at. He turned to his leader and awaited his orders with a looming sense of dread.

"Use the Maiden."

Jevan gasped and jerked her arm violently, trying to loosen Waxman's grip, but he held fast. She grabbed his arm and yelled, "You can't!"

Waxman brought his face close to hers and let his eyes travel over her features. Then he said, softly, "Would you leave my side and run to her? Is that what you would do if I let you go?"

Those words came to Kayanai's ears, but they sounded far away. It was as though his ears were not his, just as his hands were not his; they were following Waxman's orders despite his heart and mind calling out for them to stop. He raised the target rifle he'd been shouldering, closed one eye, and looked through the scope at Jet.

Magnified in the scope, she appeared as a small figure standing in the wind, arms calmly by her sides. She seemed to be looking back at him. Kayanai touched the trigger. He knew that high above the planet the Maiden would be changing position, readying to fire on his mark.

Jevan blinked back her tears and met Waxman's eyes. She held his gaze, and as she did flashes of memories ran through her mind, all of them of him, the center of her life, her ambition, her loyalty for so, so long. Then out of the corner of her eye, she saw what Kayanai was doing, and she stiffened and took a deep breath and said, "Let me go."

Not a single muscle in Waxman's face moved, but his eyes betrayed him. Pain and fury burned cold in his pale blue eyes. He opened his hand, and Jevan turned and ran.

Kayanai's head jerked up, and he watched Jevan run. She was going full tilt, using every ounce of her considerable power to get to Jet in time. She was breathtaking. Suddenly, she was down, having skidded and tumbled from a patch of ice. Kayanai leaned towards her, wanting to help, but Waxman's voice brought him back to his purpose.

"Continue. Maiden has arrived. Along with our army of Drivers…"

Kayanai reached into his vest and pulled out the firing pin. He clicked it into place and again lifted the scope to his eye. But the high horizon caught his glance. As if the whole sky was filled with falling stars, Kayanai acknowledged the arrival of the race drivers. A mob of pilots on ice to be ready for just this moment if it was to ever occur. Like the Maiden, their closing presence only jailed the moment for what lay ahead.

Back on the scope, at first all he could see was Jet's ship, large and black against the white and blue surroundings, then he saw her. Jet's pale skin and blue hair blended in so well with the background, she would have been hard to spot if not for the movement of her hair streaming in the wind. She was still looking at him.

"Fire," ordered Waxman.

"I have to get closer." Kayanai began walking quickly forward. Jevan was up again, running more carefully now. Kayanai imagined her frustration. Like being in a nightmare, he thought, when you're trying so hard to run fast, but you can't.

Waxman walked beside him taking long impatient strides, then he slapped his hand on Kayanai's shoulder, and said, "The Maiden does not require perfect aim. Do it, Kayanai."

Kayanai stopped. His shoulders rose and fell with his heavy breath. Again, he put the scope to his eye.

"She's nearly there! Do it now!" barked Waxman.

Kayanai could see Jevan waving her arms at Jet and calling to her. She was so close. "If I shoot now, Jevan will be caught in the blast," he said, over his shoulder.

"DO IT!" Waxman's voice rattled in Kayanai's ear.

Jevan was only a few strides away from Jet now. Jet didn't move, she looked straight at Kayanai.

"KAYANAI! NOW!" roared Waxman.

He couldn't shoot. He had to shoot. He heard a voice in his head. It was Waxman's. "When in doubt, shoot the enemy."

Kayanai stopped breathing. He spun on the spot and ducked low. Then he aimed and pressed the trigger on the Maiden rifle.

The force of the explosion flung Kayanai back and slammed him onto his back. For a moment, he could see, hear and feel nothing. Then the air rushed into his lungs, and his eyes blinked away stars, and he could hear the wind howling. His vision cleared and he squinted at the bright sky above. Then two things happened; the sky darkened, and the wailing wind got louder.

Kayanai sat up. Above him, the pale sunlight of Amazi's star was being blocked by three large ships coming in for a landing. He stared in shock, wondering if he were asleep, for they were ships he recognized and hadn't seen in a long, long time. The wailing was getting louder still, and it dawned on Kayanai that it wasn't the wind; it was the sound of Jevan's grief floating across the icy plain. He stood, his eyes tore away from the ships and found her in the distance. She was screaming. As he watched she collapsed to her knees, crying so loudly he could hear her clearly despite the span between them. He turned back to watch the ships land, but suddenly his view was blocked.

When Waxman stepped in front of him, his face hard and inscrutable, Kayanai's body instinctively shifted its weight, preparing for a fight. He'd disobeyed Waxman. There would be consequences. Waxman looked at the target rifle, still clutched in Kayanai's hands.

They were both frozen and waiting, till Kayanai broke the spell and slowly and deliberately removed the pin and placed it back in his vest. Then he dropped the rifle to the ground.

"Well done." Waxman regarded him with something like admiration.

Tears pricked Kayanai's eyes. It was not what he expected, and the words brought him such relief, his knees felt weak. He didn't want to fight Waxman. Waxman turned away and Kayanai followed his gaze to the sight of the three ships touching down a safe distance from the roaring fireball that was Jevan's Shriean warcruiser.

Wax tapped a circle on his cheek. "Come to my mark." Then he turned to Kayanai. "I'm proud of you for making your choice," he said. "Tell me. Why did you do it?"

The lump in his throat would have made it hard to speak, but that wasn't why Kayanai didn't answer. Why did he destroy Jevan's ship? Because he knew it needed to be done. That was it. That was all he knew.

Waxman watched him for a moment. "You don't have to answer. I know you did it because you felt it was the right thing to do." He took a step closer, then reached out and clasped Kayanai to him in a tight embrace. His tears dropped as Kayanai found his chin pressed to Waxman's shoulder.

When Waxman pulled back, Kayanai could see over his shoulder an amazing sight. Twelve giants were approaching them. As they got closer, Kayanai began to recognize them. They were part of Waxman's First Guard, some of the first ever waxen. They held important positions on planets in the outer regions, keeping Waxman's rule strong in the furthest reaches of the Alliance. Kayanai recognized some from pictures, but a couple he'd met in person. Takkade had taught him close combat, and Chaness had trained him in weaponry. It was astonishing to see them again.

Eventually, the twelve waxen stopped in a half circle around Kayanai and Waxman. Their faces presented typically impassive waxen expressions as they waited for Waxman's orders, but Chaness did glance at Kayanai and tilt her head in greeting. He nodded back, then looked at Waxman.

He was surprised to see that Waxman had picked up Kayanai's fallen Maiden rifle.

"It's good to see you all," said Waxman to his soldiers of war.

"You've come just in time to see Kayanai redeem himself and execute an order I gave him." He turned to Kayanai and held up the Maiden rifle. His eyes were like steel. "Well?" he said.

Horror crept up his spine, but Kayanai didn't move. He could feel the weight of Waxman's stare and the stares of the Old Guard pressing down on him, crushing him. But he didn't move.

Finally, Waxman shrugged and turned away. "Bear witness, you all. Disloyalty is a disease that can bring down even the strongest of us." He then raised the Maiden rifle to his shoulder and pointed it towards his original target.

Kayanai looked across to Jevan and Jet. They were together now. It looked as though they were embracing. He looked back at Waxman, his fear relaxing as he thought, It's okay. He doesn't have the pin.

At that moment, Waxman glanced at him, then said to his waxen, "Kayanai may try to stop me, he may even succeed, if he does, destroy him and the target." Then he produced the firing pin and clicked it into place.

"No," whispered Kayanai. When he hugged me… he thought?

Waxman aimed. Kayanai closed his eyes and felt the wax pulsing strong in his veins, throbbing in his temples. The feelings of despair and hopelessness and anger and loneliness rose up in him and seemed to stream out of his fingertips. He knew he had to stop Waxman. He knew it had to be done. The wax rushing through him felt like liquid lightning. He would stop him. Kayanai opened his eyes, and pointed his hand at Waxman... With a sneer Waxman pressed the trigger.

"No," said Kayanai.

Nothing happened.

Waxman looked at the rifle with astonished fury, then he looked back at Kayanai and yelled, "What did you do?" Then he threw it to the ground and to the First Guard behind him, he screamed "Destroy them!"

On his order, the circle of waxen each pulled out a weapon and began marching towards Jevan and Jet.

Meanwhile, Jevan knew nothing of what was going on. She knew only that her power, her connection to Cal, her ship was gone. Her insides felt cold and empty as if the fire that allowed her body had been extinguished. She was only dimly aware of her own sobbing. Suddenly, she felt warm hands gripping her under her arms. They pulled her up to her feet, then they wrapped around her and held her while she cried.

Eventually, Jet's voice said, "Shhh, don't grieve. I can feel the enormity of your loss, but truly, you haven't lost anything."

Jevan exploded. "I've lost EVERYTHING! I've lost Iran, and Kayanai, and Waxman. I've lost my ship and with it my power, and I've lost Cal, all for you, and I don't even know who you are!" and with that Jevan pushed away and whirled around. The warm hands caught her cold ones, and she found herself looking into the smiling face of Cal. She stared at him in wonder. It was the same old Cal—though he'd made himself her size again—he had the same shaggy dark hair, same unkempt clothes, even the same gun at his hip.

"See, you knew me the whole time," he said, encouragingly.

"Cal! It was you… is you," said Jevan. "You were Jet the whole time. But, why? Why Jet and not yourself."

"Because I wanted to fly with you again, but I figured showing up like this," he gestured to himself, "would cause a lot of boring fighting and confusion, so I came as Jet, and I can be Jet and still be myself—-see it all makes sense."

Jevan's brows were knitted in confusion, but at that, they cleared. Suddenly she laughed. She felt like a child waking from a nightmare to realize it was a holiday. "I'm not sure I understand it all, but I am glad to see you again. I'm sorry about the last time I saw you. I give you my word, give me a ship again, I'll follow you to the end of the universe!"

Cal's smile faded. "Give you a ship?" he said. "I never gave you one." He sighed and shook his head.

Jevan's smile faded as well, but she clung to hope. "But mine is gone," she said, "If you don't give me one, how can we fly together? Isn't that what you want?"

Cal didn't answer.

"Then take me with you on your ship."

"Why do you want to come with me?"

"So, we can be together!" Jevan brought determination into her voice.

Cal shook his head again.

Jevan began to feel panic. She needed to convince him. "But I need to come with you! I need to understand your power and where it comes from! I need you to teach me!"

Cal's eyes grew disappointed. He sighed, "You still don't understand." Suddenly, he dropped her hands and looked out towards the waxen in the distance. His face broke into a brilliant smile. "Now that's a surprise!"

Jevan followed his gaze. "What is it?" With a gasp she realized they were being approached by a troop of waxen with their weapons raised. "Quick! We need to get out of here!" she yelled.

She grabbed Cal's hand and tried to pull him to his ship. He just continued to grin and said, "We're fine. I don't have to do anything. Your old friend has us covered."

"My old friend…" said Jevan, confused and still afraid. Then she saw what Cal was seeing. A glowing figure was standing between her, Cal, and the waxen. It was Kayanai. He had moved to protect them, and somehow his body was now surrounded by the same aura of colours that danced around Cal. But Kayanai's colours vibrated like waves washing to a shore, reaching past where Cal and Jevan stood. Somehow acting like a working shield.

"Come on," said Cal. "There's no danger." He took her by the hand and led her closer. Jevan could hear Waxman yelling now. He was screaming at the waxen to fire. Some of them were looking at their weapons in confusion, but others had dropped them and were looking at Kayanai.

"You will follow my orders NOW!" roared Waxman. "If your weapons don't work, then smash the enemy with your hands! Are you, or are you not, my wax men??"

Three of the waxen began walking towards Cal and Jevan, one of them, Chaness, walked towards Kayanai. When she reached him, she turned around and faced Waxman, impassively. The other two had stopped and had turned onto Waxman as well. Waxman's face turned purple with fury.

"What are you doing?? How DARE you! I have given you orders, and you will obey!!" he screamed. Spittle flew from his mouth, and he waved his fists like a man possessed. Waxman's once impassive faces were now taking on varying expressions of horror, disgust and pity.

Jevan and Cal had reached them now. Cal let go of Jevan's hand then reached out and placed it on Kayanai's shoulder.

Jevan waited for Kayanai to be shocked and scared and was shocked herself when Kayanai turned and saw Cal, and joy lit up his face.

"Cal!" he exclaimed, and they threw their arms around each other, and laughed with happiness. Jevan dimly realized Cal had changed size again and grown taller still. Or maybe Kayanai had grown smaller. She couldn't tell. The colors around them glowed so brightly, Jevan could hardly bear to look at them. She was now thoroughly confused.

"So, you're no longer frightened of me?" teased Cal, slapping Kayanai on the shoulder.

Kayanai grinned. "You did say if I saw you again, you'd kill me."

"Is that what I said?"

Kayanai's face sobered as he thought for a moment, then he answered, "No, my fear made me hear that. What you said was, "I hope next time I see you again, you'll be ready to die." Slowly, Kayanai's smile returned, and he nodded his head. "Yes, I see. I understand now."

"Well, I don't," said Jevan, yelling up at them, frustrated. "I wish you could both explain it to me."

"I wish I could explain it to you too," Kayanai said, turning to meet her angry face. He knew she was still furious with him for destroying her ship. "Jevan—"

Suddenly, Waxman leaped on Cal with a roar. He landed on Cal with his full weight, bringing Cal to the ground. Jevan moved to intervene, but Kayanai stopped her. Waxman had Cal's head in his hands as though he meant to crush it, but Jevan could see tear drops falling on Cal's face.

"Kill me," sobbed Waxman quietly. "You've already taken my life from me." Cal just looked calmly back at Waxman, saying nothing.

"Kill me!" screamed Waxman.

Two of the Old Guard came forward then and lifted Waxman to his feet. He didn't struggle. Cal stood up and brushed the snow from his clothes. Then he pulled out his gun. Waxman's eyes widened, but Cal just tapped the snow from the end and placed it back in his holster. He then turned back to Kayanai.

"Ready?" he asked Kayanai.

"As I'll ever be."

Cal took a moment and looking, scoured the horizon with excitement. His smile curled wide as he saw the large army of drivers filling every part of the sky like a dome of sparkling lights. They lay in mid-air thruster hover waiting to attack on his own warships launch. If the Maiden couldn't do its work, maybe surely the race of drivers could finish the threat of Cal off once and for all. Cal laughed hard in his mind at the lunacy.

"Thanks for the present Waxman. This'll be fun." Cal chirmed already claiming the next win if he so chose to be entertained by it all.

Cal and Kayanai both turned and began walking towards Cal's ship.

"Wait!" called Jevan. "What about me? Cal! Kayanai! You can't leave me this way!"

They both stopped and Kayanai looked at her sorrowfully while Cal looked at Kayanai. "The best thing about broken things is that they live in two states: the present and the potential," said Cal.

"You're not ready," said Kayanai.

"Make me ready," answered Jevan.

Kayanai paused, then came to her and took her face in his hands. Suddenly Jevan's mind's eye was blinded by a thousand colors. Then those colours resolved into shapes, then images, then scenes. It was as though through his touch, Kayanai was downloading the whole of his experiences since first arriving on Gengaru into Jevan's head. All his thoughts and feelings, why he made the choices he did, how he felt about Waxman, how he felt about her, everything. She knew and understood Kayanai as if, for a moment, she was him. When her mind stopped reeling and she was herself again she could feel Kayanai's lips pressed against hers. Then they were gone. When she opened her eyes, Kayanai and Cal were walking to Cal's ship. As she watched, they slipped into the open hatch, it closed, and they disappeared in the Shrie Shrie flash of yellow vertical light.

Jevan would have sunk to the ground and wished for death, but for one thing. Kayanai's final thoughts were still echoing in her head. "Follow me. Find me."

CHAPTER TWENTY

There was silence for a moment in the ruined cabin of Day's ship. "But you haven't found them, have you?" whispered Day, hoarsely.

"I found you, just as I was meant to find you the first time." The Waxen pulled back the hood of her cloak revealing the famous features of the Jar of Desigar. "How did you know it was me?"

"A big clue was when you said Jevan wrote on parchment. Your underling, Aha, had parchment on him. Also, Jar Khran telling anyone her personal story, even to a fellow female waxen seems unlikely, don't you think?"

Jevan raised an eyebrow. "I shared my story with you, didn't I?" Day nodded. "Yeah, you did. Why is that? What am I to you, Jevan Khran?"

"You still haven't guessed?"

There was a pause while Day closed her eyes and let her mind travel over the long tale she heard. She'd been so rapt and caught up in Jevan's story that she'd lost sight that it was also her own.

"The baby," she answered, finally. Her eyes fluttered open and widened in wonderment. "That was me."

"Yes," answered Jevan. Jevan stood and stretched her stiff muscles.

"So, I'm..." Day couldn't finish. The magnitude of the realization was overwhelming.

Mano got it, of course. Having managed to shut down all his systems but communication, he was still listening in the corner. He could tell from her voice how Day was feeling.

He said, "All this time, lowly outpost misfit Day was actually Chief Commander Kolorov's granddaughter. Doesn't surprise me at all. You were always bossy." He knew that would make her smile.

A brief laugh shook Day, then she winced. The pain was returning in earnest now. She lifted her shining eyes to Jevan and studied the famous, beautiful face who was now looking down at her impassively. There she was, the Jar of Desigar. She was ambitious and heartless, and had caused Day great suffering, but for some reason Day felt close to her now, closer to her than anybody, even Mano. Somehow, they understood each other. "Please tell me," She gasped. "My father… what happened to him?"

Jevan crouched down next to Day, and stared at her hands, avoiding Day's eyes. "Kolorov'son's ship crash landed on Gengaru. He may have survived, though it's unlikely," she answered Day, flatly. "But your grand-mother didn't give up hope that he was alive. That's why she dumped you all the way out here and left you with a family she felt she could trust. Kolorov went to Gengaru to find him."

Days eyes filled with tears. "Tha—" She tried to speak but the words caught in her throat. She closed her eyes causing the tears to tumble down her cheeks, took a deep breath, and tried again. "That's why she left me. My grandmother went to go find her son, my father. I always thought…"

"You thought you were abandoned because you weren't wanted," said Mano.

Day sighed tremulously and looked at the ceiling. "She did it to protect me. Why didn't they tell me, Mano? Why didn't the people who raised me tell me about my grandmother?"

"I don't know, Day. Maybe they didn't know. You'll have to ask them."

Day gazed down at her ruined body, regretfully. "I don't think I'm going to get a chance to." She shifted her gaze to the waxen next to her. "Will I, Jevan?"

Jevan forced her eyes to Day's face. "No. You won't."

"But why?" Mano called out impassionedly from the corner. "Jar Khran, you could still save her! There's a medilab bed on this ship. If you get her into it, it will maintain her vitals till we make it to the Crossnor Outpost. There's no need to let her die!"

Jevan leaned over Day, her eyes still fixed on her face. Softly, she said, "I'm sorry, but your death is necessary." Day watched with surprise as a tear drifted down the Jar of Desigar's cheek.

Day said, "You don't seem to want it to happen, so why—"

"It's the last thing I want, but long ago, I sat in a ship floating in deep space, filled with dead comrades whom I'd killed to stay alive. Hope had drained from me, and I was more alone than I ever thought it possible to be. And in that moment, when I truly despaired, my salvation appeared, and a power unlike anything I'd ever felt flowed through me. But I lost it somehow when I returned to Desigar. I felt echoes of that power when I was in my ship, but it wasn't complete. I wasn't complete. Then my ship was destroyed, and I lost everything again. All this time, Day, I've been trying not to despair. I've worked tirelessly, reading, writing, learning, thinking, trying to understand what happened to me, to bring back the power I had. But nothing has worked! So now all that's left to me is to recreate that moment when my ship came to me in the first place, when I was alone and in despair.

Jevan's eyes drifted from Day's to a point on the wall. "It should be easy, right? My friends are gone - Iran is dead, Waxman is an empty shell, and Kayanai and Cal abandoned me, telling me to follow to where I can't go. Even my disciple, the betrayer Aha... even he's gone now. What's to keep me from giving in and giving up completely?"

Jevan reached down and took Day's tiny hand in hers. The heat of the wax coursing through the waxen's veins spread to Day and made her realize how cold she was on the bare ground.

"You are why I can't despair, Day," said Jevan, through a clenched jaw. "You, the baby I cared for, the little girl I wondered about a thousand times, the strong, brave, young woman I see in front of me now. You bring me hope. You make me feel less alone. With you gone, maybe that'll finally bring me to where I need to be." Jevan's tears were flowing freely now.

"You don't have to do this," said Mano. "You could trade your life for hers."

Jevan shook her head hard, her eyes were feverish behind her tears as she gripped Day's hand. "No! I need to know, Day. I'm sorry. I need to do this."

The pain was back in full, and Day groaned in agony. But she held tight to Jevan's hand and held the look they shared. "It's okay, Mano," she called to him, her voice cracking with the effort. Then she said it to Jevan too, "It's okay. I know I shouldn't feel anything like happiness right now," she gave a brief wry smile, "but I do. I know who I am now, thanks to you. In a way, you've given me my life twice. Now, I'm giving it to you."

Jevan watched, agonized, fighting to keep her resolve. "I will be alone. I will have my ship back. I will release all ties to this world," she whispered.

Day shook her head slightly and winced. "I hope it works. I don't see how you being alone will bring you to your friends. But what do I know, really? Just that I'm ready to leave this place. All I love in the universe is that broken pile of scrap over in the corner there."

"Aw Day…" said Mano.

Then Day smiled through her pain at Jevan and said, "And you. I don't know why… but you too." Then she gasped and shut her eyes.

As Jevan watched Day, she began to sob. Suddenly, she reached down and lifted Day from the floor as easily as a mother lifting a baby, and in that moment, a flash of light illuminated the room. It had come from the hole in the hull, which was now covered by the transparent filaments of sealant. Jevan froze, and her eyes widened. Then, moving like in a dream, she carried Day to the hole and looked out into space. There, blurred by the gauzy sealant, backlit by a nearby star, was the outline of a Shrie Shrie warcruiser.

"It worked," she whispered.

"No," coughed Day, "it didn't."

Jevan looked down at the girl she held in her arms and saw the face of Jet looking back at her.

"Do I still have to die?" murmured Day, her eyes screwed up in pain.

Jevan shook her head. She was already moving swiftly towards the door.

"Wait!" gasped Day. "I'm not going without Mano."

Jevan turned back to where Mano's torso lay on the ground. Then she shifted her hold on Day to free her right hand and reached down, grasped Mano's upper body and held it up.

"We'll get you some new mech legs. I'm out of hands," said Jevan, jubilantly. Her face was radiant.

"They won't have mech legs at the Crossnor Outpost," said Mano, his mouth barely moving.

"We're not going to the Crossnor Outpost," said Jevan.

The Shrie Shrie ship flashed once and was gone.

THE END

ABOUT THE AUTHOR

Jason Dowdeswell is a filmmaker and veteran pro-
ducer of visual effects for major films and episodic
shows. At an early age, Jason began storytelling to
his younger brother and sister while delivering the
neighborhood newspaper. This is his first novel.

He resides on Bowen Island, British Columbia
with his partner and two children.

Printed in the USA
CPSIA information can be obtained
at www.ICGtesting.com
LVHW090452020923
757000LV00002B/4